Pagan Heat

A deity could be anything he wanted, anything I wanted, and I shouldn't be scared. What I should do was go back into the woods, only naked, to sacrifice myself to his desire, offering myself for his pleasure. He'd be eager to take me, unable to resist the wanton girl. Hands like ivy boughs would grip me, taking me by my hips, wrapping around my body, to hold me helpless, and in he'd go, deep inside me, impossibly deep.

I lay back on the bed in the warm safety of my room, yet in my mind I was out in the woods, stark naked and powerless to prevent myself being taken.

By the same author:

Noble Vices
Valentina's Rules
Wild in the Country
Black Lipstick Kisses
Wild by Nature
Office Perks

Pagan Heat
Monica Belle

BLACK LACE

Black Lace Books contain sexual fantasies.
In real life, always practise safe sex.

First published in 2005 by
Black Lace
Thames Wharf Studios
Rainville Road
London W6 9HA

Design by Smith & Gilmour, London
Printed and bound in Great Britain by
Antony Rowe Ltd, Chippenham, Wiltshire

ISBN 978 0 352 33974 4

The Random House Group Limited supports The Forest Stewardship
Council (FSC), the leading international forest certification organisation.
All our titles that are printed on Greenpeace approved FSC certified paper
carry the FSC logo. Our paper procurement policy can be found at:
www.rbooks.co.uk/environment

1

There is something so deliciously naughty about Victorian underwear.

Having got into my combinations, I simply had to walk over to the mirror, turn my back, and pull the seam open to flash my bare bottom. I was chuckling to myself as I continued to dress, feeling just a little bit foolish and just a little bit aroused. It was fun to show off like that, and it was fun to dress completely in the style of the last years of the nineteenth century, even when the visitors were only going to see my dress, and perhaps a hint of ankle, if they were lucky.

That's the thing, you see, with Victorian clothing. How much more intriguing to be clad from neck to toe in garments that flatter and hint but do not reveal, than, say, to be in a bikini, with just about everything on show to all and sundry. I prefer it anyway, and considered myself extremely lucky to have found a job where I could indulge my predilections without being thought strange.

Hence the smile on my face as I dressed, because not only had I landed the ideal job, but also the most wonderful place to live, rent free. Most people will tell you that being a caretaker is about as low on the social scale as you can get, but I didn't care; not when I was caretaker for Elmcote Hall. I was also visitor guide, manager and chief-cook-and-bottle-washer, as the Trust didn't feel able to afford anyone else. That was just fine. In fact, it was perfect.

I did have a touch of first-day nerves, with the prospect of showing groups of visitors around and generally making an exhibition of myself. At the interview I'd assured the Trustees what a great 'people person' I was. They'd swallowed it, although it was nicer to think that it was my PhD on Elgar Vaughan, notorious occultist and the last of his family to occupy the Hall, that had swung the decision. People person or not, I did at least know what I was talking about.

With my knee-length stockings, combinations and dainty square-heeled boots on, my corset came next. Note that the boots go on first because once your corset is laced up, getting at your feet involves advanced yoga. I'd had mine tailor-made, as a treat to myself for finishing my thesis on time. It was a classic S-curve full-length corset, from my bust to halfway over my bottom. The only way to get into it without a maid, or a helpful gentleman, was to fasten the laces first, breath in deep, and do up the catches on the front, one by one as I went slowly purple.

It was worth the effort for that lovely snug feeling, and the sense of my breasts and bottom being enhanced and yet concealed. I was now encased in cotton and satin and lace, nothing revealed, and yet so naughty. After all, I was in my underwear, and all the hypothetical gentleman would have had to do would be to take me in his arms, ease my combinations open behind as he kissed me, *et voilà*!

Unfortunately it was impractical as there was no man, and I was supposed to be ready to receive a coachload of American tourists in ten minutes flat. A shame, because what I really wanted to do was kneel down on the bed and bring myself to a slow and exquisite orgasm as I watched in the mirror, but there was no time for such misbehaviour.

That was the problem of taking on the job single-handedly. I could hire outside staff – in theory I could even sub-contract – but every penny had to be accounted for and justified in terms of profit. My knowledge of accounting was slim to say the least, but I could add up, and it had been made clear to me at the interview that I was expected to save money at every opportunity. They had at least asked if I felt secure on my own, but I'd assured them I did. When it came down to it, being in sole charge of Elmcote Hall was what I wanted more than anything else.

Almost from the moment I'd heard about the place it had been a fantasy of mine to live there. As an intense, rather shy schoolgirl I'd gained far more knowledge than any of my contemporaries in an effort to impress the cool daring Goth girls. I had failed miserably, because what they were really interested in was music and make-up and jewellery, all image and no substance.

Most of them had never heard of Elgar Vaughan, or Mathers, or Crowley, or Beckett, some not even Shelley and Stoker. It was hopeless; our interests were just too divergent and I'd given up, losing touch with every single one after I'd gone to university. There I had found better company among academics and like-minded students, but somehow I'd never found the right person for me, and again had largely lost touch when I left.

Then had come my PhD, three years of intense intellectual study, with the occasional boyfriend and the occasional lover, but nobody special. Not that I was necessarily a loner by instinct; more by habit. Rather it was that I'd never managed to gather the right people around me. Now, living on my own with my parents in opulent retirement in Jersey, there was almost no connection with my early life, but that was never more than a faint regret. Now, I might not have found the company, but I had at least found my place.

I'd been lingering over every detail since stepping out of the shower, but I hurried into my petticoats and dress, cursing softly to myself as I struggled with the catches.

Once I'd finally got it right all that remained were gloves, hat, scarf and parasol, and I was ready except for my hair and make-up, which I'd completely forgotten about while daydreaming about Elmcote Hall and the erotic possibilities of Victorian clothing.

No lady of the period above the age of sixteen would have dreamt of being seen with her hair down to her waist and without make-up. The parasol was dropped, scarf, hat and gloves removed, and after five frantic minutes in front of the mirror I was ready. Perhaps not quite five minutes, because by the time I'd made my way downstairs and out onto the carriage sweep there was a large red and blue coach parked there with at least fifty tourists milling around, one of whom appeared to be starting some of the others on a tour.

It should have been my big entrance – Sophie Page sweeps majestically from the door of Elmcote Hall, curtsies and addresses the assembly in a friendly yet dignified manner in keeping with the period and her surroundings. Instead I received a few curious stares as I walked up behind the unreasonably tall man who was explaining that the reason the carriage sweep was half covered in rubble was not because we had the builders in.

'Excuse me.'

He turned, revealing craggy features under a mop of black hair, like a Roman emperor who couldn't quite decide whether to be debauched or imperious. There was also a resemblance to a face I knew very well indeed – Elgar Vaughan – but I put that down to my overactive imagination. Fortunately he realised that I was standing behind him in full Victorian gear for a reason and stepped aside, gesturing me forward with a friendly but distinctly condescending smile.

'Our guide, I presume?'

'Yes, thank you. Right, good morning, ladies and gentlemen. I am Sophie Page, and I will be guiding you around Elmcote Hall today. As the gentleman –?'

'Richard Fox.'

'As Richard – Mr Fox, was just pointing out, very little has changed since the collapse of the tower in nineteen-sixteen. Elgar Vaughan, thirty-six at the time, had not expected to die, and left no will. Or at least, no will has ever been found. Elmcote Hall therefore passed to his nearest surviving relative, a cousin involved with the diplomatic service in India. Knowing the reputation of Elmcote Hall, the cousin...'

I stopped, confused, already close to the end of my carefully prepared talk when I should have been just beginning. Richard Fox had thrown me completely, and the only thing I could do was start again from the top, or I was going to get inextricably muddled up.

'Ladies and gentlemen, welcome to Elmcote Hall, or rather, the ruins of Elmcote Hall for, as you can see, only one wing remains habitable. Elmcote Hall was built in eighteen thirty-two, on the site of the previous manor and was named by Henry Vaughan, a friend and disciple of William Beckford, leader of the Gothic revival, whose influence can plainly be seen in the architecture and the, er, collapsing tower.'

I smiled, hoping for a laugh or two, even a smile of recognition. All I got were looks of rather blank expectancy, except from Richard Fox. He gave a dry chuckle, so presumably he at least knew about Beckford and the collapse of Fonthill Abbey. He went up in my estimation as I continued, starting my walk across the carriage sweep.

'If you would care to follow me this way,' I went on. 'Henry Vaughan might have aspired to the Gothic ideal, but otherwise his life was far from romantic. He had made his fortune in the cloth trade, although in the later years of his life he did his best to cover this up. His nephew, George Vaughan, who inherited the property, was a more down-to-earth individual who greatly expanded the family fortune, and whose major contribution to Elmcote was the formal gardens, his uncle having deliberately left the grounds a wilderness, much as they are now.'

'I'm not sure that's entirely accurate.'

I turned, smiling, to find the speaker, as if I didn't know who it would be, and got in before he could make me apologise for my error.

'I know what you're going to say, Mr Fox. Yes, Henry Vaughan's so-called wilderness was far from natural but carefully contrived to express a Gothic atmosphere. Nevertheless, he planted only native species, and they were untended, just as they are today. With the exception of the follies, and what remains of the walks . . .'

I was getting ahead of myself again, and stopped, still smiling, but cursing him in my mind.

'George Vaughan laid out formal gardens, of which only the lime walk, the main lawn and arboretum remain apparent. He lived from eighteen-seven to eighteen-eighty-nine, surviving both his sons, Henry and William, and the grandson, Albert, who would have stood to inherit in due time. Thus we find a rather peculiar situation: an old man in his seventies, living alone in the house but for an elderly housekeeper and a nurse, with his great-grandson, Elgar Vaughan. To say that the child's upbringing was eccentric would be an understatement. His great-grandfather had become senile, possibly in consequence of the maze of lead piping that supplies water to the house, and would walk the halls and gardens, a shuffling, muttering figure, yet still imposing, with his great height and bulky frame. What communication he had with the young Elgar Vaughan we do not know, but it can scarcely have been conventional.'

'It's said that old George used to pursue Elgar around

the house wearing the skin of a grizzly bear, complete with head,' Fox butted in.

'It is?'

'Yes.'

'Oh, well, I wish I'd know that when I did my thesis. Thank you, Mr Fox.'

'My pleasure, Miss Page.'

He gave a little bow, polite but somehow mocking, as I went on, now at the end of the house, where we could look down the full length of the lime walk to the Temple of Baphomet at the far end. I was completely out of sync.

'As I said, scarcely conventional. The housekeeper, Mrs Rourke –'

'Mrs O'Rourke.'

'Mrs O'Rourke – thank you again, Mr Fox – appears to have been something of a *Gauleiter*, keeping whole sections of the house locked off at all times and generally wielding the rod, all too often literally. The nurse, whose name was Florence Zeals – although no doubt Mr Fox will correct me if I'm wrong?'

'No, that's right.'

'I'm glad to hear it. Anyway, Florence doted on Elgar Vaughan and did her best to spoil him. Clearly she was an influence, and may be said to be the one person of whom Elgar was genuinely fond because when she died he had her buried in the grounds, beneath what became the temple of Gaia, the Earth Mother. By then, Elgar had been through ten years of school, at Quainton Hall in Buckinghamshire, and at Eton, neither of which appear to have had any major effect on his personality, but where he did make several influential friends.'

I was finally getting into my stride, and began to walk out between the limes.

'Born in eighteen-eighty, Elgar had still been a minor when George Vaughan died. For the remainder of his childhood the estate was managed by trustees and largely neglected, while Mrs O'Rourke had a free hand with the house. On coming of age, Elgar's first act was to dismiss the trustees. He then fired Mrs O'Rourke and, when Florence Zeals died some months later, the last restraint was removed, allowing him to fully express his personality.

'This he did. Wealthy, independent and responsible to nobody, he set about making the influences of his early life flesh – mystery, locked doors and concealment, harsh discipline – or, more often, the antitheses of them. Also, the original Henry Vaughan's library remained, barely touched in decades, and it included the classics, many works of an occult or alchemical nature, stories of Gothic horror, and more. All this Elgar Vaughan had absorbed, and one merely need glance at the temples he built in the grounds to appreciate the peculiar fusion of ancient and medieval concepts. Here, for instance, set at the end of the lime walk, is one of his principal places of prayer, the Temple of Baphomet –'

'Baphomet-Lilith, thus expressing the sexual duality that forms an essential part of Elgar Vaughan's belief system.'

'You're right, of course, Mr Fox, although I hadn't planned to go into quite so much theological detail. The temple, as you see, is pentagonal in shape, made of black granite, and in an exaggerated Gothic style. The carvings you see are not mere decoration but significant, each representing an element of Vaughan's belief system. Directly facing us, for instance, is Baphomet himself, represented as the Sabbatic Goat, a winged figure with the head and lower body of a goat, after the style of Eliphas Levi, another important nineteenth-century occultist. To the right of Baphomet the, er, fleshy gentleman with grapes in his hair represents Dionysus, Greek God of Wine, while to the left we have Lilith –'

'The Green Man has to be seen,' Fox butted in. 'He's on the far side.'

I hadn't actually meant to show them the Green Man, but it was too late. Richard Fox was already moving towards the rear of the temple and a good half of the group were following. One middle-aged matron in turquoise and cerise spandex already had her mouth half open, and I knew they'd seen him. I had no choice but to join them.

Elgar Vaughan's Green Man had the conventional features: the harsh stare, the wide mouth spouting acanthus. Unlike most Green Men he also had a body, entwined in acanthus which concealed almost everything except the most enormous and grotesquely detailed set of genitals. He was also erect, very definitely erect, with the great rounded head reaching to the level of his shoulder, the heavily veined shaft seeming to pulse with life and the gigantic testicles straining with sperm. All that was bad enough, but the combination of his expression and blatant arousal made him seem at once threatening and obscene. You knew exactly what he intended to do to you.

He had shocked me the first time I'd seen him, and my visitors were no different. I distinctly caught the word 'ungodly', but ignored it, simply waiting patiently until they'd all had a good stare before continuing the tour. After all, they presumably must have had some idea what they were letting themselves in for when they'd booked the tour.

I was sure Richard Fox would make some humorous remark at my expense, but for once he held his peace and I was able to continue. Most of the other temples and follies were so heavily overgrown they were inaccessible, some barely even visible. I was supposed to clear paths to them, but intended to be selective, and so far had only had a chance to start towards Henry Vaughan's tomb, a massive white marble sepulchre now locked within a cage of thick and twisted ivy boughs.

They behaved, by and large, even Richard Fox, asking only the occasional question and nothing I couldn't answer. I showed them what remained of George Vaughan's formal gardens, those temples visible in the thick woods, and the ruins of the east wing, with the rooms still open to the outside where the tower had crashed down through them, including the study.

'... where the best-known incident of Elgar Vaughan's life occurred, his meeting and subsequent argument with Aleister Crowley and Samuel Liddell Mathers. They, it seems, expected Vaughan to join the Golden Dawn as a novice and work his way up, and to use Elmcote Hall as their headquarters. Vaughan, both proud and arrogant, refused and finally threw both of them out. Had he not made this decision, no doubt the entire history of twentieth-century occultism would have been different.

'It was after the incident with Crowley and Mathers that Elgar Vaughan began to gather disciples around him. Many junior members of the Golden Dawn, disillusioned with hierarchy and infighting, appreciated Vaughan's less rigid system, and in particular his devotion to pleasure as a form of worship. His argument, in essence, is that if we are created to take pleasure in our bodies, then what better way to worship our Creator than to indulge those senses he has given us to the full? Some of Vaughan's actual behaviour may seem to sit a little uncomfortably with this philosophy, but now, a hundred years or so after the events, it is hard to separate fact from the accusations of his detractors and mere prurient speculation.'

We'd turned the corner of the east wing, coming on the remains of the tower itself with the huge winged gargoyle still standing drunkenly among the rubble. I gave them a few facts, a few accusations and a little of the prurient speculation, the milder stuff, which seemed to be what they'd come for to judge by their pleased tuts of shock and disapproval. Once more on the carriage sweep, I finally reached the point at which I'd started.

'... an abrupt halt with the outbreak of the Great War. For all his beliefs, Elgar Vaughan was a patriot, and joined up with the first wave of volunteers, as did his male disciples in what was then his coven, Sabbat Aceras –'

'Named for the Man Orchid, which George Vaughan had cultivated here, a pun, of course, on the Green Man.'

'Thank you, Mr Fox. With two exceptions, who remained to look after the house, the female members of the cult had soon become involved with war work. Of the thirteen, all seven male members died in the war. Vaughan's more imaginative commentators, and some of his detractors, have claimed that this was the result of a curse, even divine justice. The truth, I suspect, is more mundane. Vaughan at least, and probably the others, believed that being enlightened, and having undergone certain rites, they were immortal. Certainly we know that they fought with reckless courage, the consequences of which were pretty well inevitable. Vaughan himself had joined the Royal Flying Corps and was shot down over the trenches of Ypres in May nineteen-sixteen.

'One thing is less easily explained. On the day Elgar Vaughan died, perhaps at the very moment, the tower at Elmcote Hall collapsed. It stood here, rising above the central hall, to a height of one hundred and eighty feet, a monument to Gothic extravagance. Now, only the rubble remains.

'The six female members all survived the war, but without Vaughan's patronage, the cult quickly died out and they dispersed. Of the six, the last surviving member was Alice Scott, who died a few years ago at the ripe old age of one hundred and four, which I always feel disproves the curse theory. I had the privilege of interviewing Alice shortly before her death, and may say that she was entirely unrepentant.

'Elgar Vaughan left no legitimate children, and the nearest surviving relative was a descendant of William Vaughan, one Hubert Sands, who therefore inherited, despite rumours and speculation about both a will and missing wealth. Aware of the reputation of the estate, Sands wished only to distance himself from it as far as possible, and probably never even visited. Towards the end of his life he gave the estate in trust, with the curious stipulation that no major renovation work be carried out, and so Elmcote Hall remains as you see it. Thank you.'

There were a few questions; one couple had to have it pointed out to them that it was a seriously bad move to climb on the rubble, and that was that. Richard Fox seemed content with the display he'd made of his knowledge and didn't linger. I couldn't help but feel a stab of disappointment, as it would have been pleasant to discuss my pet topic with somebody who actually knew what they were talking about, but told myself firmly it had absolutely nothing to do with his being six foot plus with a look in his eyes that reminded be irresistibly of both Elgar Vaughan and a certain Green Man.

I had no more bookings for the rest of the day, but that did not mean I had nothing to do. There was the jungle clearance for a start, hours of hard sweaty labour with a machete, which I was not looking forward to. It was also completely impractical in Victorian costume, which gave me an excellent excuse to put it off. The lower part of the west wing also needed to be cleaned up a little so that the caterers for the wedding booked on the Saturday would be able to move in easily, and at some point I had to begin recataloguing the library, checking what was actually there against the original list made after Elgar Vaughan's death. It was too nice a day to be stuck inside.

After a while spent sitting on one of the huge blocks from the tower ruins, I decided to walk into the village as I was. It was a little unnerving, as I would undoubtedly get funny looks, but it was inevitable that they'd come to regard me as reclusive and eccentric anyway. People always do.

I refuse to conform in any case. Why should I? After all, if a modern woman, Madame Turquoise-and-cerise-spandex for instance, had walked into the village in Elgar Vaughan's time, she would have been given exactly the same sort of looks I would now get a hundred years later. The only difference would be that from an objective standpoint, she would deserve them. Victorian dress is so much more elegant, on any figure.

That didn't stop me feeling both excited and strangely guilty as I set off down the drive, rather as if I was in a minuscule bikini, or hadn't bothered to put my top back on to go and buy an ice-cream on the beach. My feelings aside, I was comfortable, warm against the crisp spring day under my layers of cotton and satin, and with my parasol to shade me from the eye-watering sunlight.

In Elgar Vaughan's time, Elmcote had been a cluster of cottages set around a church; just big enough, and with just enough in the way of respectable residents to react with suitable outrage at his behaviour. It was now very different – purest gin belt, still pretty in a rustic but rather contrived way, but with even the little red-brick two-up-two-downs owned by highly salaried city types. Even the village shop was run by a couple called Antonia and Patrice, and survived by selling such things as cappuccino, organic goat's cheese and sun-dried tomato in ciabata.

Organic goat's cheese and sun-dried tomato in ciabata

was fine for my lunch, at least in the absence of roast pheasant with a little fresh watercress and potatoes from the kitchen garden, or perhaps a slice of spit-roasted goat, which was how Elgar Vaughan had disposed of his sacrifices. Antonia even tried not to look surprised at the way I was dressed, contenting herself with a polite but ever so slightly condescending comment about it being expected in my job.

There was another woman in the shop too, very tall, with strong cheekbones and a lot of make-up, also a mid-blue skirt suit so sharp it verged on the kitsch. Her accent was pure East Coast USA, a confident low drawl as she had a pastrami on rye made up for her. Her scent was strong enough to cut through the tang of roast coffee beans and exotic cheeses. Her voice reminded me of Richard Fox, the same twang, but harsher, more strident. Having decided, only half in jest, that she was a high-class hooker, that was all the attention I gave her before walking across to the edge of the river.

A bench made the ideal place for lunch, where I went to watch the swans and the boats going by as I ate and thought about Elgar Vaughan and Richard Fox. I wasn't really in the mood for company, but when the American woman came and sat down beside me it would have been impossible not to respond to her friendly greeting.

'Hi, I'm Julie, Julie Voigtstein. You new around here?'

She'd extended a hand and I took it, surprised by the strength of her grip as we shook. Her face was one big painted smile as I answered.

'Yes, I'm Sophie Page, the warden at Elmcote Hall, up the road. You?'

'Yeah, mine's the place two up from the store. Quaint.'

I turned to look, wondering how much a three-storey house facing the Thames cost to rent and telling myself that she probably wasn't a high-class hooker at all, but a money broker or something equally mundane. Making conversation with strangers was never my strong point, and I didn't really know what to say, but she had no such scruples.

'This is great, ain't it? So quiet. My old place on the East Side, it was just go, go, go, twenty-four/seven. When I came over I thought, I'll take a place in the West End, but then, when I came out to eat with the boss, well there it was, half what I'd been paying, and right on the river. I had to have it.'

'Do you work in the City then?'

'Forty-seventh Securities. The London office needed a kick in the pants and believe me, I am the girl to give it to them.'

'I can imagine. Sorry, I don't mean to be rude –'

'You English, always apologising. So what's with the outfit? Is this a theme place you run?'

'No ... well, I suppose you could put it that way. Elmcote Hall was where Elgar Vaughan lived. I do tours and look after everything.'

'You don't say? Maybe I'll look in on you one day. For now, got to run. They want me back on the floor by two. No peace for the wicked.'

She got up and made for the bridge, still eating her sandwich. I couldn't help but smile. She was everything I'm not – brassy, super-confident, on the ball and, above all, loud – but it was impossible not to like her. Just the way she walked, fast and straight, with her shiny black heels clicking on the cobbles of the river walk, radiated certainty. For one thing, I was sure she'd have dealt with Richard Fox with a great more skill than I had.

I finished my sandwich, bought a few things for dinner and a bottle of wine to celebrate my first day of work, then started back for the Hall. A crisp morning had blossomed into a warm afternoon, very warm considering there were still crocuses out in the tubs along the river. I walked slowly, thinking of how the area would have changed since Elgar Vaughan's day. The tarmac on the road, the cars, all the paraphernalia of electricity and phone lines, was new, but it was superficial. Otherwise, little had changed. There might have been more people working among the scatter of little fields and woods where the land rose from the river, but it would have looked much the same. So would the river itself, the distant downs in one direction and the tiny biscuit-coloured spires of Oxford in the other.

The double cluster of gigantic cooling towers might have come as a bit of a shock, but I could have explained them away as a temple to his new religion. He would have been immensely pleased, because for all his reputation as a charlatan I was convinced his intention had been to found a new religion, based on pleasure without guilt and seeing man as an element of the natural world rather than above it. Again, some of the things he'd actually done, or was supposed to have done, sat a little uneasily with his preaching, but I for one would have been able to come to terms with it.

I could have been one of the thirteen, I was sure, and coped as well as any, perhaps better. The thought sent a little excited shiver down my spine, as it always did, a mixture of pleasure and apprehension. Could I have coped with being naked in the company of twelve others, including Elgar Vaughan himself? The answer was yes, quite clearly. There would have been no embarrassment because I'd have been part of it. I'd have revelled in my nudity. Could I have joined in an orgy, setting aside my personal choices to allow others to enjoy me as they wished, and to take the same privilege myself? Again the answer was yes, although just the thought made my tummy feel weak. I knew I'd have to have had a fair bit of wine too, but there had never been a shortage of that. In Elgar Vaughan's time the cellar had been lined with pipes of Port and bin upon bin of bottles. Could I have coped if I'd been selected as the celebrant for one of his notorious rituals? Again, it was an intriguing thought, enough to make me bite my lip, but I knew the answer was probably no.

They had been extreme, some very extreme, the sort of thing Aleister Crowley would have thought twice about. Or so it was supposed, but to judge from some of the prints he'd had made, inspired by the rituals, the most outrageous of the rumours were no more than plain unadorned description. I might not have coped, I had to admit it, but it would have been intriguing to watch, providing that blend of shock and arousal I like so much.

Still, there was no harm in thinking about it. When I got back to the Hall I made for the Temple of Baphomet, telling myself I was making a daily inspection of the grounds but knowing full well I just wanted to daydream. Unfortunately, having brought my visitors there had taken away a little of the magic of the place; not much, but enough to tarnish the atmosphere. I walked around it, admiring Baphomet, Dionysus, the Green Man, Gaia and Lilith, but it was impossible to get my mind clear, especially of the thought of Richard Fox, so smug.

The temple was also in full view of the house, down the length of the lime walk, and I was beginning to think I might need a little privacy. In among the tangle of overgrown rhododendrons and exotic trees that had once been George Vaughan's arboretum was a smaller temple, or possibly just a folly, to which I made my way. It was more classical than Gothic, although undoubtedly part of the complex as five white marble pillars supported the roof. Above it, a beautiful Tree of Heaven cast dappled shade over the cupola, and inside a squat pentagonal cylinder of black stone stood at the centre of the little space, presumably an altar, but it made an excellent seat.

It would have been excellent for other things too. The arboretum screened it on all sides, ensuring privacy. Nobody could have seen, nobody would have known. Nobody was going to know, because the overgrown bushes had made access difficult, and approaching unheard impossible. I'd had to bunch my dress at the front to get through, and even then pause occasionally to detach bits of twig. Despite my solitude, having to walk like that, and so show my stocking-clad calves, had given me a gentle but delicious sense of embarrassment.

I couldn't not do it, that was the thing, accidental and helpless exposure, and if it was meaningless by modern standards, then that made no difference. Here there was nothing to say I was in the twenty-first century. I could let my imagination run riot, peopling the woods with fauns and satyrs, and a sense of presence, the huge, immeasurably virile Green Man lurking somewhere in the deeps, threatening and yet so compelling.

The touch of embarrassment was just what I needed too, that little naughty thrill to go with being so alone, and so out of time. There really was no difference. Elgar Vaughan could have come across me and the only thing out of the ordinary would have been to find a woman he didn't know in his temple. The explanation that I wanted to be an acolyte would have been easy.

Or I might already have been an acolyte, sitting alone in the temple imagining what would be asked of me in the same place that night. I'd be uncertain, a little scared even, but also filled with joy and desire. As Vaughan advised in his writings, I would clear my mind of all the encumbrances of modern society and become pure elemental woman, Gaia and Lilith at once.

Elgar Vaughan had loved secrets, and had been cautious of the authorities. Very little of his rituals had been written down, especially those details which might have been used in evidence against him. There was some though, and I'd read every word. I knew how the initiation ceremony had begun, and why – designed not so much for spiritual reasons, but to discourage the idly curious or anyone attempting to infiltrate his group. Of the deeper secrets there were hints, and what could be guessed from the pictures, but those were enough to set me blushing as I sat myself down on the altar stone.

I would have gone to the study, that same room now a forlorn shell of smashed brick and rotting panelling, then laid out in rich dark colours, the walls hung with his disturbing pictures and darkly erotic prints. Vaughan would have been there, with others, to hear my formal declaration of intent. He himself would have replied, telling me that to be accepted I must follow his every command without hesitation. I'd have agreed, knowing it was a test, shaken, but determined.

The first order would have been to accept a blindfold, which I'd have done, standing stock still as one of the other women wrapped a thick band of black cloth around my head and pinned it into the mass of my hair, leaving me completely unable to see. She, and one other, would have taken my hands, leading me with faltering steps out from the house and perhaps to this very temple.

Beyond that, I didn't know what would have happened, except that it would have been beyond what any woman who'd failed to free herself from the respectable Victorian or Edwardian mindset could have coped with. That was for certain because, despite what Vaughan's detractors said, his female acolytes had not been prostitutes surrendering themselves only in desperation, for money. Each and every one had been from upper- or upper-middle-class families, inevitably bringing the full wrath of the establishment down on Vaughan's head.

What would they have done to me? Impossible to know for sure, easy to imagine. Possibly it would have simply been sexual, pleasures we now take for granted, but which would have seemed extreme for a respectable girl of the time. With a dozen men and women watching, they were fairly extreme even now. So perhaps I'd have been made to kneel before the altar and provide oral sex. Elgar Vaughan himself would be first, sat just as I was, his trousers wide to expose his big smooth manhood, as shown in so many pictures, already erect.

I'd be taken by my shoulders, very gently, and eased down on him, full of shock and embarrassment as my head filled with the scent of him, but doing it, my mouth open, expecting to be filled with hot hard penis. Only it wouldn't be, not at first. First I'd be made to kiss his arse, a wonderfully lewd detail he'd borrowed from the Satanists. Only then, once I'd pressed my lips to his anal ring, would I be permitted to take in his cock.

If he was anything like his pictures he'd have been huge, long and thick and smooth, as a man's cock should be; something to worship, to adore, to lick and suck and rub until I'm ready to have it pushed deep into my body. In just moments I'd have lost myself, sucking eagerly, not in surrender but in delight, worshipping him until the compliment was repaid and he'd come, giving me his sperm deep in my mouth.

From the moment I'd decided to go to the temple I'd known I was going to masturbate. It had just taken me a little time to work myself up. I wanted to be in the same position as in my imagination, kneeling at the altar, and quickly got down. As I pulled up my dress I was already trembling in anticipation, and concern for being watched, for all my loneliness. Perhaps Richard Fox had come back and was at that very moment lurking in among the rhododendrons, his face cool and cynical, amused by my wantonness as my dress and petticoats came up, as I pulled open the split of my combinations to bare my bottom to the cool spring air.

It felt good, my bare skin tingling, bringing my mind

to focus on my very hot, very wet sex. I pushed the thought of Richard Fox from my mind, too proud to pleasure myself over him, even if he would never know. Instead I imagined being made naked behind as I sucked on Elgar Vaughan's beautiful cock, not knowing why they were exposing me, only that I had to accept it.

Once Vaughan was finished, another man would replace him. I wouldn't even know who, but I'd take him in all the same, now with my naked bottom thrust out, not knowing if I'd been bared simply for the sake of my exposure, to make me available from the rear, or so I could be beaten. Elgar Vaughan had shared the common Victorian obsession with flagellation and whippings had been commonplace, both for orgiastic pleasure and as elements of ritual.

My cheeks would be twitching in apprehension, but I'd have been ready, for caresses or for smacks. It would have been caresses, a hand slipped in between my legs, to cup my sex, to rub me gently, skilfully, bringing me up to helpless, gasping ecstasy as I sucked on the man in my mouth.

I'd reached back, curving my hand around my bottom to touch myself, teasing and stroking all those most sensitive places. They wouldn't have been content with bringing me to a climax under their fingers either. I might well even be virgin, and the man, or even woman – because I'd have no say in the matter – who was touching me would realise. Whatever they'd intended before would be forgotten because my fate would now be plain, my initiation decided.

Not that it would be quick. Each man would take his satisfaction in my mouth, one by one, until I was dizzy with reaction. By the time the last of them was done, Elgar Vaughan, ever virile, would be ready again, strong and hard in one or other women's mouths, a man's even. Nor would I be spared having to pleasure the women –

to refuse would be evidence of a closed mind. I'd have to lick, my tongue applied between their thighs, my head guided to make me lick where it gave them the greatest pleasure, until all six had come.

The others would want to explore me, to open my dress and display my naked breasts, to stroke and smack my bottom, to investigate my virgin sex, to rub me, to tease my anus. Maybe they would beat me, hard enough to leave my bottom aglow, but I'd be so far gone I'd simply wriggle in pleasure and lick all the harder. All of them would be delighted at my response, and they'd be indulging each other too, so I'd be surrounded by laughter, sighs of pleasure, moans of ecstasy.

I was moaning in ecstasy myself, right on the edge of orgasm as I pictured myself bent over the altar stone, my pretty, modest clothing dishevelled to show me in front and behind, the ring of laughing happy pagans, and Elgar Vaughan, his beautiful smooth erection in his hand, squatting down behind me as they all crowded close to watch me deflowered, except the woman who would be holding my head firmly to her sex. They'd have me trapped, helpless, but it wouldn't matter. I'd be willing and eager, squirming with pleasure as Elgar Vaughan put the head of his cock to my virgin sex, in full view, and pushed.

My scream as I came could probably have been heard in the village, certainly at the Hall. Not that I cared, with the image of my virginity being taken over the altar stone burning in my head as I shook and gasped my way through orgasm. Right at the peak Richard Fox tried to intrude himself, replacing Elgar Vaughan as the man taking my imaginary virginity, but even then I didn't care. If he'd come up behind me for real at that instant and just plunged deep inside me I'd have been unable to stop him.

2

I did wonder, once I was back in Elmcote Hall sipping a glass of Sauvignon, whether there wasn't more to my little piece of misbehaviour in the grounds than simple lust. Risking being caught masturbating is not something I normally do, and there had been a risk, small but real. Yet I had quite simply been unable to stop myself. Was it possible that there was some lingering aura which has driven me to be so rude, and to think of sex with both Elgar Vaughan and a man who I'd not only met a bare few hours before, but who I'd found intensely irritating?

It had to be at least possible. There were almost no specifics about what had happened at which temple, but if even a tenth of the rumours were true it was plenty, and often. Possibly one of Elgar Vaughan's female acolytes really had indulged a dozen men and women over the altar stone in what I'd come to think of as the arboretum temple? Maybe some beautiful wild Edwardian girl had even lost her virginity that way, the same way I'd imagined it as I came, with my mind made susceptible by where I was, by my solitude, by my ecstasy?

True or not, it was a beautiful thought which stayed fixed in my head for the rest of the day. Nobody else turned up and I spent the rest of the afternoon in the library, browsing through the Vaughans' magnificent collection of arcane books. All the really valuable ones were gone, but by no means the most interesting, and I was soon lost in a paper on the nature of angels and devils presented in a manner every bit as thoughtful and scholarly as a modern treatise on psychotherapy or economic theory.

Only the gradual shift in tone of the sunlight coming in through the high stained-glass windows marked the passage of time, and I only stopped when the sun was full on me, staining the air with a dozen vivid colours. The central window showed the same five figures as the Temple of Baphomet, although in less lurid detail, so that I was bathed in a shifting representation of Dionysus as I read; the paper and my dress tinted rich purple, viridian and soft pink.

I wanted to watch the sunset and went to the window as the great orange globe sank gently behind the temple, making its shadow grow long between the twin rows of limes like some monstrous phallus extending towards me. With the sun right on the horizon even the grass was tinged red-orange, with the shadow of the temple now touching the house, reinforcing my fantasy of surrendering my virginity to Elgar Vaughan.

Reality was rather more prosaic, but one can only wait so long, and twenty-five would have been a waste, not to mention the object of my fantasies having been dead for ninety years. Smiling for my own daydream, I retired to the kitchen to cook myself a dinner of trout and green peas with organic bread, washed down with the rest of the Sauvignon. It was dark by the time I'd finished and cleared up, so with nothing else to do, and really quite tired, I went up to bed.

It was a mistake because I woke in the early hours of the morning to absolute silence and absolute darkness, also cold. The night before I'd been dog tired, and had slept right through, so only now began to feel the night-time atmosphere of the house take effect. Most people would have found it eerie, lonely and silent, yet infused with so much. I had no such qualms, lying still in the blackness, the air cold on my face. I knew I should try and get back to sleep so that I could make a proper start on my work the next day, but I couldn't.

I might have lain like that for as much as an hour before I became aware of a subtle change in the darkness. At first I thought it was just random impulses from my eyes, but this was consistently yellow and oddly rhythmic. It also had position, on the lining where one of the heavy curtains was turned back a little. I sat up in bed, telling myself it would prove to be caused by car headlights on some distant road, but determined to investigate.

I moved to the window with my pyjamas hugged around me against the cold and peered out. At first there was nothing and I thought I might have been imagining things after all, or that if it had been a car then it had passed on. I waited, half hoping that whatever had caused the lights would come again, half hoping it wouldn't.

It did, and it was no car. A light appeared, flickering, but quite clear, in the arboretum. I immediately felt my stomach go tight. Somebody was there, with a torch, moving through the trees towards the Temple of Baphomet, perhaps more than one person. Yes, there was a second torch, somewhat behind. Possibly it was just kids out on a dare, to visit Elgar Vaughan's house at night, or vandals, or poachers. Whoever it was, my job was to get rid of them, something I'd assured the Trustees I could cope with at my interview, but which I no longer felt so confident about.

The phone was by my bed. I could have called the police – and rapidly picked up a reputation as a silly cow who started at shadows and wasted their precious time. I wasn't going to do it, not unless I had to. Instead I watched for a moment, biting my lip as the twin torches approached the temple. It was definitely where they were headed, and now I really had to do something. If the centrepiece of the grounds was vandalised on my second night as warden it was not going to look good.

Pushing open the window, I leant out. It was bitterly cold, stinging my chest as I filled my lungs with air, determined to get my voice as loud and deep as possible, then stopped, wondering what to say. 'Get off my land' would just sound silly, and it wasn't my land anyway. 'Go away or I'll set the dogs on you' was all very well, only there weren't any dogs. 'I can see you' didn't seem right, neither did 'What do you think you're doing?', which is, if you think about it, a pretty silly question.

I had to do something because they're reached the temple, their torches now reflecting off black stone. For an instant I glimpsed a figure, no more than a silhouette, but clear enough for me to realise it was no kid but a full-grown man, and quite tall at that. Once more I drew in my breath.

'Just fuck off, will you!'

The effect was electric. One of them dropped his torch. I heard the thump and a tinkle of broken glass, a curse, and another voice. The remaining torch beam appeared, in the lime walk, and for one awful moment I thought they might be coming at me. Instead they ran, not into the arboretum, but directly away from the house, scrambling through the fringe of undergrowth beyond the temple and over the fence.

I could still see their light as they moved away around the edge of the estate, right up until they reached the lane. My heart was beating fast and I felt ever so slightly sick, but I'd done it. They were gone.

I never did manage to get back to sleep but hovered on the edge, my mind wandering over all my favourite things, and yet starting at every distant noise or change in the light, either real or imagined. The local fauna seemed to have formed a conspiracy against me: rabbits thumped, foxes barked, an assortment of night birds called, and that was without every driver in Oxfordshire joining in. For maybe ten, fifteen minutes there would be total silence, followed by a selection of noises guaranteed to have me sitting up in bed with my ears straining. When the heating finally came on it was worse, with the ancient system emitting a muffled cacophony of bumps and groans that would have had your average spiritualist running shrieking down the drive.

By then the sky had begun to lighten so I got up and made myself bacon and eggs for breakfast, which I felt I deserved. It was still quite cold, even with a dressing gown over my pyjamas, and when I came out of my shower I was jumping up and down on my toes as I dried myself. That made my Victorian clothes all the more tempting, but I knew I should make a start on the grounds, while after the previous night there would be something comforting about carrying a machete.

Thick undies, jeans and jumper, my overalls on top and tough work boots seemed to be the order of the day, with my hair pinned up and a pair of heavy-duty gloves. In the shed there was not only a machete but a billhook, a sickle, a mattock and a scythe. I chose the machete and the mattock and as I started down the lime walk I was telling myself they were the sensible choice for the job in hand, and had nothing to do with my prowlers.

Not that they'd have been there anyway, but the torch was. It was a black rubber one, long enough to hold four big batteries, and with a yellow lens, now shattered on the marble of the temple floor. No damage was evident except, just possibly, a few scrape marks around the central pentagonal slab. I examined them for a while before deciding it was just my imagination, cleared up, and got down to work.

An hour later the sun had lifted above the woods and

I was hot, sticky and sorely regretting my choice of clothing. I had also completed the path to Henry Vaughan's tomb, along with a circle around it to allow people to admire the inscriptions and carvings. Clearing the bits of root, raking and seeding could wait until I had the right tools, and I moved on to do the sundial at the edge of the formal lawn, part of George Vaughan's contribution and also tourist friendly.

I thought about my problem with security as I worked. If there were people sneaking around the grounds at night I needed to make them think again, preferably with the minimum of exertion and definitely at no personal risk. The Trust wasn't going to be prepared to fund anything serious in the way of fencing, while I personally preferred to have as little as possible to do with CCTV. Possibly I could get a dog, something along the lines of the Hound of the Baskervilles, only bigger, but I could already see the headlines: 'Mrs Lowensky Eaten by Gigantic Hound'. It was still an option.

By the time I'd cleared a path to the base of the sundial I was melting. The sun was high in the sky and I was running sweat, with the occasional puff of cool air against my face only tantalising me. I badly wanted to strip off, but there were a lot of brambles and I knew I'd get severely scratched. Going in just my knickers under my overalls was a much better idea, because if I didn't get my jumper off the next person who visited the Hall was going to find me on the lawn, baked.

There was nobody about and the only windows I was visible from were my own and those of the ruined east wing. I peeled off as fast as I could, sure that a couple of hundred camera-wielding tourists would appear around the corner of the Hall at any instant. Being in nothing but knickers and socks felt absolutely wonderful, not just cool, but naughty too. It was no time for games though, and I quickly put my overalls, boots and gloves back on before wading back into the fray.

I felt better, although it was still hot work. Being near nude under my overalls also inspired some of the same feelings as being in Victorian dress, a private naughtiness I've always enjoyed. The friction of my nipples on the coarse material of my overalls as I swung the machete was also nice, at first, but quickly became too much. I decided to stop, take a shower and an early lunch, then do some cataloguing, but as I dropped the mattock and machete by my discarded clothing a better idea came to me.

According to the maps I'd seen there was a lake in the main area of woodland, beyond the sundial. Possibly it had dried out, or become choked with reeds, but possibly it was still open, and might just be a nice place to swim. At least I could investigate. I left my clothes on the lawn and walked down, taking the machete.

I needed it. The path, or what had once been a path, was so overgrown that I had to hack my way through again and again. By the time I got down to the shallow valley bottom I was hotter than ever, but one look and I knew it had been worth it. The lake was not only still there, but simply wonderful. What had once been a fringe of ornamental trees had grown so tall that it was completely hidden from view, with thick undergrowth beneath them. There were reeds, mostly dead and brown, but with vigorous, bright green growth pushing up among them. They were not a problem though, because they shielded the open water, which looked cool and clear and deep. Better still, at the very centre was an island with a folly and a marble bridge leading out to it.

For a moment I just stood, gazing at the perfectly still surface in which my form was reflected with the trees all around me. It was so easy to imagine Elgar Vaughan's people there, naked and laughing, or creatures more wonderful still, nymphs and dryads, with Pan himself, disporting themselves in the cool clear water.

There was really no option but to go in. The marble was green with algae, but I was mucky anyway, so simply dropped my clothes where I stood. My knickers came last, and I hesitated, before telling myself not to be silly and popping them off. Nude, deliciously, unrestrainedly nude, I climbed up onto the balustrade, spent one long moment stretching in the brittle sunlight, and jumped.

It was freezing, like being plunged into a vat of ice, a sudden shock that hit me even before my head had gone under, and left me gasping and shaking, also kicking my feet frantically to keep my mouth above water, because it was even deeper than I'd imagined. It might have been cold, but it was gloriously refreshing, and I knew it was going to be one of my favourite places, especially come the summer. For the moment I had a few minutes splashing about and a moment to float on my back and soak up the tranquillity of the place. Then I was going to have to get out and make a hasty retreat for the house.

Even as I hauled myself dripping onto the island I was realising that I hadn't really thought things through. I was stark naked and soaking wet, with three hundred yards of extremely rough path and a stretch of lawn between me and the house. I should really have put my overalls on, but they were sweaty and horrible, so I decided to stick with my boots and make a dash for it.

I was actually giggling as I ran back up the path, dodging the bits of bramble and nettle I'd missed before and, as I passed the sundial, really enjoying my little streak, only to stop short. Somebody was standing on the lawn, their back to me, but right by my clothes, and just turning round. For one awful moment the blood was rushing to my cheeks before I realised who it was: Julie, my brash New Yorker of the day before, who of all people I could not imagine being bothered by my nudity.

My cheeks were still hot with blushes, and it took a little courage to wave cheerfully and step out onto the lawn with a greeting.

'Julie, hi, am I glad it's you!'

She raised her eyebrows.

'Nice hooters, honey.'

'Very funny. No work today?'

'Not for me. Migraine.'

'Oh, maybe I can get you something. Hang on a minute.'

'No, I'm just fine now. Has this place got a pool?'

'No, there's a lake down the hill. I've been working on the grounds all morning and I couldn't resist a dip. You should come with me sometime.'

'In this weather? They sure make 'em tough around here.'

'Not that tough. I had intruders last night and all I managed to do was yell at them from my window.'

'Intruders? Jeez! Did you call the police?'

'No. I wanted to try and deal with it myself. Why, do you think I should have?'

'No, so long as they ran, I guess you did the right thing.'

'Hopefully, but it's not something I'd actually expected to be a problem.'

'Just kids, probably. I wouldn't worry.'

'No, they were grown men, two of them.'

'Burglars?'

'No, I don't think so. They went to the Temple of Baphomet. That's the one at the end of the lime walk.'

'Anything valuable there?'

'Not as such. I suppose the carvings might fetch a bit from a collector, but it would have to be to order. Otherwise there's nothing there.'

'That'll be it then.'

'You say that, but they're huge, and an integral part of the structure. I doubt two men could even carry them, and you couldn't just take them out because the roof would collapse.'

'Just taking a look-see?'

'That's more probable. In which case they'll presumably be back.'

'Not if you warned them off.'

'Do you think so?'

'Sure. This is what you do, you bullshit. Print out a notice saying "Police Aware" or "These Premises are Under Surveillance", get it laminated and stick it up inside.'

'Do you think that would work? I was thinking of getting a dog.'

'Dogs are a pain in the ass. They tie you down. And they smell. Keep it simple.'

As we'd been speaking I'd pulled my jumper on, and quickly gathered up my things. Julie was smiling, her red lip-sticked mouth just twitched up at one corner, and I suppose I must have looked pretty ridiculous in my pink woolly jumper with my bare bum poking out underneath as I gathered my clothes. She took the mattock and machete for me, holding them out from her body with her face set in an expression of considerable distaste as we walked back towards the house.

I left her in the kitchen with a glass of red wine and went up to change into something more practical. By the time I got down again she'd drifted into the library and was looking over one of Elgar Vaughan's more disturbing prints. She spoke the moment she saw me.

'So this is the guy who lived here? What a freak-out!'

Moving closer to inspect the picture, I nodded my head. It was one of those Elgar Vaughan had commissioned himself and showed him enthroned on the right hand side of a huge goat-headed hermaphrodite figure and surrounded by men, women, devils, angels and a dozen sorts of curious creatures. Most were nude, some were copulating, or very obviously aroused, and Elgar Vaughan had definitely had a thing about big cocks, or rather, impossibly huge cocks, like the ones Aubrey Beardsley drew for *Lysistrata*, but bigger. Julie was just amused.

'I've been at a few dos just like that, only New York guys are hung better. You not in the Scarlett O'Hara outfit today?'

'No, that's for the tours and I don't have any today. Besides, *Gone with the Wind* is set in your Civil War, thirty years too early. Fashions changed faster in Victorian times than they do today, and they didn't go in for retro.'

'No?'

It had been meant to be a joke, a pretty weak one maybe, but still a joke. Her answer was dead-pan serious. Since leaving college I didn't get many opportunities to really indulge my passion, and couldn't resist wading in.

'No. You're right in thinking that British and American fashions tended to develop in tandem, with minor differences, as did those of the rest of Europe, or at least, the majority of it. However, fashion changed year by year, and was less flexible than it is today. It also followed repeated patterns. For instance, the crinolines of the Civil War period, your Civil War of course, became larger and bulkier with time, because the leaders of fashion always needed to stay one step ahead of everyone else.'

'What's new.'

'Eventually crinolines became so vast they were impractical, at which point unsupported skirts came back. The cycle had been repeated before with panniers, and was repeated again with the bustle, towards the end of the nineteenth century. The S-curve look, which I was wearing and is created by a shaped corset, was primarily an Edwardian thing. Scarlett O'Hara would have considered it completely unacceptable, bizarre even. To make a modern comparison, imagine a woman in the 'seventies wearing low-rise jeans to show the top of her thong. People would think she was weird. That's one of the odd things about fashion, the way people see a choice of look they know perfectly well to be transient as an absolute, and it was the same then as now. People were extraordinarily inflexible about it. Note that even in Elgar Vaughan's orgy scene those who have any clothes on are dressed in the height of fashion, for all their avowal of breaking away from the restrictions of society. The same was true of hippies, of course.'

She nodded. 'You really know your stuff.'

'I'd like to think so. My PhD thesis was on Vaughan. My interest in clothing is more of a hobby.'

She was peering at the print, at a detail I'd always admired, of two figures, male and female, fully dressed, admiring the truly stupendous erection of a third, a naked satyr with the torso of a man but the lower body and head of a goat. The artist had managed to make the goat's face exude pride, while the woman looked both aroused and amused. The man was licking the monstrous penis, rather delicately, as if testing the flavour.

'He was gay, this guy Vaughan?'

'Yes and no; certainly not in the modern sense. At least, Elgar Vaughan would never have recognised himself as homosexual. He'd have laughed at the idea. No, Vaughan's sexuality, like his religion, derived from Greek and Roman concepts, from pagan ritual both real and imagined, and also from the French libertines of the eighteenth century. To him, the important thing was to take pleasure in your body, without reservation. Whether a partner was male or female would have made no more difference to him than, say, if they were blonde or brunette, tall or short, black or white.'

'Some people get well hung-up over that last one.'

'Which is their loss. Elgar Vaughan would have seen restricting oneself to the opposite sex, or the same sex, in exactly that way.'

'I've met guys like that.'

There was a hint of laughter in her voice, which I was glad of. So many people get sniffy about that sort of thing, even when it doesn't relate to them personally. I was beginning to like Julie, for all her brash attitude. She was easy to talk to, without feeling self-conscious or minding what I said, which is an unusual combination.

I asked her if she'd like a tour of the Hall and grounds, which she did, then lunch. All I could scrape together was paté on toast with a bit of salad, which she accepted as if I was doing her some great favour. By the time we'd finished we were chatting like old school friends, and I'd accepted her suggestion of going up to London at the weekend to visit a club. It wasn't normally my sort of thing at all, but with her I could imagine it being fun.

Julie didn't leave until teatime, and I walked back to the village with her to pick up more supplies. I was feeling a little guilty because while I'd worked hard for most of the morning, I'd spent the afternoon chatting. Technically, Julie was as much a visitor as anyone else, except that she hadn't paid and I had shown her around, so it could have been worse, but as I walked back I made a resolution to be more organised.

I'd bought dinner, a few things for the fridge, and more wine – three bottles this time – so by the time I got back I felt as if my arms were being pulled off. Just as I'd put everything down to open the door I realised that there was somebody coming down the drive behind me, very tall, hawk-faced – Richard Fox. It was the last thing I wanted.

He had that same condescending little grin on his face as he came close.

'Hello, Sophie. Not dressed today?'

I ignored the remark and put on my most detached professional face.

'I'm afraid I'm just closing up.'

'Good, then you'll be able to come out to the Angel with me.'

'The Angel? I already have my dinner, thank you.'

'What, eat alone when you could be wined and dined by the best-looking guy you've ever met? I don't buy that.'

It was not easy to find an answer to his sheer arrogance, so I contented myself with going indoors, only to have him follow before I could put my bags down again to shut the door. Short of attempting to throw him out physically, which might have failed, there wasn't a lot I could do, so I began to put my things way. He sat down on the corner of the table, frowning as he picked up one of the bottles of wine I'd bought.

'A Nero d'Avola? You making pasta?'

'I have a pigeon.'

'You don't want this then, much too heavy and coarse. Pigeon needs a good Burgundy, maybe Barolo if you insist on Italian.'

'Look, Mr Fox –'

'No, I can't possibly allow you to eat pigeon with this. I'm taking you to the Angel. You'll have to change, of course, 'cause they can be a bit stuffy in these parts I find. No doubt you have a little black number tucked away somewhere? Don't all women?'

'Look, Mr Fox –'

'Or perhaps something in red perhaps, something to

give you a touch of the vamp. It would suit you, that look, with all that wonderful hair.'

'Look, Mr Fox –'

'Not that I mind you in jeans, of course. You look great in jeans. I was watching that little round bottom of yours move as you walked down the drive, and I must say, I've seldom seen better.'

'Mr Fox! Will you shut up for a moment, please? Now listen. You are not the man of my dreams. You are not the handsomest man I have ever met. You do not even come close. You are arrogant, conceited, inordinately vain and generally obnoxious. Nor do I appreciate comments on my anatomy from a complete stranger. Now will you kindly leave?'

He put the bottle down and drew a long satisfied sigh.

'Ah, feisty! Excellent, I love it when they fight! Now come on, enough joking around. I haven't booked a table, so we'll need to be there early if we're going to get a decent table.'

'Mr Fox, it's not going to work. Now could you go, please?'

He didn't move, and didn't answer immediately, but shook his head and gave a brief glance to the other two bottles of wine before replying, now reflective.

'It's curious, isn't it, the way society works? I mean, how a woman always feels the need to put up a little resistance when both she and the man in question know exactly what they want. Or is it a modern thing, do you think? Perhaps cave girls were just the same? I'm a little surprised at you though, a Vaughan scholar. I thought you were more intelligent too.'

I drew my breath in, determined not to rise to the bait.

'Please could you leave, now.'

He rose.

'Oh very well, if you insist on playing teenage games.

But wouldn't it be far more adult, and far easier, simply to give in to our natural feelings?'

'Mr Fox, I know you are having some difficulty taking this in, but I am not attracted to you.'

'Oh nonsense. Look at me, six foot three, well proportioned, with a rugged masculinity you'd be hard put to match. Can you honestly say you're not impressed?'

'Mr Fox, I realise this may come as a shock, but despite what you obviously believe, women, and myself in particular, need a little more than just a set of physically pleasing contours. Personality is a good start.'

'You sound like you're quoting from *Cosmopolitan*. Come, come, Sophie, I know you're brighter than that. You know as well as I do that the reason you're trying to reject me is that accepting without a fuss will hurt your pride, and that only because our ludicrous culture penalises women who accept their natural feelings. What would you like me to do? What would allow you to save face? Perhaps I should sing the *Birdie Song* in a nasal falsetto until you give in? Or should I carry you off across my shoulder, John Wayne style? Speaking of John Wayne, I don't imagine for a moment that putting you across my knee for an old-fashioned spanking would do any good? No, you'd just run off squealing about assault and sexism.'

For a moment he'd rendered me speechless, his remarks simply too arrogant for a riposte, while the last one was truly outrageous, but uncomfortably close to my fantasy of the day before, and had sent the blood straight to my cheeks. I had to say something because there was at least a kernel of truth in what he was saying, but knowing that made me all the more stubborn. My first thought was to pretend I had a boyfriend, a fiancé even, only I knew it wouldn't make the slightest bit of difference. There was another choice, which had to work. I adopted my coldest voice.

'As a matter of fact, Mr Fox, the reason I do not want to go out with you, aside from your unspeakable behaviour, is that I am a lesbian. I prefer women, and after a few minutes of your company I am reminded why, so thank you.'

'My pleasure, always glad to be of service. So, um, given that you're a "lesbian", there's no reason whatsoever why you shouldn't come to the Angel with me. We can even split the bill if you prefer?'

He was completely unfazed, once more leaving me briefly speechless. Also, from the way he'd said "lesbian", it was very clear that he didn't believe me. The easiest thing would have been to give in and go, which I might have done anyway if he'd asked politely in the first place, but I'd worked myself into a corner. A thought occurred to me as he went on.

'Surely you must at least welcome a chance to discuss Elgar Vaughan, however obnoxious I may be?'

I nodded. 'OK, you can take me to the Angel, but on the strict understanding that this is not a date.'

He merely spread his hands, as if it was ridiculous to suggest that he'd ever had any other intention.

'Good, I knew you'd see reason.'

'If you say so. Now, would you mind waiting outside while I dress?'

The arrogance had mainly been a front, as I'd suspected, because he let me usher him through the door without protest. I obviously had to change, for three reasons. Firstly I'd just walked the best part of a mile with two handfuls of heavy shopping and wanted to. Secondly he was right about the Angel, and while I care very little for other people's opinions I don't actively court condescension either. Thirdly it gave me an excellent excuse for keeping him waiting in the rapidly chilling evening air while I did it.

I did have a little black dress, two in fact: one velvet,

one Chinese silk, also a red one just as vampish as he could possibly have wished. Both were completely out of the question. So was doing the exact opposite of what he'd suggested, and as I showered I considered by dilemma. What I needed was a happy medium, perhaps a skirt and blouse?

Having finished my shower at leisure, I dried my hair, applied a touch of make-up but no scent, selected a pair of plain, comfy knickers because he very definitely was not going to be seeing them, and began to go through my clothes. The first combination made me look like a junior secretary, the second like Mary Poppins. Neither was suitable. By then I had every single skirt I owned laid out on the bed, including a knee-length number in green tartan I seldom wore because people tended to mistake me for a schoolgirl.

For a moment I considered combining it with a white blouse, ribbon tie, knee socks and pumps, so that I could embarrass Fox by pretending he was a lecher taking his 'niece' out to dinner. Unfortunately it wasn't going to work. He wasn't old enough, the staff at the Angel were my up-market choice for catering at the Hall, and I had a sneaking suspicion that Fox would have thoroughly enjoyed the process anyway.

It would also have been too cold, because there was already condensation forming on the windows, and it looked as if there might be a frost in the night. That decided me on tights, slacks, a sweat-shirt, a roll-necked jumper and boots, which was not only warm but left me feeling armoured, and still more so with my long coat on. Coincidentally I was completely in black.

Richard Fox was standing by the rubble of the tower, his breath white in the cool evening air. He glanced at his watch.

'Is forty-five minutes the regulation wait for a boyfriend these days? Worth it though. Pretty. Very Gothic. Suits you.'

I ignored him and set off down the drive, only for him to go in a different direction completely, around the end of the pile of rubble. For an instant I was puzzled as even if he went down the service lane it was further to the Angel, which was down by the river. Only when I'd followed a few steps, meaning to ask him where he was going, did I realise he had a car parked there, a big black BMW. The lights flashed as he deactivated the central locking. I nodded.

'Pretty. Very phallic. Suits you.'

He grinned and got in. I followed suit, actually quite glad of the lift after the amount of walking I'd done during the day. One thing was odd.

'You were walking behind me as I came down the drive?'

'Oh, I'd been here quite a while, waiting for you.'

'Oh. Then why didn't I see you when I came in the gate?'

'Because I am a member of a Satanic cult intent on raising Elgar Vaughan from the dead and I was lurking about the woods hoping that you would lead me to his secret grave.'

'Very funny. No, seriously, why?'

'The real answer is too mundane to bother you with.'

'Tell me anyway.'

'I needed to take a leak, so I nipped into the woods. When I came out you were already halfway down the drive.'

'Oh. Right. You'd have been wasting your time looking for Elgar Vaughan's secret tomb anyway. He's in some unknown corner of a foreign field.'

'A large hole, more likely.'

'Very tasteful.'

He chuckled and gunned the engine to life. The Angel was only a few minutes away by car, on the river bank half a mile up from the village. We didn't speak again as he drove down, and my mind was set on a favourite but gloomy theme: Elgar Vaughan's death and the collapse of his dream. After at least one, maybe several, elaborate rituals, he had genuinely believed himself immortal, perhaps right up to the moment he hit the ground. It didn't bear thinking about, and I felt a shiver run through me as he turned onto the river road.

'Not cold, are you?' he asked, passing me a glance of incredulity.

'No,' I snapped indignantly, not wishing in any way to be seen less than prepared.

The Angel was right ahead, a dark mass against the evening sky. It had been there for some five centuries, and more or less as it was for at least a hundred and fifty years. I liked to think that Vaughan would have frequented it, perhaps approaching just as Richard Fox and I were now, in his black Grand Sport with one of his female acolytes by his side, perhaps Alice Scott, my real link with him, although I had never been quite able to make the mental jump between the pretty, bright-eyed girl in the few photos that existed of the Sabbat Aceras with the ancient crone I'd met.

I pushed the bleak thoughts from my mind as we turned into the car park, but my mood had changed. My idea of deliberately ordering as expensive a meal as possible so that Richard would be put off me suddenly seemed pointless, an act of childish pique. He was irritating, but perhaps he was right. Life's too short for bullshit.

From that moment I knew I was going to sleep with him, and that it was my choice. I needed to be held, and to share some sexual intensity with him, but mostly to be held. He had sensed the change in me, because there were no more deliberately annoying remarks as we went in to the restaurant. He'd been right about the tables too, because the majority were either already occupied or reserved. Fortunately they knew me because of their agreement to cater for the Hall, which gave me a satisfying sense of propriety, and we were given the last vacant table by the windows, overlooking the oily black surface of the Thames. The water was so still that a pair of lights on the opposite bank were reflected in perfect image instead of as trails.

I let him order, something he might perhaps have taken as a sign of surrender, but again, nothing was said. We ate lightly, scallops on their shells with Champagne and a dish of quail stuffed with white truffles and washed down with old rich claret. Both were delicious and helped to mellow my mood a little, along with the wine. We skipped dessert, and by then there was no question of what was going to happen. Nothing was said, and nothing needed to be said.

We left the car where it was and walked back up the hill, now arm in arm, in at the gates of Elmcote Hall and down the drive, the ground white with frost before us, glittering faintly under a thin moon. He steered me on past my door, but he didn't need to, because we both knew exactly where we were going. Our shoes crunched on the brittle grass as we started down the lime walk, in silence, my teeth on my lower lip, nervous, but certain.

There was no hesitation. At the Temple of Baphomet we simply stepped inside to the utter blackness of the interior. I felt his grip tighten and he was pulling me in, lifting me to himself so that as I came up on tiptoe our mouths met, his lips cold against mine, his tongue hot. For a long moment we simply held onto each other, kissing, my face lifted to his, before the pressure of his hands shifted ever so slightly, pushing me down.

I knew how it should be, as Vaughan had accepted his acolytes, on their knees, in worship and in pleasure, because they were one and the same. He knew too, or he wouldn't have been pushing me down, but it was not easy to give. Even as I went to my knees on the cold hard marble a tiny voice inside my head was screaming at me that I could not possibly do what was demanded of me, that it was inappropriate for a modern woman, impossibly undignified for me as woman full stop, unholy.

Yet it felt right, and what else could I do, kneeling on the pentagonal slab at the centre of the Temple of Baphomet, at the feet of a man who might have been the reincarnation of Vaughan himself? For him there was no hesitation. I waited, trembling on my knees as he opened first his coat and then his trousers beneath to push them down in a single brusque gesture, and turn, just as Rabelaisian as I could have wished for.

Still I hesitated, but only for a second, and then I'd done it, pushing my face between the firm muscular eggs of his buttocks and planting a single firm kiss on his anus. Immediately he laughed, and he could have been Elgar Vaughan, or Baphomet himself. I stayed down, knowing the ritual, as he turned once more and fed himself into my mouth. His flesh was cold, shrunk with the chill night, but still a good mouthful. I pulled close, cupping my hands to the firmness of his buttocks, my fingers pressed into his flesh as I mouthed eagerly on his cock which had begun to swell in my mouth.

I'd done it, I'd kissed a man's anus in the Temple of Baphomet, something I'd fantasised over so many times I'd long ago lost count. Now I had to go through with it, surrender to his will, accepting whatever he wished, and taking whatever I wished. However cold, if he wanted my breasts he could have my breasts; if he wanted my bottom he could have my bottom, or whatever appealed. What appealed to me was him in my mouth, and not just his lovely cock – which was every bit as thick and long and straight and smooth as I could have hoped for. I wanted more too, lifting his heavy balls in my hand and popping both in my mouth at once, to suck greedily as I nursed his now solid erection in my hand.

His breathing had grown deeper, punctuated by the odd little gasp of pleasure, and I stopped, wanting him to take control and not simply waste himself in my mouth. I needn't have worried. He sank down immediately, his large strong hands guiding my body, not down onto my back as I'd expected, but pushing me forward, onto all fours. I let him do it, manipulating my body so easily, into a crawling position at the exact centre of the slab, my bottom lifted, my knees wide. My coat was turned up, the waistband of my trousers taken in a firm grip and eased down, my knickers too, baring me to the cold night air.

I couldn't help but sigh, remembering how I'd been the day before in the same exposed, deliberately vulnerable state, kneeling down, available from behind, and imagining his beautiful penis sliding into me as I masturbated. Now it was real, and urgent. I pushed out my bottom, just as I felt the firm pressure of his erection between my cheeks. For one awful moment of fearful expectation I thought he was going to sodomise me, before his cock slipped lower and went deep inside.

His hands took my hips and he began to push, firm and even, slow too, and all the way, penetrating me again and again to repeatedly bring me the incomparable delight of have my sex filled with a really wide girth. My head was already full of images of what we'd done, the way I was, how his cock would have looked, and as our fucking grew faster and firmer, so they grew more vivid.

It was glorious, true ecstasy, surrendered on my knees in the temple, taken from behind after I'd kissed his arse and sucked on him, surrendering as I would have done to the Devil himself. From the moment I'd given in he had treated me perfectly, strong and certain, putting me on my knees in the temple for that crucial kiss, to let me take my pleasure in his cock and balls, to take me from behind, pumping into me, hard and deep, harder and deeper still, jamming himself in and out at a furious pace with the heavy sac of his balls swinging against me.

I snatched back, on the edge of orgasm, gasping as I rubbed myself, in time with his own ecstatic cries, and we were coming, together, in perfect blinding ecstasy that seemed to hold forever, with the junction of our bodies a blazing hot point in the all-enveloping cold, of my bare skin, of the marble floor, the marble floor of the Temple of Baphomet, of Elgar Vaughan's temple, where Richard Fox and I had fucked.

3

I was held, all night. Richard and I snuggled together against the cold in my bed after sharing two of my three bottles of wine, talking until the early hours, and there was more sex, lots more sex. When I awoke he was gone, and it was nearly noon. There was a brief pang of desertion, but it passed. He'd made his feelings very clear, not pretending that he was deeply in love with me, but displaying an open, almost childish delight in my compliance with what he wanted. It was pure sex, but then I've always thought the sex should come first. How else are you supposed to develop a relationship if you don't really know somebody?

If I wasn't worried that he'd be back, I was more than a little apprehensive about what would happen when he was. Talking about Elgar Vaughan's rituals was one thing, and it had excited me so much I'd come a second time, under my fingers, as he described what he wanted to do to me. He wasn't being arrogant with me anymore, but he was very rude and very explicit, leaving me feeling as if I was considering my first time, excited and scared all at once.

There was a lot to do, fortunately, or I'd have spent the day in bed re-running in my mind every moment of what had happened and playing with myself. With the wedding reception happening on Saturday it was out of the question. I had to call the caterers, the marquee people, various officials, and more. Even once I'd done that I had to get everything ready, such as having the kitchen tidy rather than strewn with bottles.

Working didn't stop me daydreaming, both about reality and fantasy. Having actually done something I'd thought about so many times, it was curiously hard to take in. The very first time I'd read about witches supposedly having to kiss the Devil's arse it had given me that naughty feeling which for me lies at the heart of sex. Very English, as I'd often been told, but to try and change my feelings would have been like cutting all my hair off just because a close-crop look had briefly come into style.

That image had stayed with me ever since, as embodied by a seventeenth century woodcut of a busty female figure on her knees with her face pressed to the trim buttocks of a horned fork-tailed devil with his face twisted into a look of salacious delight. Now I'd done it, or as close to done it as was practical, because I'd never met a man who better approximated to the Devil than Richard Fox.

That was reality, but fantasy was something else entirely. The resemblance between Richard and Elgar Vaughan was uncanny. He'd explained, making it seem very mundane by pointing out that it was the similarity between Vaughan and him which had first drawn my interest, but that didn't stop me speculating, my mind going off on a wonderful flight of fancy as I hurried around the grounds trying to make everything look tidy and yet abandoned.

Elgar Vaughan had died at the age of thirty-six, which was approximately Richard's age, a little more perhaps. The last recorded sighting of him, or at least his plane, was in a dogfight with German ace Oswald Boelcke. Vaughan had been shot down, crashed in no man's land north-east of Ypres, and that was that. His body had never been found, but that was hardly unusual.

What if he hadn't died? What if his rituals had been a success, perhaps arresting his age at about thirty, which fitted the timeline? It would have been awkward, staying the same age with those around him growing older, and in due course it would have become inconvenient to say the least. Perhaps he had seized his chance to disappear, which couldn't have been too difficult in the fog of war. He might have become a prisoner of war, adopted another identity. Possibly the collapse of the tower represented some complex form of energy exchange to maintain his vitality?

It was ridiculous of course, but great fun to think about and made what had happened the night before even more special. What if I had surrendered myself to the real Elgar Vaughan, a man who'd made a pact with the Devil or, as he'd have seen it, the pagan deity? Just the thought had me smiling all morning and, after dressing up after lunch for a coachload of Japanese tourists, I gave a far better performance than my first.

On a more mundane level, Richard was a New Yorker working in the City, much like Julie Voigtstein, which accounted for the flash car and his easy attitude to money. His fascination with Elgar Vaughan and the occult element of paganism was something he kept carefully hidden, which added to his appeal for me. He had read my thesis, which had played a major part in drawing him to Elmcote Hall in the first place, and, as he so rudely put it, was 'determined to have me bare'.

He was an arrogant bastard, there was no question about it, but that tends to come with the sort of confident protective man I go for. What other qualities and faults he had I would doubtless find out in due course, but he had at least been honest with me, which I appreciate. If anything he'd been too honest, unashamedly describing some of the rituals he wanted to indulge in with me, many details of which were enough to set me biting my lip just at the thought.

* * *

I'd known Richard couldn't get back to Elmcote for the night, and I didn't expect him. Even after just one night it felt lonely without him there, and I was also starting at noises again, expecting the intruders to be back. Nothing happened, and when I went out to inspect the temple in the morning there was no sign that anything had been tampered with. I even checked the five carvings, but they were as ever, and I had to conclude that if anybody intended to steal them they'd need a crane, a truck, and several skilled workmen for several hours. It was simply not feasible.

The rest of the day passed in a sort of controlled chaos. First to arrive were the marquee men, who were messing around for half an hour before discovering that the thing was roughly a foot wider than the lime walk. Then there was some busybody from health and safety who insisted I tape the rubble off, and seemed to think the tower was the result of a recent collapse. Next came the caterers, who expected facilities on the level of a school or hospital. The best man then arrived, getting in everybody's way as he tried to take over the organising.

Finally there was nothing more I could do and I retired to my room, only to realise I'd left the library open. The couple getting married presumably enjoyed the romantic atmosphere of the Hall, but that didn't necessarily make it a good thing for dear old aunt Phoebe to go looking for the loo and instead find herself confronted with a goat-headed devil sporting tits like melons and a cock to put the average elephant to shame. I went down again, corrected my mistake, pinched a bottle of Champagne from a passing caterer and was just making for the stairs when I realised the tall woman coming towards me was Julie.

With the excitement of my night with Richard, I'd completely forgotten I was supposed to be going out with her, although she looked more as if she'd dressed for the wedding than a night on the town. She was in a pink skirt suit, cut very tight at the waist, and extraordinarily garish, especially with matching heels and a huge picture hat. One of the ushers even approached her, looking polite but somewhat taken aback, by which time I was already stepping forward.

'It's OK, she's a friend of mine. Hi, Julie. I'm sorry, I'd forgotten all about you!'

'Don't sweat it. So what's with the stiffs?'

'Sh! It's a wedding, that's one of the things we do here. Look, I know I said I'd go out with you, and I was really looking forward to it, but I can't possibly leave until everything's done, and that'll be some time after midnight. I'm so sorry, I —'

'Relax. I love weddings. Let's mingle.'

'No, let's not. We're not invited, and everything's accounted for, believe me, down to the last napkin.'

She lifted one thin eyebrow.

'Including that bottle of *Cordon Rouge* you're holding?'

'Good point. Come upstairs. I've got some serious news.'

The eyebrow went up again.

'Oh yes?'

I didn't answer, but quickly snatched a couple of slender Champagne glasses and made for my room. Just closing the door behind me was a relief, and I put the catch across, badly in need of privacy and somebody who didn't regard me either as the fount of all knowledge or the one responsible for every difficulty, including the ground being too hard to hammer the huge wooden marquee pegs in easily.

Julie crossed to the window and looked out down the lime walk, now blocked by a slightly deformed marquee. I threw myself down on the bed and set to work on the Champagne bottle, peeling the foil off, twisting the cork loose, and abruptly regretting having run upstairs so quickly as a fountain of bubbles erupted all over my front.

'Shit! Look at me!'

'It happens.'

She took a towel and quickly dabbed off the worst of the Champagne, but it had already soaked through, wetting my blouse and bra. I peeled everything off, dried myself and put my robe on before going back to the Champagne, with Julie waiting patiently. Once sorted, I filled our glasses and sat back down as she perched herself on the end of the bed.

'So? What's new?'

'What is new is that I spent a night of torrid sex with that man I was telling you about, Richard Fox.'

'The condescending pig?'

'That's the one, only he's not – OK, so he is, sort of, but there's a nice side to him as well. He's really firm with me, in bed I mean, or rather – out in the temple, the one at the end of the lime walk, which is where we did it the first time.'

'Kinky! Go on, and I want the details.'

I was blushing, but something told me that whatever I might have done, it would be nothing new to her, except obviously the ritual context. It was still hard to know what to say, and I couldn't help but try and justify myself.

'We – Well, there's this thing that witches did, or were supposed to do anyway. It was one of the things they used to be accused of, a sign of devotion to the Devil, or a pagan deity anyway, to, um, kiss his arse.'

Her eyebrows went up, right up.

'Kiss his ass?'

Her voice was full of disapproval, mock disapproval. My face must have been cherry red, but she was expecting more, silent and amused, with an arch look on her face.

'Yes, kiss his arse, properly, you know. That was what was so wonderful. He just knew, as if he'd tapped into one of my deepest fantasies.'

'You fantasise about kissing the Devil's ass? I did not have you down as a bad girl, not that bad!'

I smiled, flattered and embarrassed.

'Looks can be deceiving.'

'Now that's the truth. Go on, so you kissed this guy's ass, like on the cheek, or you gave him a good rimming?'

'Sorry? I don't understand.'

'Rimming, like you licked his asshole.'

If I'd been cherry red before, I was now beetroot, but I nodded.

'You dirty bitch!'

It was no insult, more a compliment, and said in a ridiculously camp voice, which made me giggle. I wasn't going to tell her I hadn't gone quite as far as she thought, because it was obviously what she wanted and, while I didn't feel I needed her approval, I didn't mind having it either. After swallowing my Champagne and refilling my glass and hers, I went on.

'Elgar Vaughan, the guy who lived here, used to have his followers do the same, as an act of devotion, submission even, and as part of their initiation. I felt the same, and it was so special to be doing it in the temple. I suppose that just sounds silly to you?'

'Whatever floats your boat, baby.'

She didn't understand, but she wasn't judging me. I went on.

'He turned around and made me take him in my mouth. He's big, very big, and ever so smooth, like the picture we were looking at ... well, not really, but he felt like that, as if I could hold my entire body against him, and just – just lose myself in him.'

A little shiver ran through me as I finished, once more

imagining myself with Richard's lovely big cock in my mouth and hand.

'You like a big boy?'

I nodded.

'Me too. The only people who say size doesn't matter are guys with small dicks. Let me tell you, honey, cocks are like steak. You order one and you get some miserable little thing, you are well disappointed. What you want is a big juicy one, even if you know you can't eat it all.'

I laughed, delighted by the image, and the idea of just being able to order a man like a meal and send him back if he wasn't up to scratch.

'So you gave him a bj? That all?'

'Oh no. It was freezing cold, or we'd have really gone for it, but after he'd made me suck him hard he put me down on my knees.'

'You like that, don't you?'

'Being on my knees? Yes, I suppose.'

'No. I mean the way you say "I had to" and "he made me". You like it as if you had no choice, yeah?'

'Maybe. Sort of. Not forced . . .'

'Oh no, not forced, but like the guy's so horny for you, and you're so horny for him, he's just got to do it, and you just can't stop yourself.'

'That's it exactly! Not very pc maybe, but I like it, and with Richard it was like that. He's so strong, and he just eased me down, onto all fours, and got me bare, and –'

I blew my breath out, remembering how it had felt to have the full thick length of Richard's cock sliding up into me from behind. Julie nodded.

'Doggy. I like it. Say, do you think we could snaffle another bottle of Champagne?'

'I think they can afford that, for the amount of trouble they gave me this afternoon. I mean, it's spring; why is it my fault that it's a cold day?'

'You said it, girl.'

I quickly threw on a top and we went downstairs, giggling like a pair of public schoolgirls sneaking out for a midnight feast. The reception was in full swing, with everyone out in the marquee except for a few of the caterers, and it was the work of a moment for me to distract them with a question about clearing up the next day while Julie lifted not one bottle but two from the selection conveniently set out on two trolleys by the door. We were giggling harder than ever as we ran back upstairs, once more locking my bedroom door behind us as Julie opened another bottle.

We went to the window, from which we could see inside the marquee; not all of it by any means, but some of the tables and most of the area cleared for dancing. A few couples were gyrating sedately, with one or two wilder, or drunker, guests throwing themselves around to some music that was presumably playing in their heads, because it certainly wasn't coming out of the speakers. Julie laughed.

'You Brits! You have to be the worst dancers in the world.'

'That's not true!'

It was an instinctive answer because to judge by the antics of the wedding guests, the standard of dancing was appalling. It was harder to imagine anybody making a bigger clown of themselves than the tall skinny man in a pink cravat who was either attempting to break dance or was simply no longer able to stand. Julie pressed her point.

'Oh, it is! I mean, look at these guys! Same with your music, you just pinch it from us. What do you listen to?'

I spent a moment searching my mind for a favourite band who were very definitely not American. Confessing to Nirvana was out, but it gave me an idea.

'The Hellfire Club? Out of Wedlock? Coffinwood?'

'Say what?'

'You see, you don't know what you're talking about.'
She shrugged.

'Whatever. It all goes straight back to Elvis.'

I couldn't be bothered to argue but took another swig of Champagne, tilting the bottle carefully to my mouth to make sure there were no disasters. Julie took it from me and for a while we simply stood there, silent save for an occasional remark on the dancing or the increasingly amorous behaviour among the younger guests as they, like us, grew gradually drunker.

Only when the first of the taxis had begun to arrive and the wedding was beginning to break up did we step away. I had to go down to make sure everything was running smoothly, but the caterers had everything under control and I was simply in the way. Pinching yet another bottle, I made my way back upstairs, knocking to be let in.

As Julie threw herself back down on the bed I opened my bottle, more carefully this time. I poured and lay down next to her, feeling pleasantly wicked and not a little aroused. Talking about Richard had got to me, and I wasn't the only one.

'So come on, what's he like this Richard guy? D'you do anything else?'

'Yes, of course, lots. Not outside though, it was too cold. We came back and drank, and talked, and had sex, and more sex, and lots more sex, right in this bed and with me bent down over the kitchen table. Now that was rude.'

'How many times?'

'Four in all, before we went to sleep. He's got stamina, no question, but the last time – the last time, it took him a bit of time. He made me crawl around in the nude so he could watch me and get himself hard. He made me suck his balls too.'

I stretched on the bed, wishing Richard was there to

make me do it again, in front of Julie, maybe even to fuck us both. She'd have been game, or I could easily imagine her being game, but I couldn't decide if the idea made me more excited or jealous. Julie slapped my leg.

'Dirty girl! So he likes your ass, yes?'

'He adores my bottom, yes. He adores me full stop, but some of the things he wants me to do . . .'

'Oh yeah, like what?'

'All sorts, things Vaughan is supposed to have done, like whip me, and – and put it up my bottom.'

'Nasty! You like that?'

'I don't know. I've never done it. I don't mind trying, with him, but I'm scared it might hurt.'

'You've got to do it right, take your time, slow and easy.'

'Have you done it?'

'Sure, it's cool.'

She was so completely casual, about something so dirty I'd always kept it for my darkest fantasies. Yet for Richard it would just be the start, and I was sure some of his wilder ideas would shock even Julie.

'There's more. He wants other people to watch too, maybe even join in. I can handle that, I think – maybe, only not somebody who's been paid to do it. A friend maybe, somebody who understands.'

'Is that an invitation?'

I hadn't meant it as one, not consciously, and I immediately found myself blushing again, despite the Champagne. She laughed when she saw my face.

'Hey, take it easy, I don't mean to push in.'

'No, not at all. I mean – that is – well, if anybody was to watch, I'd like it to be you.'

'Say, thanks. That's kind of sweet.'

'I mean it, but who knows. Let's play it by ear, yes?'

'You got it, girl. So what else is this horny pig into, huh?'

'Anything and everything, believe me. One thing, he wants to take me into a church and watch me masturbate on the altar, with one of those big candles.'

'Well nasty. Going to do it?'

'I don't think so.'

'You religious?'

'Not in that way. A lot of churches have CCTV now.'

She laughed and swallowed the rest of her Champagne. As I refilled her glass I was wondering if I dared tell her Richard's more extreme fantasies, or my own. She'd been completely accepting, and yet everyone has their limit. I was going to speak when her mobile rang. She swore, fumbled in her pocket, pulled it out, dropped it, and at last managed to get it to her ear. The first word she said was 'no', in a serious, businesslike voice quite different to her usually brash drawl, before she turned to me.

'Hang on, honey, right back. Work.'

I relaxed back against the pillows as she moved to the door, really quite glad of the interruption. There are some things best kept in one's own head, or shared with the most intimate of lovers. Frankly, there are some things best kept in one's own head full stop. Some of the ideas I'd picked up from Elgar Vaughan's rituals, and more especially his drawings, definitely fell into that category, as did a few of those Richard Fox had suggested.

Julie was taking forever on the phone, and seemed to be involved in a serious and really quite heated discussion. Presumably some crisis had come up, something that couldn't wait for the Monday, which I suppose is one of the drawbacks of a high-pressure job. Not that I really cared, so long as she sorted it out and came back to talk to me. I felt warm, relaxed, pleasantly drunk, the Champagne glass oddly heavy in my hand, and I must have been asleep before my eyes had closed properly.

* * *

I woke up in total darkness, and near total silence. There was a moment of confusion before I realised I was in bed and that it was the middle of the night. Next came a touch of panic as I remembered the wedding and the things I should have done once it was over. Muttering under my breath, I threw my legs out of bed and only then realised what else was wrong.

All I had on were my knickers. The night air was cold on my legs and chest. Somebody, presumably Julie – hopefully Julie – had undressed me and put me to bed. I couldn't remember her doing it, but she obviously had, which was embarrassing to say the least. Falling asleep drunk was bad enough, but there was something acutely humiliating about being stripped down to my knickers and put to bed by a woman I'd only met a few days before, especially when I should have been working.

I bit my ill-feeling down, telling myself Julie had only done what she thought best. Maybe she slept like that, I didn't know, and she certainly felt no embarrassment whatsoever at the sight of other women's bodies. Far more important was what had happened with the wedding, and I had to go down and check.

Only when I tried to stand up did I realise that I was still drunk. It was odd, because my mind was perfectly clear, but I was having serious trouble balancing. I at least managed to get the light on, and after a moment figured out that my clothes were in the wash basket. By then my teeth were chattering with cold, and I dressed as quickly, and as warmly, as I could.

I was really cursing myself as I tugged on my boots, and when I'd finally managed to find my watch I discovered it was 3.30, the dead hours of the night. That was at least better than coming down when there were a few drunken guests still around, but not good. Having managed to open my door I immediately turned the heating on, so my room would be warm when I came back in, before staggering downstairs to survey the wreckage.

The first thing I found was a note from Julie, weighed down under a salt cellar on the kitchen table. She said she sorted out what she could and 'dismissed' the caterers, before putting me in bed. My earlier irritation instantly faded to gratitude. What she hadn't done was tidy up, which meant the reception room was in chaos. Not that I could possibly have expected her to, and besides the caterers were supposed to return in the morning. She wouldn't have locked up either, and that had to be done. Sunday was the day Trustees were most likely to turn up unannounced, and if they found the whole place wide open they were not going to be happy.

The most obvious thing was the front gates. Not that shutting them made the least bit of difference, when there was no lock and anyone who wanted to could get through the fence anyway, but I had to do it. I went out into a clear frosty night with the sky a dome of star-sprinkled black cut by the bulk of the Hall. I glimpsed the ragged fringe of the woods, and a low crescent moon. I was swaying slightly as I walked down the drive, but the night was so beautiful and I was too drunk to really notice the cold; there was only the faint ghost of my breath in the air and the feel of the crisp frosted ground under my feet.

I closed the gate, smiling at the grotesque black iron goat faces, horned and glaring, but fast becoming like old friends to me. With the frozen latch at last in place I turned back, walking more slowly still, and imagining how the Hall would have looked with the tower still standing, a great phallic shaft of stone standing erect in defiance. Elgar Vaughan would have seen it just that way many times, but he'd gone beyond the mere symbolism of his ancestor. With his imagery there was no doubt, no mere suggestion, but open glorious display, lewd and virile, like his wonderful Green Man.

The service gate hadn't been opened, so that at least I knew was still locked. Both doors had to be done, but that could wait. I didn't want to go inside, not just yet. Instead of making for the Hall I crossed the carriage sweep towards the lime walk and around to where the marquee stood open, a dull flickering yellow light within. It should have been Richard, or Elgar Vaughan, or some strange night spirit from the woods ready to ravish me on the cold ground. Instead it was just a pair of candles carelessly left burning to illuminate the double row of empty tables, each still set out, with every glass reflecting a double spark.

I moved down the row and blew out the first candle. The second I picked up, lifting the heavy black candlestick. Both the huge blow heaters were off, the wires leading out under the back to the silent generator. I told myself I'd check it anyway, but I knew exactly where I was going. Behind the top table a flap in the marquee let me out again, into the open night with the limes towering high to either side. I walked forward in my little pool of light, the candle turning the woods to utter blackness on either side.

As I approached the temple I knew what I wanted to do: to play out my encounter with Richard, down on my knees on the central slab, cold marble and cool skin, bare as I brought myself up to ecstasy. Not immediately though, not until I'd thoroughly immersed myself in the lingering echo of Elgar Vaughan's creation, of which I so badly wanted to be a part. Lifting the candle high, I stared up at the Baphomet figure, evocative of so' much of Elgar Vaughan's belief, and yet ultimately undeveloped.

He, or she, had a goat's head, yes, and horns, and

wings, the pentacle on the forehead, breasts even, but little round breasts, a virgin's breasts, not the magnificent heavy bountiful globes I would have given him. The serpent staff rising from his lap was wrong too, a coy euphemism for what should have been there, a huge straining penis. I moved on, walking around the temple with my candle held high, to admire the figures of Lilith and Gaia, and on, to stand beneath the Green Man, my belly tight in anticipation as my eyes feasted on what he had to offer.

My mouth had come a little wide and I swallowed, wishing I could take him into me, just as a breeze touched my candle. Instantly I was plunged into complete darkness, my eyes dancing with yellow and green after-images which cleared slowly to show the stars and, against them, towering over me to an impossible height, a huge half-human shape, intensely male, his craggy figurehead harsh against the stars, arms outstretched to catch me and, thrusting out above me, a monstrous impossibly virile erect cock.

I screamed and ran, blundering into the side of the temple to sprawl headlong on the grass, and for one terrifying instant I truly expected wood-hard fingers to reach down and grip my body, pulling at me, tearing off my clothes, lifting me up, and putting me onto his great log of an erection. Even as common sense kicked in I was rolling over to make absolutely certain that what I'd seen was simply the outline of a dead tree against the stars and not the Green Man in his most primitive and masculine form.

My heart was beating furiously as I pulled myself to my feet, my fingers tingling with reaction and my stomach weak. I tried to force a smile, to laugh at my own foolishness, but it wasn't easy with that image still burning in my mind. It had been a second, two at most, from the moment the candle blew out to the realisation that what I thought I'd seen wasn't real, but I knew it would stay with me forever.

I was still shaking as I turned back for the Hall, all thoughts of playing with myself gone, along with my courage. As I walked I was sure there was somebody behind me, but I was not going to turn around. My fingers were still locked tight around the candle stick, with the broken stem still in place, at an angle, and if Richard, let alone anyone else, had decided to play a joke on me by jumping out from behind one of the limes I swear I'd have brained them.

Only back indoors did I really calm down. I felt a little silly, but scared too, and badly in need of a drink. There was no shortage of that, but Champagne was too weak, and I made myself a coffee with a heavy slug of brandy mixed in. I was sipping it as I made my way up to my room, still clutching the candle stick. It was foolish to be frightened by something I at once knew to be an impossibility and longed to be real. I would have surrendered myself, completely.

I went to the window and pulled the curtain aside to stare out into the night. The woods showed black against the sky, the branches like fingers reaching up, clutching for me. I'd always been sensitive to the feel of the place, but it was now stronger by far, and for the first time I began to really understand not so much what Elgar Vaughan had created, but what he had worshipped.

Possibly it had been real. Possibly my reaction, fear instead of surrender, had broken the spell, or my near instantaneous disbelief. Perhaps he was still out there, stalking through the woods, disappointed in me but still wanting me. The thought sent a fresh shiver through me, and I moved away from the window to sit down on the bed, biting my lip in uncertainty. He was too big, impossibly big, for all that I've always wanted a cock I could hold to my body as I'd hold a man.

No, a deity could be anything he wanted, anything I wanted, and I shouldn't be scared. What I should do was go back into the woods, then and there, only naked, to sacrifice myself to his desire, on my knees in the leaf litter, my haunches lifted, offering myself. He'd be there, out in the woods, eager to take me, unable to resist taking me. Hands like ivy boughs would grip me, taking me by my hips, wrapping around my body, to hold me, helpless, and in he'd go, deep inside me, impossibly deep.

I lay back on the bed in the warm safety of my room, but in my mind I was out in the woods, stark naked and powerless to prevent myself being taken by the Green Man, chased and caught and fucked and made pregnant. My jeans came open and down, my knickers too, all the way to my ankles, to leave myself open. The candle went where it belonged, inside me, hopelessly small in comparison to what I was thinking of, but quite enough to do the job, to bring home to me the glorious sense of being filled.

He was with me as I began to stroke myself, on top of me and deep inside, then behind as I flipped myself over to crawl a little way up the bed, imagining myself after I'm tripped, trying to crawl away. That was how it had to be, a chase, a chase I could never win, and did not want to win. Yet I had to be chased, and caught, falling to my knees as he came up behind me, towering over me, with bark for skin and ivy for hair, so strong, so virile.

I'd try to crawl away but fingers of ivy would catch my body, pulling me back. His cock would touch me, a wood-hard shaft, long and smooth, and oh so, so big, impossibly big, big enough to hold my body to, to ride on. Still he'd fit, perfectly, and it didn't matter how, so long as I could feel him deep in me, all the way. His fingers would writhe around me, like the ivy boughs on Henry Vaughan's tomb, and I'd be held tight, utterly helpless, as I was penetrated with a ferocity befitting only a demon.

It was perfect, and I held the image in my mind as I began to come, of myself down on my knees, still trying to crawl as he caught me and filled me with his glorious impossible cock, and fucked me hard, at last to fill me and leave me lying in the leaves.

4

In the morning I felt better than I really deserved to, perhaps because I'd been out for some night air. It was just as well, with the marquee people turning up before the caterers and finding they couldn't start work until a good deal of clearing up had been done. I did my best to help, also to smooth ruffled feathers once the caterers did arrive, picking up litter and searching for missing glasses, two of which I found by a tree halfway along the lime walk.

Once again there had been a sharp frost, and the grass was a sheet of the palest scintillate green showing every footprint, including mine, going towards the temple and back. They weren't the only ones. Two more sets led the same way, up between the limes to where the temple stood. My first thought was of intruders, and to wonder how closely I'd missed running into them in my drunken state. There were no prints to where I'd found the two glasses, which meant the frost had formed after the wedding guests had dispersed.

I put the glasses down and set off towards the temple, following the prints and doing my best to think like Sherlock Holmes. Both sets were a lot bigger than mine. One was clearly feminine, with a neat triangle at the front and a sharp hole where her heel had pressed down. The others were as clearly masculine, larger still, with a grip pattern, perhaps work boots or walking boots. The two tracks ran side by side, but not that close.

The obvious answer was that a couple had walked up to the temple at the very end of the reception, once the frost had formed, but after the other couple had left their glasses. Presumably they'd wanted somewhere private to talk, maybe to have sex, although it would have been pretty cold, as I knew from experience. Sure enough, they led to the temple steps, and inside were two glasses and a Champagne bottle still with some wine in the bottom.

I ducked down to pick everything up, relieved and amused by my flight of fancy. There was nothing suspicious going on, just sex, perhaps between the best man, who'd been tall, and one of the bridesmaids. Both had been considerably taller than the bride, which had amused me because even in their dresses it had looked as if she was being guarded by them. I smiled at the memory – of that and at how it felt to have a full dress turned up for sex – and was going to leave, but stopped.

The scrape marks left by the men I'd disturbed before were still visible around the pentagonal slab. In fact they were more severe than before, definitely. There was even a chip mark, about an inch across, as if somebody had tried to force a crowbar into the crack. Somebody had tried to lift the pentagonal slab, without question, and by far the greatest probability had to be that it had been my two visitors of the night before.

It was alarming, to say the least. I'd been there at nearly four in the morning, alone and drunk. They might have come before me, or after. Possibly they'd even been there while I was, and my stomach went tight at the thought of going into the temple in the pitch black, intending to play with myself, and stumbling right into them. I shook my head, trying to push the thought away. I had to be practical, to work out what was going on, and why.

A thought entered my head, only to be dismissed as too ridiculous. Besides, it was the wrong slab. Still, somebody wanted to lift the slab, and presumably under the misapprehension that there was something of value beneath it. There were certainly enough rumours about Elgar Vaughan, perhaps most importantly what had happened to the bulk of his wealth.

I knew, because I'd calculated what it would have cost him to keep the place up for fifteen years, build all the temples and live the life of Riley with his acolytes. Not only that but by then the original business, the source of the Vaughan wealth, was being run as a company. Still, it was just the sort of thing conspiracy theorists love to get their teeth into.

That made me feel a little better because I could picture an intense bearded man and a ditzy-looking girl instead of the hard-faced professional thieves I'd imagined might be after the carvings. It was still a problem, and made worse by the fact that I was ninety-nine per cent sure the original intruders had both been men, while the second pair had been a man and a woman. Yet if there were four people involved, that made it seem more likely still that some sort of conspiracy theory was going around.

There's really only one place to check out all sides of a conspiracy theory, and that's the internet. I didn't have a connection. I didn't even have a computer. At college I'd used it all the time, at first, but very quickly exhausted all the information on Elgar Vaughan. The majority had been erroneous, and as I walked back towards the Hall I was trying to think of which of the many rumours and misconceptions might lead to people trying to lift the central slab of the Temple of Baphomet.

I'd only gone a few steps when I saw a very welcome sight indeed – Richard Fox, walking towards me with that same knowing superior smile I'd found so infuriating at first. Now it was rather different, as we were lovers and he was the person I most wanted to see. I kissed him as he reached me because I'd stopped, intent on showing him what I'd found.

'Richard, hi. I want to show you something. Come into the temple.'

'Should we, with all these people around?'

'Not that! You're obsessed, Richard, not that I'm complaining. Look, here, somebody tried to lift this slab last night.'

He bent down, frowning, to run his fingers over the tiny chips in the marble as I explained what I knew, and suspected. From the look on his face I half expected him to take out a magnifying glass or start putting tiny objects into an envelope with a pair of tweezers, but he soon stood up again.

'Whoever it is has to be pretty serious about it. Obviously they think there's something worthwhile under the slab. Perhaps we should lift it ourselves and see?'

'No. I'm supposed to look after the place, not wreck it! Besides, I've seen the plans. It's a solid base, laid down by George Vaughan for a folly, but never finished. Elgar Vaughan laid the floor directly on the old base.'

'Oh. I thought there was something in your PhD thesis, from the interview with Alice Scott, about Vaughan concealing his most important papers under the central stone of the temple before he left for the war, and possibly more?'

I hesitated before answering.

'Yes, but not here. This is the Temple of Baphomet, specifically. The Sabbat Aceras temple as such was the space under the tower, now covered by a couple of hundred tons of rubble.'

'Could somebody have misunderstood?'

'Only if they didn't read through properly. I define my terms in the introduction. Or maybe if they'd only read the paper my supervisor and I published, although again, there's a map.'

'I see. OK, so let's look at what we know. Somebody, at least two people, want to lift the slab. Therefore they think there's something valuable underneath it. Could you possibly be wrong? Could Elgar Vaughan have hollowed out a space beneath the stone, or raised the floor up a little to create one? Let's look.'

He went outside and I followed, watching as he ducked down to where a fringe of long grass had grown up around the base of the temple. Pulling the grass away, he revealed the pale stone of the base with the black granite directly on top, separated by no more than a fraction of an inch of mortar. He chuckled.

'So much to that theory. I still say we should lift the stone.'

'No, definitely not. It's set tight and we'd be sure to damage it. Which is a good point, as it goes. How would Vaughan have lifted it without damage? I'm sure there's nothing under there.'

He gave a reflective nod.

'There's something else I want to show you. Come around the back.'

He followed me to stand beneath the Green Man, waiting patiently as I tried to figure out how I'd managed to transform what now looked like a perfectly ordinary dead tree into my gloriously over-endowed wood spirit. It wasn't obvious at first, but as I moved a little to the side there he was, arms outstretched, erection thrust out above me, only to disappear as suddenly. I turned to Richard.

'Stand here. Tell me what you see.'

I moved to let him take my place and he peered up at the foliage, just as I had done, puzzled. The tree was now set against the sky, and it was hard not to merely see the details of bark and ivy rather than the full shape. After a while Richard shook his head.

'Nothing.'

'Nothing at all? Look again. Maybe duck down a little.'

He tried, but once again shook his head. So did I.

'Maybe it's because you're a man.'

'What is?'

'That you can't see the Green Man.'

'What Green Man? Not Vaughan's?'

'No. Not Vaughan's. That dead tree, with the ivy around the top. When I came out last night to do my rounds, my candle blew out as I was standing here, and I really thought he'd come to claim me.'

'The Green Man? Elgar Vaughan in the form of a Green Man?'

'I didn't stop to think about theological subtleties. Do you see the projecting branch? Can you imagine that as a penis, eight feet long?'

He laughed.

'You'd love that, wouldn't you!'

'I was scared! But – yes, I got off on it afterwards. Can you really not see him?'

'Now you mention it, maybe, but I'd never have thought of it myself. Like you say, I think you need to have it in your head first.'

'And you don't?'

He grinned. 'I'd be the Green Man.'

I nodded my understanding and we walked out from behind the temple.

'So what do you think I should do about the intruders? I really ought to tell the Trustees, but it's not going to look too good when I've only just started. What do you think?'

'Keep it to yourself. Rub a little dirt in, and if they do notice, say it was like that already.'

'That's pretty much what I was thinking. If there are rumours going around, it might be possible to pick something up on the net. Are you online?'

'Of course. Do you want to come back to London with me?'

'I'd love to, but I have to wait until this lot's cleared

up. Technically I'm supposed to be here on Sunday as well, until six. My day off is Monday.'

'Come back with me tonight then.'

'What if they come back? They seem pretty determined.'

I was biting my lip again, torn between responsibility and the possibilities offered by going home with Richard, of which surfing for conspiracy theorists was the least appealing. Twice whoever was doing it had tried, and twice they'd failed, the first time because I'd warned them off, the second, presumably, because they hadn't been able to do it. They'd used a crowbar, and both of them had been quite big, at least to judge by their footprints. It had started to thaw, but the prints were still visible, and another idea occurred to me.

'Put your foot there, Richard, in that print, the male one.'

He didn't hesitate but moved to the lines of footprints and placed his foot neatly in one of those made by the man. It didn't fit. It didn't touch the sides.

'Bloody hell! What size are your feet?'

'Eleven.'

'And how tall are you, six-two?'

'Six-three.'

'Shit! His feet must be . . . I don't know, but huge! Hers aren't exactly small either!'

'There we are then, they should be easy to spot.'

He was joking, but it was true. It was also yet more disconcerting, to think of a woman who had to be six foot tall, and a man who could have given Frankenstein's monster a run for his money, lurking around the grounds in the dark. I'd been out there too, and it looked as if my fear of the Green Man hadn't been all that far off the mark. Suddenly I'd made up my mind. They could try and lift the slab until they were blue in the face. I just wasn't up for tackling gigantic intruders.

'OK, I'll come back with you, but late. Latish anyway.'

'Perfect. I can take you to the Angel again, get you dead drunk, and spend the night amusing myself with your body.'

'Sounds good to me.'

The rest of the day was spent working, and trying to justify my own choice. What I should have done was inform the Trustees, and the police, but I couldn't see it achieving anything, and certainly nothing that was to my advantage. The Trustees might put a caretaker in, which I definitely didn't want, or even replace me. The police would come round, peer into the hole – so to speak – and maybe give me an incident number if I was lucky.

It was better to leave it and hope that either they'd give up, or manage to raise the slab and find out there was nothing underneath, hopefully without causing any conspicuous damage. Meanwhile, I had other things to worry about. The wedding party had made a lot of mess, but it was nothing to what the marquee people had done, with the soil churned up and the ground full of holes.

I also had a call asking if the Hall was open that afternoon, and I had to reply that it was. Putting Richard to the most male of uses with an assortment of garden implements, I went up to change. I do like to do things properly, and so worked from the ground up: make-up, hair, stockings, boots, combinations, corset, petticoat – which was as far as I'd got when Richard came up.

'Hi, Sophie, I found some glasses by ... hmm, how delectable, come to Papa.'

He stepped towards me, and it was quite obvious what he wanted.

'Richard, no! There are people coming.'

'Yes. Us.'

'No!'

I was trying to sound serious, but I couldn't keep the laughter out of my voice. He caught me by the wrists as I tried to back away around the bed, and sat down on the edge, pulling me after him. I thought I was going to be put on my knees and let out a squeak of mock alarm, then another, very real, as I realised he had something else in mind. He didn't want me on my knees, but over his.

'Richard, no! That's not funny!'

'Oh yes it is. At least, for me.'

'You bastard! Get off! No!'

There was absolutely nothing I could do because he was just too strong and I couldn't stop giggling. I was pulled down across his lap into a thoroughly undignified position, with my bottom stuck up in the air and my arms held up in the small of my back, protesting like anything, and I meant it.

'Ow! Richard, no! You're hurting, Richard!'

'Oh, sorry. Is that better?'

'Yes – no! No, it is not better! Let me down, you oaf!'

He merely chuckled, then gave a happy sigh as he reached for the hem of my petticoat. I'd been kicking my legs around, but I realised I was only making myself look silly and stopped, resigning myself to taking a spanking.

'You're a pervert, Richard Fox, you know that?'

'Oh, absolutely. Would you have me any other way?'

'No, but this is really undignified. You're not supposed to do this sort of thing to women nowadays.'

'True, perhaps, although an area in which our predecessors definitely had the right ideas. And think about it, if you want to fully enjoy the authentic Victorian experience, then a good spanking now and then is a must. Now, let's see just how authentic you are.'

As we'd spoken he'd had my petticoat half-raised, but now he pulled it right up, exposing the seat of my combinations, at the sight of which he gave a pleased click of his tongue.

'Splitters! Excellent! I should have known you wouldn't let me down, and what pretty lace.'

'They're original. Be careful.'

My voice sounded more than a little sulky in my own ears, but it was impossible not to feel a touch of pride too. I'd never before met a man who could even begin to really appreciate Victorian underwear. He began to touch, using a single finger to stroke me gently through the baggy cotton around my bottom as he answered me.

'I will, although I cannot promise the same for what's underneath.'

I tried to answer him, but all that came out was a little sob as his fingers delved in among the rear folds of my combinations. He found the edge and pulled them wide, unveiling my bottom. His hand touched my flesh, and I thought it was going to start, only for him to start stroking me, very gently, and talking.

'Glorious, a true peach ... no, a nectarine, because your skin is so smooth, like cream. What is it about a pretty bottom that's so utterly delectable, so irresistible? The shape, I suppose, the way the split mimics another charming piece of female anatomy, which, incidentally, is peeping out ever so sweetly from between your thighs. Yes, delectable indeed ...'

As he spoke his finger was tracing a slow line between my cheeks, driving me to distraction, just as his words were bringing my sense of frustration up to boiling point.

'Just do it, you bastard.'

He laughed, his hand lifted, and the next instant I was earnestly wishing I'd kept my mouth shut and let him carry on with his fondling. It stung like anything, and had me kicking and struggling again immediately, undignified or not. He certainly found it amusing because he was laughing his head off as he spanked me, a demented cackling noise that broke off only when the doorbell rang. Not that he stopped spanking me.

'Visitors. Never mind, no doubt they can keep themselves amused.'

Somehow I managed to find my voice.

'Richard, no! Stop it, they'll hear.'

'Don't make such a fuss then.'

'I can't help it. Now stop!'

He stopped and let go, so suddenly I fell on the floor, drawing fresh laughter from him. I got up, refrained from slapping his face with some difficulty, and quickly began to rearrange myself as the bell went for the second time.

'You're an utter pig, Richard.'

'So the girls always tell me.'

I threw him a dirty look as I smoothed my petticoat down. My bottom felt hot and tingly, delightful in one way, but utterly frustrating in another. I needed sex, badly.

'Did you have to do that? I said there were people coming, and now I have to show then around with a warm bum. How embarrassing is that?'

'Perfect! I shall think of you as I peruse one or two of old Vaughan's more salacious prints to keep myself ready.'

'Maybe, but for now you can go and let them in while I finish dressing. Honestly, look what you'd done to my hair!'

He was still chuckling to himself as he made for the door. I was left to make frantic repairs to my hair and make-up, haul my dress on and rush down, still trying to do the catches up as I reached the ground floor. Two minutes later I was out on the carriage sweep where Richard, looking cool and immaculate, was pointing out features of the Hall to a group of people. He turned as I approached, smiling, but absolutely certain that all six of the respectable and studious-looking visitors were going to know that I'd just been put across a man's knee.

They were a local history group and, while they didn't know a great deal about Elgar Vaughan himself, they knew the history of the Hall and of the surrounding area. One old lady was particularly interesting, as she'd lived nearby all her life and could remember playing in the grounds as a child. Richard had come with us as we started around the grounds and was as interested as me, immediately asking her a question.

'Have there been many changes?'

'Oh no, not to speak of. You couldn't go in, that was all. There was a keeper, then, had been there since the Great War, I'm told. He used to chase us with a stick, he did, if he saw us, threatening all kinds of things. We believed him too. Not that it stopped us. We used to go all the more, if anything, down to the lake mainly. Is that open now?'

'I've opened the path, yes, but it's very overgrown.'

'In my day we used to come in at the back, otherwise you'd get seen. We didn't like to come too close to the house at the best of times.'

There was amusement in Richard's voice as he answered.

'Because it's supposed to be haunted?'

'Oh no, because of the keeper. Mark you, it was a brave lad who'd come up here at night. They say you could hear Vaughan and his cronies chanting from under the rubble of the tower.'

'How about the woods? Any giant tree men?'

I gave him a dirty look, but she merely laughed.

'Nothing like that, no, but his carvings used to give me the creeps. Taught me a bit though.'

She laughed at her own joke, more ribald than I'd

have expected of her, and as we rounded the corner of the house the conversation switched to the condition of the formal garden. I continued with the tour, but my heart wasn't really in it. What I wanted to know was who'd been out in the grounds at night, and what they expected to gain by lifting the temple slab.

Given Richard's comments about my thesis, it was just possible that they'd got the wrong slab, but that was an avenue of investigation I was really rather eager to avoid. Not that there was much to be done about it anyway, without the aid of a team of building contractors. The hall temple was well and truly buried, and was going to stay that way, with the tower protected as a ruin, both by government and according to the terms of the Trust.

It's so easy to be paranoid. I couldn't even completely eliminate Richard from my suspicions, because while his feet didn't match the man from the night before – or rather, his shoes didn't – he might still be involved. Possibly his job was to keep me safely out of the way by seducing me? That meant they'd now know it was the wrong slab, possibly, so if he was involved there would presumably be no further investigation of the Temple of Baphomet.

Richard wasn't the only suspect. Anyone else who'd ever worked on Vaughan had to be considered, anyone who'd seen my thesis or the subsequent paper, including my supervisor. Not even the Trustees could be automatically discounted, nor anyone else for that matter, including Julie. If it had been worth checking Richard's feet for size, it might also be worth checking hers. After all, she was tall enough and she had certainly had the opportunity. Possibly she'd asked me to go clubbing to give her accomplice a free run at the temple, but the wedding had spoiled her plan. Possibly she'd never meant to go clubbing at all but had got me drunk so they could visit the temple safely. Possibly she'd even drugged me, because I'd gone out like a light.

No. It was just another flight of fancy, scarcely more credible than Richard being Elgar Vaughan. Julie was a successful New York businesswoman, and knew nothing about Elmcote Hall beyond what I'd told her. The truth was that I didn't really have any suspects as such, and could only hope that my internet search would turn something up.

By the time we'd finished with the grounds, the group were complaining about the cold and making hopeful remarks about tea. I obliged, serving it in the reception room of the west wing where they could admire the Vaughan family pictures, as opposed to the ones in the library. It was already beginning to get dark by the time they left, and I sat down gratefully in the kitchen, feeling I'd done my bit. Richard even made me coffee before sitting down with his legs stretched out and his chair tilted back, grinning.

'What are you thinking about?'

'You, the way you behaved with the visitors, so wonderfully English, and all the time with a pair of pink buns under your skirt. I wonder what they'd think if they knew?'

'I'd forgotten all about it.'

'Oh no you hadn't. I could tell your mind wasn't on the job.'

'No, really. I was thinking about the people in the temple.'

'What, do you mean I have to warm you up again?'

'No, you do not. I'm fine, thank you, and would like an hour's peace, a leisurely glass of wine at the Angel, then dinner. After that you can do with me as you please.'

'That sort of offer might tempt a man to rush his food. Very unhealthy.'

'Then don't do it. Restrain yourself.'

'That wasn't actually what I had in mind.'

'Oh yes?'

'Yes. What was that wonderful piece of philosophy from *Personal Services*? Oh yes, that it's best to get your man de-spunked before you go out, because then he won't rush dinner. It's entirely true, although it perhaps fails to take into account that there are those of us quite capable of being de-spunked – wonderful phrase that – both before and after dinner.'

'You're a hound.'

'I'd rather be referred to as a goat, if you must keep comparing me to animals.'

'As you wish. You're a goat, a satyr.'

'That's better. Now, why don't you crawl over to me on your knees, take a good mouthful of coffee and pop this in with it?'

As he'd spoken he'd unzipped, to pull himself free. There's something about a man like that, fully dressed except for what really matters, and I felt my tummy tighten a little, but responded only with a slight lift of my eyebrows.

'And what do you expect me to do with that?' I asked, gesturing to his lewd display.

'As I said, although if you prefer to change a detail here or there I'm not one to be fussy. For instance, you might take the upper part of your dress down around your waist. In fact, I'd like that.'

'I bet you would. Seriously though, I ought to change.'

'Change? No, Sophie, you can't do that to me! I want you as you are, either now or later.'

'I can't go to the Angel like this,' I said.

'Why not? What could be more respectable?'

'They're not going to see it like that, are they? Although I suppose I could.'

'You should, but you should also come to me now. Imagine I'm Elgar Vaughan if you like, and you're an acolyte, or even a maid. Get on your knees, Sophie, that's an order.'

I made a face, but he'd got me. Bunching my skirt and petticoat up, I got carefully down on my knees. He moved a little forward on the chair and opened his legs, offering himself to me as I crawled across the floor. As I reached him his hand came out, taking me gently by my hair and steering me down into his lap. I closed my eyes as my mouth filled, with my naughty feelings rushing back to fill my head.

It was rather a nice thought, being a servant girl, a tweenie perhaps, made to go down on my knees to suck the master of the house. No doubt I'd have been terrified of Elgar Vaughan and done just as I was told, taking him in my mouth to the delight of the other cultists, both male and female. I'd be enjoying it, of course, because I wouldn't be able to stop myself, but my feelings would be very mixed, and very intense. He was beginning to get properly hard when he spoke again.

'Now the coffee. Go on.'

My head was pulled back by the hair, not hard but very firmly, brooking no resistance. He was holding the mug, and put it to my mouth as I knelt up. I took some in, hot and sweet, the way he liked it, and held it carefully as I returned to my task. He gave a pleased sigh and began to tickle the back of my neck, sending shivers down my spine. Once more I pictured myself as a tweenie, being made to perform lewd tricks for the master's pleasure, my body responding despite myself.

I really couldn't help it, all my feelings flooding back as I enjoyed what I was doing to Richard, the way he'd spanked me, the way he just expected me to do his bidding, gentle but firm, and completely in charge. My hands went back, to throw up my skirts and pull the seat of my combinations wide, baring myself behind. Richard gave a knowing chuckle as he saw, adding a fresh pang to my sense of helpless excitement. My hand burrowed in under my petticoats and I was teasing myself, my pleasure rising quickly.

My eyes closed and I was there, a maid on my knees on the scullery floor, my bottom bare and pink from spanking as I sucked on my master's penis. The image held, locking in my mind as the delicious shivers running through me grew stronger, and stronger still. Richard came, just as I did, together in a long glorious moment of perfect, uninhibited intimacy. Only when it was well and truly over did he ease me up from his lap to take me into his arms, my head cradled on his broad chest. At last he spoke.

'There, that's better, isn't it? Now we can enjoy dinner at leisure.'

Dinner was even better than the time before: oysters and turbot, washed down with Champagne and followed by slices of thoroughly indulgent chocolate cake. Richard had to drive back to London, so I ended up drinking almost the entire bottle, which left me pleasantly tipsy. As we drove through the darkened countryside towards the motorway I was daydreaming as usual, thinking of what we'd done and imagining what we might do. Already I had realised several of my darkest, most private fantasies, while Richard was quite capable of providing his own input, opening a road to places I hardly dared consider.

I even felt a little guilty for my maid fantasy, because Elgar Vaughan's extraordinary turnover of servants had been a major element of the scandal surrounding the Hall, although to the best of my knowledge none of them had claimed to have been molested. It was more often a case of coming downstairs in the morning to find a goat in the main hall, not to mention the nightly screams of laughter and ecstasy and general 'ungodly goings-on'.

Presumably with six willing and liberal-minded female acolytes, he hadn't felt the need to abuse his staff. Possibly he'd even considered it immoral. With Elgar Vaughan it was always hard to tell.

Then again, what went on in my head was nobody's business but my own, and possibly Richard's. Nobody would come to any harm, so why should I restrict myself to pc fantasies, or behaviour? No, I could be Richard's maid, or get turned over his knee, or be chased through the woods by the Green Man. It was in my head, my concern.

I was also eager to see where Richard lived as, when it came down to it, I knew next to nothing about him while he now knew a great deal about me. As he worked in the city I assumed he was doing fairly well for himself, but I still wasn't expecting the top floor flat in Soho, just off Golden Square, complete with roof garden. It was amazing looking out over the London rooftops, just yards above the bustle of the streets, but with a wonderful sense of detachment.

Richard had immediately begun to make coffee and I began to wander around, a little surprised at his taste. Given that he presumably entertained colleagues from time to time I hadn't expected the walls to be decorated with Elgar Vaughan prints, but there was not so much as a hint of his interest. When I asked he simply laughed.

'Oh no, this isn't mine. It belongs to a friend of mine, a barrister. He's in New York, I'm over here, so it made sense to swap rather than going to all the trouble of finding suitable accommodation, never mind paying for it.'

'I see. I thought it looked a little, I don't know, Spartan?'

'That's deceptive. Bruce is gay, but he's careful not to be too in-your-face about it with work. Like me, he prefers to indulge his dark side in secret.'

He gave me a wicked grin as he began to grind the coffee beans, filling the air with a delicious bitter-sweet smell. I waited for him to complete the ritual, which he had down to a fine art, far more elaborate than my own, and even including warming the cups. A single small spoonful of Muscovado sugar went into each, although I don't normally take it. I didn't protest, and had to admit it was delicious.

Coffee in hand, he steered me into the study and we sat down at the computer. Again he took charge immediately, running up a search engine and feeding some terms in. The results were astonishing. In the four short months since the publication of my paper, people from the driest historians to the most extreme cultists seemed to have latched on to Elgar Vaughan. The total number of results still fell far short of those for Crowley, but he'd almost caught up with Samuel Liddell Mathers. An impressive, but slightly alarming, number also mentioned me.

In most I was simply credited as co-author of my paper, and in a few cases as living at the Hall, despite having been there for a matter of days. Several commented on my interview with Alice Scott and the inference that important papers and possibly some unspecified form of wealth remained hidden, but there was nothing telling. Some were more unusual, referring to me as a Vaughan acolyte, a witch and a 'known pagan', whatever that implied. There was even a preacher in Cincinnati calling me a 'blasphemous Devil worshipper', which was a little strong as I was only really getting started in that direction. Only a very few carried the feel of conspiracy theory, notably one claiming that Vaughan's cult was being revived and that a 'strange, long-haired woman of indeterminable age' had moved in at the Hall.

'What do they mean "indeterminable age"? Cheek!'

'I think the implication is that you're one of the original female acolytes. Let me check to see if I can get an address for the service provider.'

He could, which was more than I'd have been able to do. The site was based in Wisconsin, which made it seem unlikely that they had anything to do with the people trying to raise the slab. Nor were they very mysterious, with plenty of photos of them indulging in their investigations of pagan or supposedly Satanic goings-on. There were no exceptionally large men among them, and no women at all. Nor could we find any other worthwhile leads, either on websites or among discussion groups.

Richard was enjoying himself anyway, amused or fascinated by the content of the sites. Three coffees later and I was beginning to get bored, with very little of interest coming up anymore, while I learned nothing, or at least nothing about Vaughan or the intruders. I had to squeeze Richard's crotch before he finally got the message, and even then he just sat back, grinning broadly.

'Do you know, we ought to revive the Sabbat Aceras. We could make a fortune.'

'Don't be sordid. How do you mean?'

'There are endless possibilities. For instance, you like the idea of being watched while we have sex. How would you like to have to suck me off, just as you did before, only with a group of men and women to watch? We could charge –'

'Richard! Absolutely not!'

'I thought you liked being watched?'

'Not charging for it! Besides, it has to be the right people. If we charge, all we'd get would be a bunch of dirty old men, so you can put that idea right out of your head.'

'Hmm, pity. We could even have set up an internet site, with webcams in the temples, and – OK, never mind, I take your point.'

He had, the point of my shoe on his shin, but despite a grimace of pain he was still laughing as he went on, amused by my reaction.

'OK, no dirty old men, and no webcams, I promise. I'd undoubtedly get the sack anyway, although I suppose I could wear a goat mask...'

'I'd get the sack too.'

'Yes, I was going to say your Trustees might not approve. How do they see the Hall? They allow weddings, how about pagan rituals, festivals even?'

'I doubt they'd permit a festival. Most of them see it as a responsibility, a piece of heritage. Only a couple are interested in making money above what's needed for upkeep.'

'And how often do they turn up?'

'Officially? Twice a year. Unofficially, any time they like.'

'But presumably not in the middle of the night?'

'No. It is a good idea, Richard. In fact I feel quite serious about it, but we must have the right people, exactly the right people, my choice.'

'Fair enough, but you want to do it, yes, for real, in front of them?'

'Yes. That would be an integral part of it, if we're to follow Elgar Vaughan's lead, which we must. It scares me a little, but I want to do it, yes.'

5

Richard's suggestion had me full of nerves. It was the sort of thing I'd have thought about, fantasised over, but never dared do. The organisation was easy enough, time and again I'd imagined exactly what I'd do and which temple I'd use for what, but invariably my ideas quickly outstripped the possible, involving hermaphrodites, mythical creatures, demons and more, in impossible numbers and doing impossible things, mainly to me.

My real concern was the Trustees. I wouldn't technically be in breach of contract, at least so long as the cult members paid their four pounds fifty entrance fee or their discounted one year membership at twenty-five pounds. Nevertheless, it was a stipulation of Hubert Sands' original agreement that the Hall was not put to improper use which, while vague, presumably covered pagan and/or Satanic sex orgies.

It had to be secret, and that meant taking extra care in choosing who was involved. Richard wanted the full thirteen, and felt that anyone with an appreciation of Elgar Vaughan would do. I knew that I could never do what was wanted of me unless I found the watchers attractive, something he didn't really understand, perhaps a male thing. Fortunately he accepted that it was my decision, and also that while thirteen was the right target to aim for, we couldn't expect to get so many together initially. Even Vaughan hadn't managed that.

He was remarkably confident, and keen to get things going. So was I, although even the thought of taking him in my mouth with people watching was enough to make me feel weak at the knees, and very, very aroused, never mind some of the other possibilities he'd raised. As I went about my work during the next few days I was constantly on edge, moving between worry and a state of arousal so strong I simply had to bring myself to ecstasy in order to calm down again.

It was on the Wednesday that I did it in the Temple of Baphomet, on my knees, and so horny that it was only afterwards I realised that the pentagonal slab had been tampered with again. This time they'd tried to conceal what they'd done, rubbing dirt in to conceal the marks just as I had. By the look of it they'd tried to hammer a wedge into the crack, but had failed. It had to have been noisy though, so had probably happened on the Sunday night, while I was at Richard's.

My immediate reaction was shock, and to look over my shoulder, expecting to find a seven-foot-tall man looming over me with his erection in his hand and his female accomplice watching from behind with a know-ing leer. Relief followed, because having explained to Richard why the slab couldn't possibly conceal anything thicker than a few sheets of paper, he could safely be excluded as a suspect.

On the way back to the house I realised that the slab itself might be hollow, and nothing would do but to find a hammer and test the whole of the floor. There was no difference between the pentagonal slab and any other.

Again I considered purchasing a dog, and realised that there was another drawback. I couldn't just go to Batter-sea and purchase a monstrous slavering hound which I could then unleash to roam the grounds by night – the Hound of Elmcote Hall. The whole idea rested on the beast treating me as its mistress, and I couldn't really see it working. Alternatively, I could buy a puppy which might reasonably be expected to grow up into a mon-strous slavering hound, but that wasn't much use in the short term. The Puppy of Elmcote Hall just didn't have that ring to it, and I couldn't see my seven-foot man being impressed.

I also reconsidered CCTV. After all, I would be in control of it, and could make very sure that only what I wished got caught on camera. It went rather against my principles, but I reassured myself that had the intruders simply wished to indulge their passion in the temple, perhaps even conduct a sacrifice or two, then I wouldn't have minded. It was damaging things that was the problem.

Julie had called on the Monday, to make sure I was OK, and to tease me about falling asleep. She'd also been moaning about how dull life was in the village and that I was the only person she'd met locally who was any fun. I suggested coming over for a drink and she jumped at the idea, bringing a bottle of heavy Californian red which we shared, drinking and talking until the small hours.

Richard was coming down on the Saturday, but rang on Thursday to say he had put together a list of possibilities, picked from appropriate internet groups. For the sake of secrecy we'd agreed not to invite people to the Hall because there were sure to be problems with those we rejected, and that meant we had to go to them. He'd chosen eight, which either suggested a lot of hard work or that he wasn't being too particular. Of the eight, two were female, and both preferred to meet with another woman.

I agreed to do it, although a touch uneasily in case either Davinia or Lilitu turned out to be a thirty-stone man with a thing about axes. Richard was full of enthusiasm, and by the time he came down he had another five, including a third woman, complete with pictures. Once I'd finished showing my second coachload of the day around the Hall we sat down in the kitchen to go through them, with the printouts spread across the table and a bottle of Sauvignon between us. Some were impressive, some not, but as Richard laid the last one out my eyes opened wide.

'I thought you might be interested in this one.'

'He's enormous! If that's an ordinary door he has to be, well, pushing seven foot.'

'Six-ten, I estimate, judging by the bricks, which are a uniform size.'

I nodded. Men that size are not commonplace, and he might have been substituted for the image of the male intruder in my head and no questions asked. Not only was he tall, he was bulky, with tree-trunk legs, a massive chest and a heavy paunch, also a huge tangled mop of tawny-gold hair, beard and all. He was dressed casually, sloppily even, with worn jeans, a leather jacket and a sweatshirt advertising some band the details of which were invisible beneath his beard. There was also a great deal of jewellery, rings, a piercing in one eyebrow, several chains around his neck. My eyes had gone down though to his feet, and the heavy rough work boots, boots that might very well have left the footprints I'd seen on the lawn.

'Who is he?'

'He calls himself Magog, after the giant. That's his online name anyway. I didn't want to get too close for fear of arousing his suspicions.'

'Absolutely. So what else do we know?'

'Quite a lot. There are plenty of posts from him on groups dealing with the occult going back quite a while, but he's only recently picked up an interest in Vaughan. Whatever he's up to here, he's keeping it to himself, but I'm sure he's your man.'

'Well I certainly hope there aren't two like him!'

'What do you suggest we do?'

'I suggest we take him on board.'

'Take him on board? You have to be joking!'

'Not at all. Look at the guy. Would you rather have him on the inside or the outside?'

I looked, but my thoughts had gone off on a different track. Instead of considering the problem of confronting him about the damage to the temple, I was thinking of how it would feel to be semi-naked at Richard's feet with a man like that watching me. My stomach was tying itself in knots, and I couldn't stop myself from nodding. Richard went on, oblivious.

'I knew you'd see sense. We could even lift the stone to show good faith, and to prove there's nothing underneath it.'

'How? We can't damage it, and that would mean giving away that we knew it was him.'

'Would that matter?'

'Well . . . no, I suppose not.'

'As for lifting it, I've been thinking about that. The slab is fitted flush, without mortar, and if it was meant to be lifted, it can be lifted. Does that make sense?'

'I suppose so.'

'So either it's mortared down, in which case there can't be anything there anyway, or it's not, in which case we should be able to lift it using a suction device. You can hire them.'

'It's worth a try I suppose.'

'Absolutely. I'll approach Magog then, OK?'

'OK. How about his girlfriend, the woman who left the prints of her heels?'

'There are one or two references to a girlfriend, but she doesn't seem to post herself, or not that I can see. But that should be OK. After all, they already know about the Hall.'

'That's true.'

'How about the others?'

* * *

Among the remaining nine men there were only two I was even prepared to consider. The other seven were simply wrong. Richard had at least made some effort to suit my taste because they were all reasonably tall, but they lacked a certain quality I found it hard to define, and which he couldn't understand at all. Even with only their pictures to go on there was a lack of presence, or aura perhaps, which made them unacceptable, and the information Richard had collected on them only reinforced my decision.

Even with the remaining two I was doubtful, but had to admit they were at least worth interviewing. One, who called himself simply the Magus, was a devout Crowleyite, although to judge by what Richard had learnt he had put little if any of his theory into practice. He was very tall and thin, with dark piercing eyes that projected a disturbing gaze. Like Magog, he was a little worrying, but I could picture him in the Temple of Baphomet without difficulty.

The other was definitely intriguing, an outwardly straightforward man called Nathan who was pictured standing by a Land Rover on his farm in Lincolnshire. Physically he was very much my type: tall, well built, with that rough edge which so appeals. The reason he was suitable was that he left votive offerings out in his woods to ensure a good harvest, a form of paganism with echoes of the writer Saki, who had been a contemporary of Elgar Vaughan and met him on at least one occasion. Nathan even mentioned Saki in some of his posts, which helped to sway my opinion.

My three women were harder to assess. Davinia was simply unworldly, tall, very slim, with hair even longer than mine, down to her thighs. Her beliefs centred on the Earth Mother, and she made little stone dolls like those found in ancient sites, exaggeratedly feminine, with heavy breasts, a swollen belly and full buttocks, the exact opposite of her own figure. She lived deep in Cornwall, near Helston, and if it hadn't been for her obsession with fertility and impregnation I'd have dismissed her out of hand as too wishy-washy.

Lilitu was scary, at least, if she was to be taken seriously. She modelled herself not on Lilith as first wife of Adam, but on the Babylonian demoness, and certainly looked the part. Her picture showed pale skin, hair dyed jet black, elaborate black and green make-up, and fingers sheathed in artificial talons of silver filigree work. She seemed a touch artificial, but she did know quite a lot about Elgar Vaughan, and it was easy to imagine her as an enthusiast.

The third, Sarah, was relatively mainstream, a wiccan and a herbalist, but also a great believer in restoring pre-Christian festivals, her versions of which involved nudity, although more as a way of casting off the restraints of conventional morality than any sexual reason. That might not have been enough, but her picture looked promising. She was thirty or a bit more, with an abundance of auburn hair and a serene maternal face. Around her neck was a long chain with a pendant hanging between her breasts in the form of a classic Green Man.

Sarah was the closest, living a few miles along the river at Whitchurch, so it made sense to visit her first. I went down on the Monday, after a weekend of rude and passionate sex with Richard during which we attempted to shag in every one of Elgar Vaughan's temples. We very nearly got caught in the shrine to Artemis, escaping only because I was riding him and so saw Lorna Meadows, the secretary of the Trust, as she approached across the lawns. Had I been in doggy, as usual, she'd have walked right in on us, and I determined to be extra careful in future.

That meant giving nothing away until I was absolutely sure it was safe, and I was trying to work out how to go about it as my all-stations train rattled slowly through the Thames Valley. I got off at Pangbourne and crossed the bridge over the river, quickly finding Sarah's shop a little way up the hill on the far side. The window display included everything from culinary herbs to corn dollies, with little of overtly pagan significance and nothing to do with the occult. Feeling somewhat doubtful, I pushed in at the door to find Sarah herself seated behind the counter.

'Hi, Sarah, I'm Sophie Page. Richard Fox said I'd be coming?'

'Yes. Come in, sit down. Tea?'

I accepted, and sat down in a wicker chair to one side as she went to prepare it. When she came back it was with two mugs of something hot and floral, with a faintly astringent taste I didn't recognise. She explained what it was, and how she blended different herbs for different occasions, also incense, which appealed rather more. Incense had also been something Elgar Vaughan made extensive use of, which allowed me to put something into the conversation instead of just listening, and to get to the crucial topic.

'... it would be perfect, I'm sure. Do you celebrate Samhain with a group?'

'Oh yes, of course. There are several well-organised festivals. The most important thing is that everybody works together. That's why I feel we must be accepting of everybody's broad beliefs, to avoid the risk of schism. Are you with the National Association?'

'Er, no.'

'Oh, you must sign up, you really must. Hang on just a moment and I'll get the forms.'

I left twenty minutes later, twenty pounds poorer and a fully paid-up associate of the National Association of Natural Worship. Elgar Vaughan had not even come into the conversation. Sarah was a very nice woman, a woman who believed in sisterly affection, unashamed nudity, free love and lots of incense, but would have been horribly shocked at the idea of watching me in supplication at an altar to Baphomet, never mind the naughty details.

With the rest of the day free I was at a loose end, and having failed once I was keen to try again. Cornwall was plainly impractical, but Lilitu was in London, and I could be there in maybe an hour. I had her internet details and I'd passed a library in Pangbourne, so it was at least worth a try. It worked too. Not only was she online, swapping messages about Crowley's infamous Sicilian farm, but she was delighted to have me visit.

By midday I was outside her flats, a huge anonymous block in Gospel Oak. I hesitated only briefly and went up, doing my best to ignore the atmosphere of urban decay. Her flat was on the third floor and outwardly no different to those to the left and right, a plain red-painted door leading off a passage, with the only evidence of individuality provided by pot plants. I knocked anyway and a moment later a rich female voice asked me to wait, accompanied by a metallic clanking.

Finally the door swung open to reveal the massive chained security gate within and Lilitu, in all her glory, taller than me, in a dress of clinging forest green velvet that matched her elaborate Gothic make-up and her talons. She was more than a little daunting, but her painted mouth was curved up in a happy guileless smile as she looked at me.

'Dr Page, yes?'

She wasn't supposed to know my full name, and I was a little taken aback but there was no point in denying it.

'Yes, I suppose so. I never use my title though, or people start talking about symptoms. Sophie's better. You must be Lilitu, hi.'

'Lily, just now. Come in, it's great to meet you!'

I stepped forward and to my slight surprise she kissed me, no more than brushing my cheek with her lips, but distinctly friendly and enthusiastic. She had to shut the door behind us, fixing the heavy-duty chain back in place, which gave me a chance to glance around her flat.

It was hard to imagine a greater contrast with the drab exterior. There wasn't much space: a single bedroom, a long living room with a kitchen beyond a screen at one end, and a closed door which presumably led to the bathroom. The difference was in the decoration – black iron, brass, screens of carved wood, velvets and satins in rich dark colours and an immense amount of gauze, creating an atmosphere of baroque indulgence. Even her telephone looked as if it might have been pre-war, and the only nod to modernity was her computer, a sleek and expensive-looking laptop.

'I love your flat!'

'Thank you. I appreciate that, coming from someone who lives in Elmcote Hall. That is so cool.'

'Oh. I didn't know Richard had said anything?'

'He didn't, but it doesn't take a genius to figure it out.'

She jerked her thumb at the computer and flopped herself down on a pile of cushions upholstered in old gold plush. I sat down too, opposite her, as she went on.

'Like, I've read you're stuff, and how many Sophies are going to be into Elgar Vaughan? It had to be you.'

'I suppose so. So that's how you knew my full name?'

'Sure. All I got from the boyfriend was that you wanted to meet other people who're into Vaughan's stuff. I love it. Here, look what I found on Portobello Road.'

She reached out to a pile of old books that looked as if they'd been arranged for dramatic effect. At the bottom was a slim folio, bound in tatty shagreen, which she drew out and passed to me, still talking.

'They were printed and bound in Paris, in nineteen-twelve.'

I opened the book, expecting maybe one of Vaughan's rather rambling papers on the occult, and my mouth came open. The very first print, foxed at the edges but undamaged beneath its transparency, was one of those on the walls of the library, showing Elgar Vaughan and his acolytes standing in the hall beneath the tower. At the centre of the circle stood a brazier, with smoke from the burning incense rising to form the goat-headed hermaphrodite Baphomet figure who had been so important to his beliefs.

'Beautiful. I have the original in the library at Elmcote, and prints, but not bound like this.'

She was absolutely glowing with pride as I turned the page, and I was wondering what I'd done to inspire such devotion. The second print was the one of Vaughan enthroned beside Baphomet-Lilith which I'd shown to Julie, and the others from the same series, all commissioned together. There were only ten, and several copies of each were in the library, but it was still a wonderful thing for her to have, while the others belonged to the Trust. Already I was warming to her, but I didn't want to rush my decision.

As I went through the prints she watched, curled on her side among the cushions with her chin propped up in her hand. Her feet were stretched out, encased in seamed tights, or maybe stockings. Given her height, it occurred to me that she might just be a candidate for the female footprints in the frost, and I decided to ask her more or less straight out.

'Have you been to Elmcote Hall?'

'Not inside, no. I went last year but it was closed up, and one other time.'

'It's not hard to get into the grounds.'

'I know. I've been. I sneaked in the back, just by the Temple of Baphomet ...'

I really thought I was about to get a confession, but she carried on blithely.

'... but the place was full of workmen so I couldn't really explore. I've been in the woods, all round. Do you actually live in the building?'

'Yes, in the west wing, on the first floor. The workmen you saw would have been doing the conversion, but they weren't allowed to change much, fortunately. My room is the one at the end, overlooking the lime walk and the temple. Did you know there's a rumour that Vaughan hid his most important documents under the central slab?'

For a moment she looked puzzled.

'I thought that was the other temple, the Sabbat Aceras one, under the tower?'

'Either one, depending who you're talking to.'

'But in the interview with Alice Scott in your paper –'

'Oh yes, if it's anywhere it's the Sabbat Aceras temple. Sorry, I was referring to the rumours rather than what Alice Scott hinted at.'

She was innocent, or a very good liar. I relaxed a little more as she pulled herself to her feet.

'I'm being a crap hostess, aren't I? Would you like some wine? I won two bottles of Aussie red in a tombola at the church hall yesterday. You should've seen the looks some of the women were giving me.'

'I bet, and some of the men, if you were dressed like that.'

She knew exactly what I meant, and grinned in response. Not only was she beautiful, but exotic, and to me she exuded sex, with the velvet of her dress clinging to her womanly figure. Everything about her was sumptuous: her voice, the way she looked, her manner, and also her perfume, which I recognised as the same as Julie's.

'What's your scent?'

'Persephone. Don't you recognise it?'

She stepped close and held out her wrist, letting me draw in the deep spicy scent, which also had just a touch of something like autumn leaves. It suited her, and she wore a lot of it.

'Yes, a friend of mine wears it, but I didn't know what it was.'

'Oh right. You get it mail order, from this place in the States. They do all sorts of good stuff. I'll give you their address.'

'Thanks.'

I went back to looking at the prints as she opened the bottle and poured wine into two large green glasses, but closed the folio and put it carefully back before accepting mine. The wine was heady and strong, with a spicy taste, but deliciously smooth, tempting me to take a hearty swig instead of a sip. I watched as she curled herself back onto the cushions, asking myself the crucial question: how did I feel about her watching me submit myself to Richard?

The answer was simple. I didn't mind at all and, unless I was badly misjudging her, she'd revel in it. It still took me a moment to find the courage, and the right words, but I'd made my decision.

'Lily ... there's a bit more to it than simply wanting to meet other people who appreciate Elgar Vaughan. Richard and I want to try and revive the Sabbat Aceras, and we're wondering if you'd like to be involved. Would you be interested?'

Her eyes were shining immediately.

'Would I? Does the Pope shit in the woods? I'm in!'

'Good. I thought you might be.'

'Believe me, you couldn't keep me away! So what are you planning?'

I responded cautiously.

'We're not one hundred per cent sure yet. First we need the right people.'

She had no such reservations.

'That's for sure. Tell me you're not going to wimp out, Sophie. Tell me you're going to recreate Elgar Vaughan's rituals, please?'

I could feel the blood starting to rise to my cheeks as I responded, but I couldn't help but be infected by her sheer enthusiasm.

'Yes, that's the general idea. You see why it's hard to get the right group together?'

'Do I! And you're asking me?'

'You seem perfect. Obviously we'll have to work the details out between us, so nobody's being asked to break their personal boundaries, but you seem – I don't know – confident?'

'A dirty bitch?'

It took me a second to respond, but she was smiling.

'You could put it like that I suppose. The thing is with Elgar Vaughan is that we don't have detailed records of his rituals, and it's hard to separate fact from rumour and speculation. Even what we do have sometimes seems to contradict itself, such as never being sure if his principal deity is the Green Man or Baphomet, and whether or not Baphomet is analogous to the Christian Devil.'

'Then we can suit ourselves, as long as we're true to his ideals.'

'Absolutely. Richard and I have plenty of ideas, most of which involve me as – as the subject. Some are quite hard to get my head around, as it goes.'

'Like?'

I paused, extending my glass for more wine to give myself a chance to think. She was so open, so frank, apparently so experienced, despite being maybe three or four years younger than me. I had a sneaking suspicion taking a man in my mouth in front of other people was going to sound pretty tame to her, but I didn't want to admit to any of my more bizarre ideas, let alone Richard's, for fear of horrifying her and spoiling the whole thing. I changed the subject.

'He claims to have summoned spirits, of course . . .'

She had caught the doubt in my voice, and broke in.

'He did, didn't he? As egregores.'

She stopped, waiting for me to answer, and again I hesitated, caught for the second time. I had always found it hard to bridge the gap between enjoying the fantasy of the occult and accepting it as reality. Lily evidently had no such trouble, and I thought back to the information Richard had gathered on her, and how she'd introduced herself, before doing some vigorous bet hedging.

'I've never seen it done, that's all, and for my thesis I had to toe the rational scientific line. So, when you're Lilitu, it is as an egregore?'

'Yes.'

There was complete conviction in her voice, no shade of doubt. It was something I'd read about in depth, but never been able to form a conclusion on largely because it was next to impossible to find an unbiased commentator one way or the other. Vaughan, among others, claimed to have drawn in various spirits to the bodies of himself and his acolytes, thus creating the egregore of that spirit. He'd believed it, with every bit as much certainty as his detractors had believed it was either out-and-out fraud or some sort of psychosomatic reaction. I could at least give an honest answer.

'That I'd like to see.'

'You will.'

With those words there was a subtle shift in her;

greater confidence, as if she'd found the balance between us. There was a wistful tone in her voice as she continued.

'That would be so perfect, to create an egregore and simply let go. That way anything can happen.'

I smiled and nodded, but it was impossible not to rationalise. What better way to explore your darkest needs than to surrender your responsibility? To be held down or tied helpless by the man you love, and simply enjoyed at his will, or in this case to take on the spirit of some being, full of primal lust and energy. A thought occurred to me.

'Richard Fox, who contacted you, is very similar to Elgar Vaughan: tall, with a slightly harsh face, and harsh in more personal ways too. Would it be feasible to draw Vaughan's spirit into him?'

'If he's receptive.'

'He will be, I'm sure.'

Like me, Richard had a residual streak of cynicism, but if it could be done it was going to be wonderful, and it wouldn't really make much difference if I fully believed or not. If Richard did, he would behave towards me as Vaughan would have done, or at the least, how he perceived Vaughan would have done. As I took another deep swallow of wine I began to understand how it worked, and how important faith was.

Lily poured again and we settled down to talk. It was very easy to open up to her and I explained my theory of how Vaughan might have feigned death in order to disappear. She not only accepted it but latched onto it with enthusiasm, pointing out that the theory explained the supposed gap in Vaughan's wealth, which I didn't have the heart to point out was pure speculation. Despite that, by the time we'd finished the bottle she very nearly had me believing it herself.

Outside, it had begun to rain, creating a dank grey

veil over the concrete flats and dingy red-brick houses visible from her window. I knew I should start back, but couldn't bear to face the raw weather. She lit candle lamps and closed the curtains, shutting out the mundane and leaving us in rich incense-scented warmth. We opened the second bottle, now laughing together over the Vaughan prints, side by side on the floor.

When her arm came around my back I didn't think to stop it, and before I really knew what was happening we were kissing. For all the things that had gone on in my mind, I'd never given myself to another woman before, but in that hazy half-real state it was easy. I just gave in and she took me, teasing my neck and stroking my face with her talons as we kissed, so that the urge to let my legs come open or push my bottom up had grown strong before she even touched my breasts.

Nothing was said, we simply closed the book and crawled onto the pile of big golden cushions. There she undressed me, taking off every scrap of my clothing to leave me naked and open in front of her. Only then did she start to kiss me again, on my mouth and neck, on my chest and on my breasts, and as her tongue and teeth worked gently on my nipples my back was arched and my eyes closed in need.

As her mouth went lower I took my own breasts in my hands, stroking myself as my tummy jumped to the touch of her lips. When the tip of her tongue burrowed into my belly button my thighs were already wide, welcoming her to do exactly as she wished. She did, taking me by my legs and burying her face between them. As she began to lick me I felt a tiny touch of guilt, but it had vanished in an instant, swept away by the joy of surrendering to her, and sheer physical pleasure.

She made me come in just moments, with my back arched tight and my hands locked onto my breasts, and held me as I shivered and gasped in her arms. Only then did she begin to undress herself, standing over me as she peeled her green velvet dress off to lay bare the full firm curves of her body. She was in stockings, the lace tops tight around her thighs to leave low swells of soft pale flesh between them and her knickers.

I watched, knowing I had to do whatever she wished, deeply aroused and a little apprehensive. Her bra came away to show full heavy breasts, made to seem fuller still by the curve of her waist. My eyes fixed on them, wanting to touch as much from curiosity as from lust, until she had pushed her knickers down to bare the soft plump swell of her sex. As I saw what I knew I was going to have to lick my mouth came a little wide and the knot in my tummy tightened.

Yet I stayed put, surrendered, as she came to stand over me, looking down at my naked body with her hands on her hips for a long moment before sinking down, straddled across my middle. I was pinned beneath her and it felt wonderful, helpless, with the heat of her sex pressed to my belly as she moved down, her full breasts lolling forward into my face.

I took in one hard nipple and began to suckle, quickly losing myself in the pleasure of her body. She fed me from both breasts, holding them to my mouth, until my tummy had begun to jump once more and the urge to touch myself had grown strong. It was as if she knew, because only when I was fully ready did she move up my body and swing around, seating herself on my face even as I began to masturbate.

Smothered in the warm softness of her bottom, I was licking eagerly, as I liked to be licked myself, without restraint. I could hear her sighs as I did it, encouraging me to be naughtier still, licking in places a girl's tongue is never normally expected to go. Lily simply gave a pleased sigh, wiggled her bottom in my face, and with that I was coming. So was she, together in an ecstasy as intimate as anything I'd shared with a man, perhaps more so, and no sooner was it over than she was cuddling me and stroking my back to soothe away a guilt I didn't feel.

6

Travelling back to the Hall on a rainy Tuesday morning with a headache was no fun at all, but I had a lot to keep my mind busy. Lily and I had slept together, beneath the gauzy awning of her black iron bed, and pleasured ourselves silly until the early hours of the morning. I'd woken sprawled nude across the sheets, with a throbbing head and the realisation that I was supposed to be in Oxfordshire. She'd been asleep, and I'd dressed quickly, waking her only for a purely sisterly kiss goodbye before leaving.

I was happy about what we'd done, because I wanted to give my sexuality free rein, and it would have been senseless to deny that I'd enjoyed it. It had also been very easy to give in, to what I knew were genuine feelings within myself rather than simply the lack of will to resist Lily's gentle yet uncompromising approach. There were still nagging voices at the back of my mind, telling me that I would now have to come to terms with myself as a lesbian, that I'd been unfaithful, that it was just plain wrong. They contradicted each other and I knew, rationally, that they derived from all the different social pressures I'd been subjected to over my life, but that didn't make them go away.

My response, as always, was a stubborn determination to accept my deeper feelings, and not the voices of social disapproval. One thing Lily had mentioned, as we talked between bouts of sex, was how much she enjoyed my ability to cope without getting in a fuss over it. I was determined to make that true, to accept her as she was, without guilt. She was also the perfect person to have as a member of our group, the new Sabbat Aceras, not only because she was genuine and beautiful, but because with Richard and other very strong male personalities Lily would provide a very necessary balance.

It was getting on for eleven by the time I arrived back at the Hall but there were no messages for me and, with a steady drizzle falling from a sky the colour of old pewter, I couldn't imagine anyone turning up to be shown around the grounds. There wasn't a great deal I could do either, except get on with cataloguing the library, which kept me busy for the rest of the day. Richard called in the evening to say that he'd signed up both Magog and Nathan who would be coming down with him on the Saturday.

I'd never had any doubt at all that he would ask them, and accept them if they proved suitable, but the prospect of actually meeting them brought what had been a fantasy into reality, and a very immediate reality. They were only coming to meet me and to look around the Hall, while Richard would not have given out any details of what was intended, but that did very little to prevent me from becoming increasingly nervous throughout the rest of the week. Even the presence of a film crew using the Hall and grounds as a set for some elaborate Gothic fantasy failed to distract me completely.

Inevitably, being male, he was delighted by my confession that I'd been to bed with Lily, which made him more enthusiastic still about our chances of success. He simply assumed that she and I would be willing to go together in front of him and the others. It was something I did want to do, even what I soothed myself to sleep over that night, with my eyes lightly closed and one hand slipped in down my pjs. It was also something that set my throat tight and every nerve in my body tingling whenever I thought about it.

For all my determination, I felt I needed somebody to talk to. Lily was no good, as I didn't want to let her know I was nervous, and all my old friends would have been completely horrified. The only person I could think of was Julie, who was at least open-minded rather than judgmental, and far from naïve. She called before I did, the following morning, suggesting that I come down to the village for some pasta and a drink later on, and I jumped at the offer.

It had finally stopped raining, leaving a fresh scent in the air beneath a tumble of fast-moving clouds. I walked down as soon as I'd closed the Hall up, enjoying the clean crisp air and giving myself a decent appetite. Julie was as ever, her tailored red skirt suit both smart but distinctly brash. Even with her heels kicked off as she worked she was considerably taller than me, adding a lot to the air of assurance that made her such an easy confidante.

The house was already full of delicious smells: frying onions, fresh basil and other herbs, puréed tomatoes, and wine from a bottle of southern Italian she was both drinking and using for the sauce. I accepted a glass and settled down at the table, watching her elaborate preparations with a little surprise. Somehow I'd imagined her using convenience food, given the stresses of her job. Far from it; she was full of enthusiasm, not even working from a book, but explaining what she was doing as she went along.

'... but the real secret is in the timing. Some people seem to reckon you can just stick it all in the pan and leave it. That is not good. First fry the onions, but not the garlic, or it burns. And it has to be good olive oil, with just a little butter melted in. The meat has to be good too, not mince. We've got veal and pork, which I need to cube and seal. Would you stir?'

I accepted, glad to have a chance to get my thoughts

in order and a little wine into my system before bringing anything heavy into the conversation. Moving close to Julie at the cooker as she began to heat oil in a frying pan, I caught her scent, the same Persephone that Lily wore, bringing to mind something else I wanted to talk about; two things in fact.

'Is it Persephone you wear?'

She hesitated a moment before answering.

'Persephone? I don't get you, honey.'

'Your scent. Isn't it Persephone?'

'No, but maybe that's a brand name over here. They do that sometimes. I wear Montmartre.'

'Oh. I would have sworn it was the same, but Persephone is from the States.'

'You may be right. It's a marketing thing maybe, like they make one product to keep the costs down, but sell it under different names, and at different prices, so they can catch more people.'

'I see. I mentioned it because a woman I met earlier this week wears Persephone. She –'

'Hang on, honey. You need to keep those onions moving, they shouldn't start to brown.'

'Oh, sorry.'

I'd almost said it, that I'd slept with Lily, because I badly wanted to get it out, even if it was perhaps too soon. There was also the problem of having a frank and open conversation without admitting that Richard and I were intent on reviving Elgar Vaughan's cult. Julie, after all, was no pagan, for all her open-minded attitudes, and Richard and I had agreed to keep the number of people who knew to an absolute minimum.

Once she'd got the sauce fully underway my help was no longer needed and I went back to my wine, sipping and talking as the smell grew slowly richer and more enticing and my appetite rose from good to ravenous. The conversation stayed on food too, with Julie extolling the virtues of the shops in New York and New Jersey, where she'd spent most of her early life.

I listened in fascination, to a story completely different to my own, and which made me feel both sheltered and privileged. All my life I'd known my parents would support me in a crisis, and that I could chase my dreams without fear of ending up on the streets. Julie had left home in her late teens, after some row she obviously didn't want to go into, or wasn't ready to divulge. From then on she had been focused on money and security, with a determination and success that left me in awe.

By the time the sauce was ready, after a full hour, I felt I could have eaten a horse. I was also pleasantly drunk, having happily gone on to the second bottle. Julie had fresh penne, so it was the work of only a moment more to serve up, and I had a gloriously scented plateful in front of me. For a while neither of us made a sound, save the occasional murmur of appreciation, until I'd taken the edge off my hunger. I'd just decided how to avoid giving too much away while talking openly about pagan orgies and lesbian sex when Julie got in first.

'You were going to tell me about this woman you met, Lily?'

'Yes. She's a – a Goth I suppose you'd call her, and she knows a lot about Elgar Vaughan. I went to look at some prints she'd bought in Paris, like the ones I showed you in the library.'

'Uh, huh?'

'Yes. She's really nice. Sensual. I found her sensual, that is, right from the start.'

'Uh, huh?'

'Yes. She's very beautiful too, and she likes warm rich colours and scents, like your perfume.'

'Uh, huh?'

'Yes. And ...'

'You're going to tell me you went to bed with her, aren't you?'

I'd gone red, but I nodded. She simply smiled, a little knowing, a little amused, as I began to stammer.

'I – I don't know how it happened really. It just seemed so easy, so natural ...'

'Was it good?'

'Great.'

'Got a problem with it?'

'No, not really. It – it's just that it was my first time, like that, and I wanted to talk. I told Richard, but he's a man. I don't know, maybe I just feel I need a little moral support for my decision.'

'You go, girl. Whatever rocks your world, you do it. Just take care.'

'I will. Thanks, Julie, I really appreciate this. There's another thing too. You know I was saying that Richard had a lot of fantasies, about being watched together for instance? He wants to do it now, for real.'

'Do you want it?'

'Yes, I think so.'

'You think so, or you know so?'

'I know. Just thinking about it makes me so aroused, but still ...'

'Then what's stopping you? Go for it.'

I nodded, part reassured, part more nervous than ever. Something within me had wanted her to be strongly against it, to be outraged and to advise me to back off and drop Richard like a hot brick. Now that last possible route to safety had been removed, and all that was normal, and mundane, had been removed. I was really going to do it.

If I'd thought I was nervous before, I'd barely understood what the word meant. Richard had taken to calling every evening, full of enthusiasm and new ideas. Most were excellent, or at the least worth talking over, but it was all a bit much to take in. I had a coach party on the Saturday, and was very glad indeed of the distraction as I gave them the tour. As usual I was in full Victorian dress, from my combinations outwards, and for the first time that year I felt a little too warm.

Richard arrived while my party was still there, tagging onto the group as I showed them the ruined east wing and the tower.

'... with the curious stipulation that no major reno-vation work be carried out, and so Elmcote Hall remains as you see it. Thank you.'

I half expected Richard to come in with some difficult question, but he held his peace, merely watching me with his knowing smile. One or two of the group would have lingered, but the driver was in a hurry to get on and soon had them shepherded back aboard the coach. Richard and I watched them go before he kissed me, a peck which quickly grew in passion until I really thought he was simply going to turn me over the rubble and take me then and there without a thought for who else might turn up. I broke away.

'Richard! Not here. At least come indoors, or down to the temple.'

After allowing his hand to linger on the seat of my dress for just a moment more, he stood back.

'A fine offer, but not right now, thanks. I want to keep you warm.'

'For what, exactly?'

It was a deliberately arch comment, and he chuckled.

'For whatever the day may bring. Still, I told them not to turn up before six, so we have an hour or so if you really insist?'

I shrugged, and if he'd hauled me up over his shoulder

and carried me off to the nearest convenient spot I'd only have protested enough to make sure I was held down while he did it. As it was he merely smiled and took my arm, drawing me towards the lime walk.

'Later then. For now I shall hold myself back, and all the better for when the time comes. As I said before, both my men are suitable. They are also strong personalities, with their own concepts, their own ideas. While it's very important to accommodate everybody involved, we also have to make it very clear that what I say goes.'

'As long as it's agreed, of course, but only when it comes to details of what we actually do. If it's anything to do with the Hall, I have to have the final decision.'

'Absolutely. That goes without saying. What I meant was as far as our relationship is concerned. I think what I'm trying to say, Sophie, is that I don't want to lose you to another man.'

I paused to kiss him.

'Don't be silly. I'm yours.'

'Or another woman?'

A pang of guilt hit me, given that I'd gone with Lily without even thinking of Richard's reaction. It had never even occurred to me that he might be jealous.

'Not in a way that excludes you, I promise.'

'Thank you. I can live with that.'

For the first time it occurred to me that his certainty, or arrogance, might not be quite as cast iron as it seemed, and I might not be alone in having qualms about what we were doing. He spoke again as we reached the beginning of the lime walk.

'So long as that's clear.'

'Absolutely. I've been checking the temple, but nobody's been there. Did Magog admit to it?'

'Not in so many words, but yes, effectively. Like me, he'd misinterpreted your paper. I think I've managed to convince him. At least, he was impressed by my offer to try and raise the slab, but didn't want to take me up on it.'

'Did you find out about the woman, or the other people?'

'Oh, it was his partner, but she's a little wary. Or having trouble getting her head around it, I'm not sure which.'

'I can understand that. And Nathan?'

'He had nothing to do with it, I'm ninety-nine per cent sure.'

'Hopefully it doesn't matter any more. So we have three men and two women. I think we need another woman before we can start in earnest.'

'One woman, and one man, not only because seven is a more auspicious number, but if I'm to take the place of Elgar Vaughan, we should reproduce things as accurately as possible. Still, it wouldn't be a bad idea to get a little practice in beforehand.'

I knew exactly what he meant, which gave me a hot flush before I went on.

'I still have Davinia to visit. Do you have anyone in mind for a man?'

'Not yet, unless you'd like to take back your objections to any of the original group.'

'No.'

We'd reached the temple and began to walk around it. As always my eyes were drawn to the Green Man, also to the dead tree which had given me such a start, but as we came around the temple it was as if my thoughts had been made flesh. Somebody was coming towards us across the carriage sweep, and he could only be Magog, a vast man in every way, long-legged, his torso like a barrel, his face staring from hair the colour of autumn leaves.

As we came closer even Richard seemed to be dwarfed,

and when Magog spoke it was in a bass rumble, but brief, a trifle shy even, simply his name and a greeting. I responded in kind and we turned for the house, Richard talking easily of this and that, Magog answering with terse responses, me silent with my nerves tingling.

I badly needed a drink, and opened a bottle as they sat down, pouring myself a glass and draining it before serving them. Both accepted their glasses without comment, easing me naturally towards the role I'd agreed to take, and the only way I could accept what I really wanted. Whatever Richard's earlier misgivings, he now seemed completely casual, discussing a dozen aspects of paganism, witchcraft, Satanism and more, with Magog seldom speaking save to provide a gruff agreement.

Occasionally I would add a comment, or correct some minor mistake, but I was really content to simply let it wash over me, watching the two of them and thinking of how in the same house, something over a hundred years before, Elgar Vaughan must have held just such conversations. He, and those who'd come to join him or visit him, including Aleister Crowley himself, would have sat as we were sitting, perhaps even covering the same ground. Now it was happening again, and with Richard as the focus.

Watching Richard's face as he talked, it was easier than ever to imagine him as Vaughan, while Magog was quite simply elemental. Both were perfect. I had chosen well, and so had Richard, bringing together the nucleus of a group I'd be proud to be with, and more. Later, I would be at Richard's feet, as Magog watched. Perhaps, if Richard deemed it appropriate, the big man would even join in and I, I would do as I was told, irresponsible in my pleasure.

I was still daydreaming when the doorbell went again. By then it was dark outside, and I opened the door to find Nathan looking down at me from his dark piercing eyes. He was taller than I had realised, and dressed in black, providing me with a brief and exquisite image of answering the door to the Devil before he spoke.

'You are Sophie Page?'

His voice was even, upper-class, but with a touch of the accent of his home county, and ever so slightly harsh. Even before, he had appealed to me, but as I accepted his hand I was wishing all the good ones didn't tend to come at the same time.

'I am. Come in. Everybody else is already here.'

He simply nodded and came in, walking across to the open door of the kitchen. As I followed I was stung by a touch of resentment because he'd immediately made me feel like a maid. I bit back the feeling because I knew where it came from, within me. He carried all the effortless panache of a man with absolute self-assurance, an echo even of the young aesthetes of Saki's England.

Richard rose as Nathan entered the kitchen, as did Magog, the three of them tall and purposeful. They shook hands and sat once more, Richard picking up the conversation where he had left off.

'We were discussing modern paganism, and whether beliefs should reflect the times.'

Nathan considered, very grave and thoughtful, before speaking.

'They have always done so, and if we are to accept that man and his gods are linked, then it is inevitable they always will. Nevertheless, I feel many people have taken a wrong path.'

'How true.'

'Take the National Association of Natural Worship, for example. They seek to bring people together and believe that everybody should be able to worship in his own way. So far so good, and yet their own creed – to see the spirits of the corn and the wild as inherently benevolent, indeed, to see nature as inherently benevolent – is self-evidently wrong. No, as Vaughan saw, and I believe, we may control to an extent, we may appease, but it is a cardinal mistake to assume that if we only embrace nature she will always respond kindly. Anybody who has worked the land knows this, but very few wiccans and such are in touch with the land, whatever they may claim.'

Richard nodded. Magog produced a deep grunt of what was presumably agreement. I couldn't help but respond, and attempt to steer the conversation in the direction I knew it must go.

'Absolutely. Look at Vaughan's concept of the Green Man, essential to the cycle of the years, and yet frightening, and aggressively virile.'

Nathan nodded.

'The perfect example. The Green Man of the National Association of Natural Worship is emasculated, a feeble creature, like one of those peculiar fish in which the female is large and the male tiny, also, after mating, completely dependent on the female. Vaughan realised that there must always be an exact balance between the male and female principles.'

Again Richard nodded.

'Christianity, of course, has the principle reversed, with the stress on the male element and the female very much a minor key.'

'True, although with the Church now allowing priestesses, perhaps the imbalance is beginning to redress?'

'The Church is still inherently patriarchal, with an omnipotent male creator as primary deity.'

'There is a long way to go, yes.'

They were going off at a tangent again. I drew an inward sigh and once more tried to steer the conversation my way.

'Another strong point of Elgar Vaughan's beliefs was the attempt to draw together pagan and Christian concepts, although with his highly sexual version of the occult I doubt he would have got very far. I somehow don't see the late Victorian or Edwardian Church accepting orgiastic festivals in place of Christmas or Easter.'

Richard laughed. Magog produced a bass rumble. Nathan's mouth very briefly twitched into a wonderfully evil smile before he spoke again.

'A fine idea! Was that his aim?'

Things were going my way.

'His dream perhaps. He was surprisingly practical about how long it would take to make a serious difference, but he was convinced that if enough groups incorporated sexual elements into their rites it would eventually come to be seen as a normal way of worship.'

'Incorrectly, I fear. He merely provided an easy way for the Church to condemn him. There he was wrong. Church dogmas are too firmly established for so radical a change to work from within. The answer is to offer a new and more appealing belief system, as he did, but it will inevitably be in antagonism with the old. Take any schismatic movement across the history of religion and you will see it has always been the same...'

I drew another hidden sigh as he went on, illustrating his first point with the Protestant movement and then with the rise and fall of the ancient Egyptian Aton sect, while I listened and waited for another chance to bring the focus around to me. It was hopeless with Nathan and Richard deep in debate, Magog seldom speaking but fascinated, a feast of reason which would have been just fine except that I'd spent so long in anticipation of what might happen.

There was nothing to be done because ultimately Richard had to take control. We'd finished the second bottle and I opened a third, hoping that a little more alcohol might help. As I came to place it on the table, Richard hugged me to him, his hand on my bottom, and at the realisation that it was about to start all my feelings came rushing forward, leaving me blushing and weak-limbed as he spoke.

'How about some food, darling?'

I nearly hit him with the bottle, but it was an order, and that was what I needed. He did at least give me a squeeze and a pat as he sent me off towards the work surface, but it only served to bring my feelings close to the boil. Being made to cook as they talked and drank was a very poor substitute indeed for being taken out to the Temple of Baphomet and put on my knees to take Richard in my mouth as the others watched. It was at least something; as I began to put together a risotto I was imagining myself as Elgar Vaughan's maid, preparing food as she listened to three men discuss the details of disturbing sexual rituals and wondered if she would end up as the subject of them.

They were at least in agreement, with very few differences in opinion between them, and nothing insurmountable. Both the others were clearly developing a lot of respect for Richard, and *vice-versa*; also for me, with frequent references to my work and questions too. It was all very flattering, but I didn't want their respect. Well, I did, but not if it prevented them from being rude with me.

I soon had the risotto ready and I took a little pleasure in serving them, deliberately curtseying to each as I gave him his plate. All three thanked me politely, bringing my frustration higher still, to the point where had Richard said the food was no good, whipped me across his knee and given me a bare-bottom spanking in front of them I'd have been grateful. He didn't, and we continued to talk as we ate, the men complimenting me on the risotto before sitting back in their chairs looking replete. I had to do something.

'Shall we go into the library?' I suggested. 'I don't suppose either of you have seen the full collection of Elgar Vaughan's prints?'

Magog patted his stomach.

'Perhaps in the morning, love.'

Richard nodded sagely.

'Perhaps a coffee. I'll make it. You relax, Sophie.'

'No. I mean to say, I'd prefer a brandy. Anyone else?'

'Coffee for me, please, Richard.'

'Coffee, yes.'

I'd got the brandy in specially, thinking I might need it, but never imagining they would. Maybe Richard was doing it deliberately, in which case I had to play the game and wait while my need rose and rose. When the time did come, it would be all the better, but if it didn't I swore to myself that Richard would not have the benefit of what was rapidly becoming desperation. He'd teased me so badly, telling me what he'd make me do, in detail, to keep me on a high of nervous apprehension for what seemed an age, and now it looked as if he didn't have the courage to go through with it.

Richard was making the coffee, in his usual elaborate fashion, and slower than ever because he didn't know where anything was in the kitchen. I went out into the reception room and across, to where the wall had been repaired after the collapse. Nothing was visible of the arch which had led into the space beneath the tower, Elgar Vaughan's main temple, now strewn with blocks of rubble.

I wanted to see it, and walked to the door and outside, to climb onto one of the tumbled granite blocks. The whole heart had been torn out of the house, the floor with each slab beautifully inlaid with symbols now covered in rubble. I moved closer still, cautious as I stepped from block to block, but sure that after so long no further collapse was likely. One great cube of granite provided a perfect seat, or an altar, and I lowered myself onto in, in deep shade, sipping my brandy and trying to let myself calm down. After a few moments' meditation I heard the door open once more and caught Richard's voice.

'I think she went upstairs. Sophie?'

Rather than answer him I stood up, hoping they'd come for me. Richard appeared in the pool of pale light beside the rubble and Magog, who spoke as he turned to the ruins of the tower.

'I can do it.'

He stopped as he saw me, surprised. Richard had seen me too, and raised one booted foot to the top of the nearest stone. Nathan had not been with them, but appeared a moment later, to put his fingers to his chin, his intense gaze fixed right on me. Richard spoke.

'Gentlemen, we should celebrate, to seal our pact, and also that I may show you we lack nothing of Elgar Vaughan's spirit. Sophie, kneel at the block.'

I inclined my head, obedient yet serene, despite the instant tightening of my muscles and the sudden rush of blood to my face. It was perfect: not a request but an instruction, and one I was eager to obey. They could see me only as a grey shape, I knew, which made it easier as I got slowly down to my knees before the heavy block on which I'd been sitting. The granite was hard and a little cold, but I didn't care. It was a good place for my first experience, and a little discomfort was a small price to pay.

Richard scrambled up to seat himself where I had been a moment before, and I turned to him. We were right under where the tower would have been, perhaps six feet above the true floor, and so where Elgar Vaughan would have stood as he led his rites, his head where mine would be as I took Richard in my mouth. Richard spoke.

'She will take in my seed, and yours.'

I hung my head in mute acceptance of his decision. Neither man spoke, and Richard reached out, briefly caressing my hair, a soothing touch before his hands went lower. I stayed still, given over completely to his will, glad and eager that it would be me who was first, and who gave each of them the ecstasy that was so much a part of Elgar Vaughan's worship.

First I was to be bared. Richard's strong fingers slowly tugged open the fastening of my dress until it could be pushed down, baring my shoulders and trapping my arms, my breasts pushing up under the thin cotton of my combinations. I closed my eyes as Richard touched them, stroking gently before his hands eased down the front of my corset to lift them free. A tug and the lacing at my chest was loose, the sides of my combinations fell away and I was bare before him. Again he touched, teasing my nipples to excitement, and a sob escaped my throat.

'Come forward.'

I thought he'd do it, and pressed my face to his lap, but his hands went back to my skirts and I realised that I was to be spared nothing. It was right, modesty utterly inappropriate to what I was doing. I closed my eyes tight, focused on my exposure, my pleasure building fast. My whole body was shaking as my skirts were bunched slowly up onto my back, inch by inch, my dress and petticoat together, to lay bare my stockinged calves, the lace trim of my combinations, and the seat.

The cotton gathered over my bottom hid me completely, but I felt exquisitely naughty, and naughtier still as my combinations were eased wide, my bottom unveiled, to leave me in a delightfully dishevelled state, completely dressed and yet with everything showing, for their pleasure and my own. One of the watching men gave a murmur of appreciation and I felt myself flush as

I thought of what he could see and what I would shortly have to do for him.

First came Richard, his cock already a large hot bulge against my face through material, then hot and bare as he freed himself. I nuzzled him as his hand closed firmly in my hair, to pull me back, and feed me. As I began to suck I was already dizzy with pleasure and I knew I had to come. Showing inhibition was as wrong as modesty, and my hands went back, burrowed under my up-turned skirts, to find the warm ready flesh of my sex.

I touched myself, easing a finger into my body to make it completely obvious what I was doing. Nobody spoke, not a word, both men watching in silence as I pleasured myself and Richard grew slowly hard in my mouth. My head began to fill with images as I gave myself over completely to lust, of Elgar Vaughan, of Baphomet, of the Green Man, of Satan himself, all waiting in line to enjoy me, their monstrous cocks hard in their hands, ready for my body.

They would take their turns as I knelt to them, holding each glorious erection in turn, licking and kissing and sucking in glorious abject worship until I was given their seed in my mouth, or better still, inside me, to leave me pregnant, incubating the Devil's child. I came at that exquisite thought, sucking urgently on the smooth beautiful cock in my mouth as my body shook and trembled. Richard came, full in my mouth, my body still wracked with ecstatic tremors as I swallowed down what he had to give me.

If he was Vaughan, then Nathan was Satan, lean and dark, cool and mocking as he replaced Richard, seating himself to feed his penis into my open eager mouth. I was still masturbating and in my head I was sucking the Devil's cock, utterly wanton and utterly liberated in my need. In moments I'd come again, and a third time, rising to a plateau of abandoned ecstasy I wanted to go on forever.

I was lost completely, coming over and over again, my body possessed by three men. As Richard's finger took over what I'd been doing I took hold of Nathan's balls, feasting on him and, as he came, moments later, feeding myself from his cock. Magog replaced him immediately, huge and heavy in my mouth, my Green Man, as hard as wood and impossibly big. Yet I took him in, what I could, my body bucking and writhing in Richard's hands as he took me to one blinding peak after another, orgasm after orgasm, perfect ecstasy, until at last Magog fed me his seed. With that, as I finally let my body go limp, the Sabbat Aceras had been reborn.

7

Sunday passed in a haze. We had made it real, and it was only the beginning. Breakfast was cheerful, with even Magog quite talkative, and a pleasing intimacy between us for what we'd done. Unfortunately I had work to do and was unable to linger, but had to get dressed and ready by nine.

It was a beautiful spring day and I had a steady show of visitors, mostly alone or in small groups, but including two coaches. I left Richard to show Nathan and Magog the Hall and grounds, wishing I could join them, but with barely a moment to spare for the entire day. They spent a good deal of the time in the library, and discussing how the Hall would have been laid out before the collapse of the tower.

By the time the last of the tourists had gone Nathan had already left, needing to make for Lincolnshire, and Magog followed soon after. Richard at least left late, after a last passionate moment together, and as I walked back to the Hall after shutting the gates I was feeling at once elated and empty. I was also dead tired and went straight to bed, drifting quickly to sleep with my mind full of images of orgiastic pleasures with men and demons and spirits, who then came to populate my dreams.

I was up early on the Monday, intent on Cornwall and Davinia, Earth Mother fanatic and possibly acolyte to our nascent cult, now officially called Sabbat Aceras. I wanted her to be right, but was determined not to compromise. The one thing that united the five of us so far was that we looked back on the past as a good thing, something to be revered rather than changed, and it had become the measure against which we needed to judge other people's suitability.

Richard had arranged everything, including paying my fares, which was a relief, my less than wonderful wages being the only drawback of my job. It was quite a journey for one day in any case, down to Reading to catch a fast train for the West Country before doubling back from Penzance by cab, which was the only way to give myself the time I needed.

Helston I knew vaguely from a single visit as a child, but all I could remember was the twin streams flowing down the stone gullies to either side of the main street. It didn't seem to have changed, and Davinia's shop was easy to find, close to a large arched memorial at the bottom of the hill and unmistakable, with the Earth Mother figures in the window.

Davinia herself was behind the counter, a little older than I'd imagined her, and with her hair piled up in a great glossy bun on top of her head. She was in a lilac dress, something like a kaftan, and so loose on her slender body it was as if she was in robes. Two other people were in the shop, so I spent a moment examining the smaller Earth Mother figures. Most were clay, but a few of the smaller ones were carved in local serpentine, with the twisting red and green patterns of the stone enhancing the swollen forms of bellies and breasts and buttocks. I chose the prettiest, one patterned with tiny golden flecks of fool's gold, took it to the counter and introduced myself as the other customers left.

'I'll have her please. I'm Sophie Page. You should be expecting me?'

'Yes ... yes. You are the girl with concerns about the Satanist, Vaughan?'

A little taken aback, I didn't answer immediately, and she went on.

'You will need her in beryl, not serpentine, dear, if you want a ward against evil. On the next shelf down, by the window.'

I looked down to where she was pointing at a tray of pendants, green and pink. Peering closer, I could see the outline of the Earth Mother figure on each, but I was already beginning to think I'd made a mistake. She continued to talk as I pretended to choose among the pendants, buying myself time to think.

'Has Vaughan appeared to you?'

I struggled for something convincing to say.

'I think so, yes. As an egregore.'

She'd looked concerned. Now she looked horrified. I hastened to correct myself.

'Not that I'm at all sure. That was just what somebody said, after –'

I broke off, because it wasn't getting any better. She looked deeply shocked, and there was real fear in her voice as she spoke.

'You have been involved in a ritual, to summon the spirit of Elgar Vaughan?'

'No, no, not at all. It was just that – that my friend and I were playing – pretending really, and – and he said he felt something, and the name Elgar Vaughan came into his head, and made him want to – want to . . .'

I shut up, because I really thought she was going to collapse. When she did speak there was a harsh edge to her voice.

'You are a very foolish young woman. Never, never think to play with such forces!'

She was shaking her head, seriously agitated, to which my reaction was pure embarrassment. I paid for the pendant and the Earth Mother, then left. I'd only been in the shop a few minutes, making my decision seem yet more sudden after my long journey, but there was no choice. All too clearly she was unsuitable, although it was hard to understand why she, a professed pagan, should think so badly of Elgar Vaughan. True, there were Satanic elements in his belief system, but he'd never gone in for anything actively unpleasant, just unrestrained sex. At least I'd given nothing away.

I was also in Helston, with a couple of hours to pass before I even needed to think about starting back. It at least made sense to return to Penzance, rather than risk a problem with cabs, so I did, and walked down to the promenade to dangle my feet over the edge above the gently moving sea and eat a tub of chocolate chip ice-cream, which I felt I deserved.

It looked like a wasted day, but her attitude had made me more determined than ever, so after finishing my ice-cream I began to browse the junk shops, hoping for some ritual paraphernalia. I'd known Penzance had a reputation as somewhere you might hope to find almost anything, but I hadn't realised just how many shops there were, or how diverse.

In no time at all I had a beautiful Stansfeld Jones tarot, a leather-bound symbology from the late 'twenties and a brass chafing dish complete with a seriously bizarre fresco of goats, satyrs and other strange creatures not easily identifiable. The man who'd sold me the bowl had some idea what he was talking about. I asked, slightly cautiously this time, if he had anything relating to Elgar Vaughan, and immediately he produced a pentacle in worked brass and enamel showing the same five figures who decorated the Temple of Baphomet at the five points.

I had to have it and met his extravagant asking price by telling myself I'd live on crusts for a month if necessary. It was beautiful, perfect, and as I admired it I was already thinking of myself kneeling over it to take Richard and others into myself, or perhaps serving as a human altar, with it placed on my naked back. The possibilities were endless, and as I left the shop to hurry for the station I knew the day was far from wasted.

One thing did nag at my mind intermittently all the way back to Reading. Except in the unlikely event of the pentacle having left Elmcote Hall before Elgar Vaughan's death, it had been stolen. Quite a few things were known to be missing, mainly vestments which had presumably gone with those who owned them, but also a number of carvings, various pieces of apparatus and a few books.

Most, if not all, had gone with the cult members. Alice Scott had even had a small onyx statue of a dryad on her mantelpiece, half woman, half tree, between a china figurine of a Pierrot and a photograph of her daughter. I'd said nothing, obviously, but that and everything else had still, technically, been the property of Elgar Vaughan, therefore of Hubert Sands, and ultimately the Trust. One of the stipulations of the Trust was that nothing be sold off, especially anything that might be of significance to other cultists.

The pentacle belonged at Elmcote Hall in any case, but the question was whether or not to inform the Trustees. I did at least have a receipt to show that I'd bought it, and would presumably be reimbursed, but it was the only Sabbat Aceras artefact I could in any way at all claim as mine, and I didn't want to lose it. By the time I was waiting for the connecting train to take me up the Thames Valley I'd managed to find an excuse to put off my decision by waiting to ask a lawyer where I stood.

I might not have gained us a new member, but things were definitely coming together. Richard, Lily and Nathan all rang me during the week, and I found myself wanting to organise a fully fleshed ritual even if it did involve only the five of us. After all, Elgar Vaughan had allowed his group to build up slowly and never once compromised on the membership, even turning Crowley and Mathers away. His group had taken years to come together properly, and we'd only had weeks. Others could be found in due time.

With the weather a great deal warmer than it had been I was also kept busy, both showing people around and with larger events, including another wedding reception, also attempting to keep the estate in some kind of order. It was really too great a task for me alone, especially the gardens now things had begun to grow, but when I told Richard I was planning to ask the Trustees if I could employ a part-time gardener, he had a better idea.

Magog lived close enough, thirty-odd miles away towards Swindon, and worked for a plant hire company some of whose equipment might even come in useful. He also had enough spare time to come in on Saturdays, allowing me to tell the Trustees I'd found a volunteer, while providing the perfect cover for our activities. He was good at it too, despite taking a rather wholesale approach, including using a small tractor to clear the paths in to the temples. When Lorna Meadows visited she was delighted, commenting on how neatly the job had been done and complimenting me on saving money. It never seemed to occur to her to wonder why Magog was prepared to travel so far to do hard unpaid work, or perhaps she suspected that he was playing Mellors to my Lady Chatterley and was just being tactful.

She would have been right, at least in part, because on the Saturday night we'd used the same temple, Wayland's, she'd been so complimentary about on the Tuesday, with me on my knees to Richard and Magog turn and turn about. It was hard to keep the smile off my face as I showed her what else I'd been doing, although I did feel a little guilty for what it was hard to see as anything else but deception. She was at least pleased, but I determined to have another heart-to-heart with Julie, who made the perfect neutral voice.

Julie had treated me and so I determined to treat her in turn, inviting her up for a meal. She accepted happily, and I took a few minutes off in the afternoon to get a brace of pigeon from a neighbouring farm, which I stewed in red wine and thyme, creating a scent every bit as delicious as her pasta sauce to greet her when she arrived. This time she was in green, bright mid-green, another tailored skirt suit cut to exaggerate her bust and hips, along with heels to match, which she was seriously regretting keeping on to walk up the hill. As soon as she'd come in she kicked them off and padded across the reception room in her stockinged feet to greet me with a kiss.

'You'd think I'd learn, no? Oh no, not Miss Julie. But then, I've got nothing to go with sneakers. What's that wonderful smell?'

'Stewed pigeon with red wine and thyme, shallots, mushrooms, fried red cabbage and the best bread and butter I could get.'

'Grand! You're spoiling me.'

'Just returning a favour. Wine?'

'Sure. Do I ever refuse?'

I poured, not from the bottle of cheap Merlot I'd been cooking with, which had already gone down my throat during preparations, but a St Emilion which Richard had brought up at the weekend, undrunk due to the three of us being otherwise engaged in Wayland's Temple. It was good, and after just a sniff Julie gave a nod of appreciation and turned the bottle to show herself the label.

'Château Fonroque, a favourite. You have taste, girl, definite taste.'

'Not me, Richard Fox. I don't suppose I could even afford it.'

'It's not cheap, that's for sure, but then, what is that's worth having?'

'The best things are free, including sex, which I wanted to ask your advice about.'

Her eyebrows rose.

'Again? What is it this time!? I mean, you've been with another girl, and that's OK, so –'

I broke in hastily.

'Nothing bad – well, not really. It's more to do with my job. I told you about Richard wanting other people to watch, well ... we did it, two men, and I – you know, did them too ...'

She broke in.

'You are one bad girl, Sophie Page, and you are making me jealous! There's nothing wrong with taking on two guys, honey, or ten, only it's plain damn greedy, that's what it is! This I've got to hear too, so spill it.'

'Hold on, that wasn't my question. Do you think I'm right to use the Hall for things which the Trustees might disapprove of? We did it outside, you see, and –'

'Come on, girl, you are killing me! Do you know how long since I last had sex? Never mind, just say it's a long time.'

'No? I'd have thought you'd have men running after you?'

'Not any I wouldn't run away from, and a sight faster. Don't mind that. So you reckon your Trustees might not like you getting nasty on the lawn. This was night-time, right, the place was closed?'

'Of course.'

'Then it's none of their goddam business! This is how I see it, Sophie. Say one of the Trustees was a real tight-assed bible-thumping son-of-a-bitch, right? Some of those guys reckon you should stay lily white 'til your wedding night and then do it through a hole in the sheet, no joking! Now he's not going to like it whatever you do, is he?'

'No, I suppose not.'

'And are you going to let him tell you what to do?'

'No, obviously . . .'

'And say maybe there's another one, a homophobe. What's he going to say if you bring your Gothy girlfriend up for a piece of pussy pie? He's not going to like it!'

'True.'

'True's right. There's only one person who can judge your morals, girl, and that's you. Just so long as you're not hurting anybody, you do whatever rocks you.'

I nodded. She was right. I'd only thought about it from what I imagined as a typical moral viewpoint, not my own. We weren't going to damage the Hall. We weren't going to hurt anyone. We weren't going to indulge ourselves while the Hall was open, especially after Richard and I had nearly been caught. I reached out to chink my glass against hers.

'Thank you, Julie. You always manage to make me feel good about myself.'

'Anytime, honey, but there's a charge. I want to know what happened with you and the three guys, and I mean all of it, every nasty detail.'

I gave Julie all the detail she wanted, enough to leave me blushing and very wet. She was barely out of the door before my hand was down my knickers, and I made myself come then and there. I knew she'd felt the same, and when I went to lock up the library I found myself looking at a portrait of Elgar Vaughan, who seemed to be asking why I hadn't taken my friend to bed.

The only obvious answer was that I wanted to stay friends with her and she'd probably have run a mile. After all, she knew I'd been to bed with Lily, and if she'd wanted to take me to bed in turn, she could have asked. She was the confident, in control one. There was more to it than that, I knew, but not anything I could put my finger on. Physically, she and Lily weren't that different, both were tall well-built women, statuesque as my mother put it. Both had confidence, both were very easy to relax with. Both even wore the same perfume, whatever it was called.

My conclusion was that with Lily there was a ritual element to the sex, as there was with Nathan and Magog. That somehow made it acceptable, taking it outside the boundaries of normal behaviour. Even Vaughan seemed to have restricted himself to his acolytes, despite preaching unrestrained lust, although his choice might well have been purely for the sake of convenience.

I felt ready to go and the others agreed. All that was needed was a time when all five of us could be together at the Hall. Unfortunately we lacked Elgar Vaughan's luxury of having the Hall to himself and no calls on his time. Saturday was the sensible choice and really the only practical one for Richard, although it meant making sure we left no evidence for the morning, which was essential anyway. Unfortunately neither Lily nor Nathan could make the next weekend, so we set it for the following one, and a ritual to celebrate spring and the rebirth of the year.

Only details remained, with everyone keen to have their own input. I didn't mind so long as I got plenty of attention, and that was now inevitable. Richard was also inclined to be flexible, using his position to bring things together rather than to impose his decisions on others. His only stipulation was that he should lead, taking the place of Elgar Vaughan, something I was also determined on.

Nathan's input was that there should be some form

of offering, preferably a sacrifice, which I was prepared to accept but wasn't entirely comfortable with. Even if you ate it afterwards, sacrifice had always struck me as a bit unfair on the animal, who could hardly be considered a willing participant, while for me the most shocking thing about Crowley's infamous goat ritual had been that the unfortunate beast didn't make it through to the end.

Lily was determined on some form of summoning, preferably creating the egregore of some suitable spirit. I was keen too, and fascinated to see what actually happened, both for personal and more detached reasons. Richard was equally keen, and obviously fancied her, so she was given *carte blanche* to arrange it.

Magog's request was more down to earth, just as I might have expected. He wanted both me nude, and preferably Lily too. No mention was made of the men, but I was happy with that, preferring to relinquish my control. Lily was less sure, but once Magog had seen a picture of the way she intended to dress he immediately accepted her choice. Lacking email, I didn't see, but it sounded magnificent. What she and I might, or might not, do together, was left to us, along with one or two heavy hints.

By the weekend I was walking on air, and desperately keen for Richard to come up. He arrived on the Saturday, but too late to do more than share a brief kiss and a hug before I had to start work. Magog also arrived, and the day was spent alternately doing my proper work, with no fewer than three coach parties of German tourists, and arranging things for the following week.

We chose Wayland's Temple, which was set deep in the woods and sheltered from all sides except where the path Magog had cut approached it from the lawn. Even then nobody would be able to see unless they approached from the path down to the lake, and at night that had to be extremely unlikely. We also considered applying to install CCTV on the main gate, but eventually agreed that recording anything was likely to backfire on us in the long term.

There were people around right up to closing time, and Magog had to get back, so Richard and I were left to our own devices in the evening. He took me to the Angel again and eventually persuaded me to come back to London with him and stay over on the Sunday night. Once there, we more than made up for our abstinence during the days in his bed, indulging ourselves into the early hours and fantasising together over what we could do as a group.

When I woke up, Richard was long gone. Vaguely I remembered the brush of his lips against mine as I lay half asleep, but that had been hours before. It was now getting on for noon. Not that I had anywhere to go, but it seemed pointless just lazing in bed for the rest of the day, even his bed. Only as I was brushing my teeth did I think of having lunch with Julie, who could presumably be contacted easily enough.

Unfortunately all I could remember about her company was that the name had related in my mind to the names of New York streets, and that she was involved with Securities, whatever those were. My knowledge was far too vague to get anything out of directory enquiries, and so I sat down with Richard's directory. The only company that sounded even vaguely right was one called Forty-seventh Securities, in Bishopsgate, but they denied any knowledge of a Julie Voigtstein.

No other company rang a bell at all, so I gave up and spent my afternoon shopping for incense candles in China Town instead. There were plenty to choose from: big ones, little ones, long-lasting, extra-drippy, in dozens of colours and with dozens of scents. I kept going until my arms were beginning to feel the strain of carrying my bags before making for Paddington and home.

It was getting late by the time I got back to the Hall, and the weekend had really caught up with me. I downed a carton of milk and retired to bed, although my mind was still racing with thoughts and images as I drifted towards sleep – of the temples, of Lily and Magog and Nathan, but most of all of Richard and Elgar Vaughan, now two faces of the same coin.

In the morning I was up bright and early to unlock the Hall and the gates, before making a brief inspection of the grounds. I checked the slab in the Temple of Baphomet, just in case Magog and his mysterious girl-friend weren't solely responsible for the disturbances, but there was nothing amiss. Evidently I had been wrong in assuming there had been four rather than two people involved.

Everything else was also as it should have been, and as there was still half an hour before I was technically supposed to be open I treated myself to a quick dip in the lake, this time with a towel convenient to hand. When I got back to the Hall, it was to find Lorna Meadows in the library, examining the pentacle I'd bought in Penzance and had foolishly left on the table, meaning to check it in the catalogue. She looked some-what puzzled and I hastened to explain.

'Ah, yes, that's a piece I'd been meaning to ask you about.'

'Yes? I don't recognise it.'

'No? I'm rather concerned, as it happens. I was in Penzance on my day off and found it in an antiques shop. It's unmistakably a Vaughan artefact, and the best thing to do seemed to be to buy it and check in the catalogue to see if it's listed. I have the receipt.'

'Good. Let's see.'

I went for the catalogue, a large book put together for Hubert Sands and annotated when the Trust took over. It listed everything from the house and temples down to the few sad remnants of personal property sent back from France, approximately in order of value, which was all very well, but made using it a serious headache. If the pentacle was listed, it had been in the Hall when Elgar Vaughan's lawyers began going over the estate a few weeks after his death, and was therefore the property of the Trust. If it wasn't listed, it had left the Hall prior to Vaughan's death and was therefore mine.

Almost the entire book had to be searched to be sure it wasn't there, but by good fortune a group of visitors arrived a few minutes after we'd begun. They belonged to the minority who were more interested in George Vaughan's garden than either Gothicism or the occult, and I did my best to demonstrate how it had been set out and the way the landscape would have worked. By the time I got back Lorna was beginning to get impatient, her gaze narrowed to a frown as she peered at the lines of copperplate handwriting through her glasses. She spoke immediately.

'I can't find it and, frankly, I haven't time for this. You'll have to look through in your own time and check for references elsewhere. Meanwhile, I trust you're happy to have it stay here?'

'Absolutely. How far did you get?'

'Down to the damaged porcelain from the east wing, so if it was listed I'd have expected to find it. Still, as you know, occult items with no practical use tend to have relatively low values set on them, so it may still be to come. Let me know what you find out, and if it has been stolen from the house we'll have to institute some kind of investigation.'

She'd stood up, giving the nearest print a glance of fastidious distaste before she made for the door. I saw her out and returned to the library, intent on checking the catalogue and praying the pentacle wasn't listed. She had left one of our promotional leaflets on the page, at a broken Japanese money toad valued at seven old pence. I couldn't imagine the heavy brass pentacle being less than that, but continued anyway, down through the items valued at approximately sixpence, approximately thre'pence and approximately a penny, to where the long list began of those things considered of no appreciable value.

It wasn't there. I started at the beginning again, with my hopes rising, but while there were several pentacles listed, none corresponded to mine. One was valued at a shilling and it sounded a great deal less impressive, and so it seemed mine really had left the house before Vaughan's death. That in itself was fascinating, infecting me with the same determination to get at the facts which had driven me through three years of work on my PhD.

I kept going the next day as well, not only because I wanted to be absolutely certain, but because it was the best way of calming my nerves for what was coming at the weekend. Having double-checked that the pentacle was not listed in the catalogue, I set about trying to find a reference to it in Elgar Vaughan's irritatingly sparse notes from the active period of the cult.

There were also photographs, mostly innocuous, and the prints, highly graphic. I knew that several of the objects depicted in the prints were real, including the chair in which Elgar Vaughan was enthroned next to Baphomet and which I was now sitting in as I went through my references. There were also plenty of pentacles, some drawn from life, and pentagrams, which were not always easy to distinguish.

I drew a blank, but there were also a great many real objects not depicted in the prints, so it was impossible to reach any conclusions. Having examined the last of the prints I got the photographs out, without a great deal of hope, and beginning to wonder if it wasn't something he'd commissioned but which for some reason had never been delivered.

As always the photographs fascinated me. There were studio portraits of Vaughan as an infant and a child, always very still and serious, and as a youth, first in conventional Victorian attire for his age and class, and then suddenly in loose black robes. Then came the ones from the high days of the cult, with his looks changing from youth to maturity and slowly gaining that same craggy confidence which so reminded me of Richard, and *vice versa*. Last of all were the wartime ones, two taken in France and one apparently just before he left, with his baggage piled up on the carriage sweep, including my pentacle, leant against what appeared to be a hat box for a topper.

He'd taken it to France, but it hadn't come back. I double-checked the catalogue, but I was right. So how had it come to be in an antiques shop in Penzance?

There were sensible answers. He might have left it after all, perhaps giving it as a parting gift to one of his acolytes. He might have taken it, but lost it at some point over the following two years. It might have been with his things but been left behind after his death, either by mistake or out of distaste for occult matters. It might even have been in the plane with him, and found again later, but that seemed unlikely.

Or, he might have set aside a few important personal possessions somewhere he could retrieve them later before deliberately faking his death.

8

It was an extraordinary flight of fancy, and yet it exactly fitted the known facts. I went through them again and again, but aside from flying in the face of current scientific opinion, there was no fault. Flying had also flown in the face of current scientific opinion, so to speak, not much more than a hundred years before. So rather than dismiss the idea out of hand I determined to treat it as a formal hypothesis: was Richard Fox in fact Elgar Vaughan?

Simply to ask him was pointless. It raised four possibilities. He could be Vaughan and admit it. He might not be Vaughan but pretend he was. He might be Vaughan and deny it. Or he might not be Vaughan and admit he wasn't. As I could never be sure he was telling the truth, it made no difference which answer he gave.

Nor was it easy to pick at his background. He was from New York, that much I knew, but he would presumably have a story prepared to cover his past. Or there was his employers, who might well have records to cast some light on things, but were hardly going to open them for casual inspection. The matter needed careful thought, and the only thing I could think of to do immediately was write a letter to the Penzance shopkeeper, as I'd left in a hurry, asking if he could provide any further information about the origin of my pentacle.

There had been something approaching awe in my attitude to Richard from the first, despite my initial resentment. I tend to be like that, wanting men I can look up to, although so far in my life every single one had proven to have feet of clay, or more usually, just be clay full stop. That was another good reason for not voicing my suspicions to Richard. If he was Elgar Vaughan, I could lay myself completely and utterly at his feet, both metaphorically and literally. If he wasn't, he was still far above any other man I'd met, but to know for sure might break the spell, and that had to last at least until I had experienced complete devotion to him in a full-scale pagan ritual.

Not that I had long to wait – just days – with everything coming rapidly together and no reason it should go wrong. We had the perfect place, we had the perfect people, and if seven or thirteen would have been better than five, then no doubt that too would come with time. I was as eager and apprehensive as ever and took to going out to Wayland's Temple every day, as if to check that it was still there.

The temple was one of Elgar Vaughan's more peculiar flights of fancy, built as he had envisioned an ancient smithy, and yet also designed for rituals. Essentially it was a square of heavy granite blocks with an elaborate roof carved as if crude beams supported a thick layer of thatch. There were no windows, only a large square door, with a huge stone anvil at the exact centre and a bench running around the inside.

Nobody pinched it, and I was standing in the doorway on the Thursday afternoon when a familiar voice called out my name from the direction of the lawn. It was Julie, and I called back, asking her to join me. After a moment she appeared on the broad mown path. She was wearing yet another skirt suit, this time turquoise, with matching heels as usual. I was a little surprised to see her, but she seemed to have highly flexible work hours and didn't remark on it as she joined me, planting a peck on my cheek before looking around the inside of the temple.

'Weird! What's this place for?'

'Rituals, to celebrate the Horned God in his aspect as the smith, Wayland.'

'If you say so, honey.'

'He was a Saxon god originally, and part of the Teutonic cycle, but the concept goes back long, long before Christianity.'

'You don't say?'

She looked around, her face set in what I'd come to think of as the 'tourist expression', which most of my visitors would wear if they were magically transported back in time to view the Hanging Gardens of Babylon, or watch the Great Pyramid being built. I wanted to tell her, at least something, although I knew I shouldn't. She sat down on the anvil.

'Cool, like one of those olden-day cottages. So how was the weekend? Any more four-ways, girlie fun, orgies?'

'No more since I last spoke to you, only a couple of great nights with Richard, but I'm on a promise.'

She lifted an eyebrow.

'You're going to tell me, right?'

I hesitated, then decided what really mattered was that I kept the ritual element to myself, and Julie wasn't interested in that anyway. She was still looking at me, and I was blushing despite myself as I answered her.

'Five of us this time – Richard, the two guys and my friend Lily.'

'The one you slept with?'

'That's her.'

She sighed.

'Some girls get all the luck.'

I shrugged and smiled, wishing I could invite her to join in, but knowing it would be completely inappropriate. It was a little awkward, because for all her looks and confidence she was obviously feeling down about relationships, or at the very least her sex life. Unfortunately, as I was about to indulge myself with four people at once, it was a little hard to know what to say. I had to try.

'Cheer up, Julie. You're beautiful. I know what it is with you, you're just too fussy. Half the men in your company are probably after you but oh no, none of them are good enough, are they? I know you!'

I was trying to make a joke of it, and she did smile, just about, before replying with a sigh in her voice.

'Not this girl, honey. There's only one person for me.'

'Oh. I know I shouldn't stereotype people, but I've always had you down as more the Sex and the City type, you know, having who you please, when you please, and daring anyone to criticise you. So, you're in love with somebody? Back in the States?'

'Not in the States, no.'

'Here then? What, is he married or something?'

'Something like that, yes.'

'Oh, right. Can I just say then that I think you're doing the right thing. I mean, I can't believe you couldn't get him if you wanted to, and a lot of people would just do it.'

'It's nothing like that.'

I could see she didn't want to talk, which hurt a little when I'd come to her so many times, but I reached out and took her hand.

'I understand, but if you do need someone to talk to, I'm here.'

She smiled and returned the pressure of my hand, unfortunately hard enough to make me wince.

Julie was in my thoughts a lot over the next day, but there was nothing I could do. I spent most of Friday on edge, checking and rechecking every little detail and trying to think of things that could go wrong. Short of an out-and-out disaster, there was nothing, but that made no difference to the way I felt, fussing and fidgeting, and still in the library long after I should have been in bed asleep.

On the Saturday morning I was late up and still in my pyjamas when Richard arrived. He was wonderfully calm, and amused by the state I'd worked myself into, telling me to get dressed while he opened up the Hall. I let him take over, feeding myself after a shower with cereal and a bacon sandwich before going up to dress. For the evening I wanted to be in just my Victorian underwear, so contented myself with my dress and petticoat for the day.

By the time I got down Richard was out on the carriage sweep contemplating the rubble, and I had a moment to study him in profile without him knowing. One of the portraits of Vaughan in the reception room was close enough for me to see both it and Richard if I took just a small step back. I did, comparing the two faces and trying to find a difference. It was a late picture, and Vaughan's face was more mature, or perhaps just fleshier. His hair was also a shade or two darker, but then, it was a painting, and nearly ninety years old at that. There was nothing to say that the picture inside might not have been painted with the man outside as the subject.

A thought occurred to me: to discover Richard's precise height and compare it with Vaughan's, which I could probably work out from photographs. If they differed it would weigh heavily against my hypothesis. Not that I could do anything immediately, so I stepped out to join him and his arm went around my shoulder as I came to his side.

'Are you ready for tonight?'

'As ready as I ever will be.'

'That's my girl. Magog should be here shortly. The others are coming later.'

Even as he spoke a car appeared at the gates. My tummy tightened at the thought of the huge man and what I might find myself obliged to do with him, but it wasn't his car, just a black 4x4 bringing the first of the day's visitors. I stepped forward to greet them, happy to have a distraction.

It was the same for the rest of the day. Magog arrived while I was giving a tour, and set to work on the gardens, trimming the laurel and rhododendron at the fringe of the lawn. Just knowing he was doing it partially to make the bushes thicken and provide even better concealment was a thrill, adding to the feel of being naughty that for me was so important a part of it.

Nathan arrived in the late afternoon, as poised as ever in his black suit as he admired the house and grounds. Last came Lily, looking beautiful in a sheath of crimson velvet, her hair wound onto her head and set with feathers and glass beads in the same rich shade. If the others were unlikely to draw comment, the same was not true of her. Everything about her spoke of secretive and erotic goings-on. She was unashamedly friendly too, kissing my mouth as she greeted me, and steering me indoors with a hand on my bottom.

Fortunately there were no visitors at that point, but a last group arrived just as I was about to shut up for the day. I was obliged to show them around, leaving the others talking in the kitchen. When I finally managed to get free, and had closed the main gates with a padlock and chain, they were already through their first bottle of wine and deep in discussion. Lily was holding the floor, the others intent on what she was saying.

'...thinking you can do it isn't enough. You must know you can do it.'

Magog glanced briefly at Richard, then answered simply.

'That I can.'

I poured myself a glass and came to the table.

'What are you talking about?'

Richard reached out an arm to pull me down on his lap as he answered.

'Tonight. Lily suggested that Magog would be the perfect person to take on the Spirit of the Wild, the Green Man.'

I glanced at Magog's huge bearded form.

'Yes. No question.'

Lily gave me a smile that was pure wickedness. As she went on she was serious, but her eagerness showed through.

'I know you aren't playing at this, and it's just as well. You appreciate that when possessed he, the Magog we're talking to now, won't be there at all. His body will, but his mind will be given over completely. He won't be responsible for his actions at all. That is why you never ever summon the egregore of a malign spirit, at least not without confining the subject. As Lilitu I claw and bite, and I wear a chain on my ankle to stop me getting out.'

I could imagine it, an image both frightening and compelling, but no more so than Magog. Here, on Elgar Vaughan's estate, I wanted to experience what it meant to be taken by the Green Man. Also, we needed Lily. Richard agreed.

'We must do that, Lily. For tonight, we need you to lead that part of the ritual. Later you can teach us.'

'I will.'

'Have you brought everything you need?'

'Incense, yes, and some candles, but I could use more. I'll need a chafing dish, and a tripod if there is one.'

'There are seven. How big?'

'Whatever. Three foot tall?'

I nodded and ran off upstairs to fetch a tripod from the store room and my own chafing dish with the goat design. My candles were there too, and I brought everything down. Outside, the sun was already behind the tops of the trees, throwing long shadows down the lime walk and extending that of the Temple of Baphomet towards the house, once again making me think of penetration by an impossibly large penis. By the time the sun rose again, I knew I would have shaken off any claim to be a mere student of alternative religion and immersed myself thoroughly in Elgar Vaughan's blend of the pagan and the occult. There would be no going back, but going back was the last thing I wanted.

'We are safe to go outside now. Let's prepare.'

We went out, each knowing what he or she had to do. Magog had brought a ladder and I propped it up on the stone beams within Wayland's Temple, to allow me to set candles out. Lit, they created a golden light above us and bathed the interior of the temple with a soft glow. Everything else I left for Lily and went outside to help set up the twin lines of torches to make a processional way to the temple.

The path led down to the lawn and I walked back towards the house to make sure nothing showed, with the sun falling behind the woods turning everything briefly to gold before dusk set in and the colours slowly began to fade. Again I thought of my final chance to preserve what remained of my Christian upbringing and to turn away, and again I rejected it out of hand.

With the torches burning and the others drinking red wine on the lawn as they watched the sunset it was time for me to change. I went up to my room to lay out my clothes as I wanted to be at first, a Victorian girl in dishabille, partially naked and receptive to every deliciously naughty temptation my decadent friends had to offer. With everything ready I began to strip and I felt my third and final moment of choice.

I might have simply walked away, towards everything mundane and proper and safe. Nobody would have stopped me. Nobody would have realised I was gone until it was too late. I never even hesitated but stripped stark naked, washed, dried my hair, twisted it onto my head and fixed it with pins in the style of a hundred years before. I perfumed my body, applied the merest touch of make-up to enhance my eyes and yet do nothing to conceal the nature of my face, and began to dress.

I'd ordered new stockings which went on first, black and tied above the knee with scarlet ribbon. In those alone I felt intensely sexual, a girl from some rude and very private cabaret laid on for wealthy decadents. With my black square-heeled boots on the feeling was much the same, but more intense, with the muscles of my legs and bottom tighter to show me off.

My combinations changed the theme, concealing me, and yet leaving me in what would have been considered a thoroughly improper state in which to be seen by gentlemen. That was more like how it would have been for Elgar Vaughan's acolytes, not mere playthings for men but half stripped for action on their own account. My corset followed, adding a rich sensual touch, and I was ready.

As I picked my way down the stairs I was wondering how many other women had come the same way, in the same attire, or stark naked, ready for whatever the night might bring. There had been at least ten, some of them many, many times, and as I crossed the reception hall I was telling myself that come what might, I would do my sisters proud.

Outside it was now dark, the lawn lit only by the light

streaming from the library, just enough to make my way down until I could see the flicker of the torch lines on the processional way. I could hear the others and stepped boldly forward to join them, taking the big pewter goblet full of rich red wine as Richard offered it to me. I wanted to be drunk, outrageously drunk, not because I needed to be, but in celebration of immoderate bacchanalian pleasure. Lily came to me as I swallowed a mouthful, smiling, to trace a finger from my neck, down across the swell of my breasts and over my corset, following the curve at the side.

'Beautiful. I shall have you, Sophie, later.'

'Of course.'

'First, though, I believe you are to be the focus of our dedication. Are you ready?'

Her hand had continued to move lower, to the front of my combinations, and inside, one finger stroking the mound of my sex, then lower still. My thighs came a little apart and a soft gasp escaped my lips as she touched me, first between my lips, then slipping her finger into my body. I closed my eyes and my mouth came a little open as she toyed with my sex, melting to her on the instant. She withdrew, her finger went to my mouth and I was tasting myself, my eyes still closed as she spoke.

'Very ready, now go away, before I lose control and have you on the floor.'

I went, shaking at her openly sexual approach. With her there was no reserve, no indecision. She wanted me and she took me. Outside I stood to drink my wine, staring down the twin lines of torches with my tummy fluttering. Richard came to stand beside me, his arm around my shoulder. I leant close, drawing in his scent and the strength that seemed to come from him. For all my wild imaginings, it was him who'd made it real, and could draw me deeper still.

As the first waft of burning incense caught my nose he turned, and I with him. Lily had set up the tripod and chafing dish a little way in front of the great stone anvil. Already thick bluish smoke had begun to curl up from the smouldering powder, filling the air with a tang not unlike her perfume. Nathan was sat to one side, watching intently. Magog stood behind the anvil, his great arms folded across his chest. Lily addressed him.

'You should be naked.'

He simply nodded, accepting on the instant.

I watched as he undressed, very casually, shedding his clothes to lay bare his great barrel chest and bulky belly, grown thick with russet hair, his huge legs, sheaved in corded muscle, his massive, rock-hard buttocks and at last the heavy mass of his cock and balls. Clothed he was forbidding, naked he was elemental, raw masculinity, with nothing of the coy or civilised. As he kicked his clothes to the side and stood as before, I could already imagine him as the Green Man. Lily rose and turned, beckoning us inside.

'We are ready. First, do any of you doubt what we are about to do?'

Richard shook his head and I likewise. I meant it, because already there was a sense of presence stronger by far than anything I'd felt in a church or cathedral, even among ancient sites or at Crowley's now abandoned farm in Sicily. It could be done, I knew, all it took was belief. Nathan also responded, the smallest inclination of his head, but not Magog. He didn't need to.

I sat down as Lily continued, moving about the temple to place candles on the floor, five of them, set out in a circle. Taking a piece of red-coloured wood, she pushed it into the chafing dish, chanting softly under her breath as she waited for it to start to char. Richard had also sat, he, Nathan and I as points of a triangle with Magog standing as before.

With the wood now starting to smoulder, Lily stood straight once more to shrug her dress from her shoulders and push it down to the floor. She had nothing on underneath, and stepped stark naked from the puddle of crimson cloth, her full breasts and the fertile curve of her belly made more plentiful still by the curved highlight of orange flame light.

She pulled the piece of wood from the incense and began to draw on the slabs, curves and lines, joining the five candles to form a pentagram with the stone anvil at its heart. As the sign formed, Richard stepped to its upper point, opposite the door, folding his arms across his chest as he watched Lily work. Only when she had finished and risen to stand at his right hand did he move, gesturing to me.

I stepped forward to climb onto the anvil, kneeling awkwardly with my face to the door. Richard lifted my pentacle and placed it on my back, his strong sure fingers quickly tying it into place with the laces of my corset. I thought of how I was, kneeling on the altar in place of the sacrifice, as the sacrifice. Quickly my combinations were opened at front and rear, baring my breasts and sex, as was proper, my body exposed for entry, nothing concealed.

Richard began to read out the dedication, his voice loud and even, commending us to Elgar Vaughan as the new Sabbat Aceras, to his deities and to the principles of wisdom and freedom in body and mind. I found myself following the words, as each and every one of Elgar Vaughan's acolytes must have done, dedicating myself, renouncing the authority of the Church over my body and my soul.

'. . . as Eve took the apple, to gain wisdom not shame, to flower not to wilt, and so brought Adam with her into the light, to show that humankind might rise above servitude to the patriarchal god.'

He went quiet and absolute silence took over as I closed my eyes, waiting for what I knew was to come. I was being watched, by four people, but it felt as if there were a thousand eyes on me, all those he had summoned and more, the spirits of the corn and the wild, looking in from the night, each eager to see me dedicated to them. As Richard spoke, I was ready.

'Accept this, the pleasure of your handmaiden and of myself, in sacrifice.'

On the final word his penis touched the open mouth of my sex. My mouth came wide in an ecstatic gasp as the full thick length slid inside me. The others moved close, Nathan to feed his penis into my open mouth, Lily and Magog to worship my body, stroking my breasts and belly, my back and hair. As Richard found his rhythm inside me, so Lily had opened me to her fingers, masturbating me to help me towards climax.

My pleasure was rising, already far above the simply physical. I was to have my ecstasy dedicated to Elgar Vaughan as I knelt dishevelled and penetrated in his temple, and it was singing in my head. My muscles had begun to tighten, my mind focused on the two hard men inside me and the fingers caressing my body, and what it meant, approaching my perfect moment, to be given in sacrifice.

When my orgasm hit me I would have screamed the temple down had I not had half the length of Nathan's cock in my mouth. As it was I went tight on both him and Richard, and with that both came, filling me with seed at the perfect moment, so that all three of us were coming together, directing our orgasmic energy to the spirit of Elgar Vaughan. Nor did it stop there, my ecstasy rising again and again, peak after peak, as they held themselves in me, both spent as shudder after shudder passed through my body. At last Lily withdrew her fingers and I stopped, so weak they had to hold me up to stop me falling, and help me from the altar once the pentacle had been taken off my back.

It had been done, the dedication made without flaw, the first act of worship there in ninety years completed, and I had been the subject, the sacrifice. Standing back at my point of the pentacle I was still dizzy with elation, for what I'd done, and what was coming.

Briefly we stayed, our hands folded in our laps in meditation, each standing silent at their point of the pentagram, the night pressing in on us, and Lily began to chant. Magog knew how to react and stepped forward to seat himself on the altar, his great legs wide, his manhood and testicles hanging heavy between, already stirring with arousal as his eyes rested on Lily's naked body. Her head was lifted, her eyes lightly closed, then abruptly bright as they met mine, each dark pupil reflecting a dozen candles, and full of arousal, maybe also fear.

'He is here. It can be done. Watch, and concentrate. Think on your image of the Green Man and he will come.'

My head was already full of just such thoughts, and swimming with sex, wine, the heady incense, the scent of the candles, of Magog and of Lily. I let my eyes come wide, watching the orange flames dance on their bodies, naked or clad in black, and thinking how I'd come out from the house to the Temple of Baphomet, how for one exultant terrifying moment I'd seen the huge woody figure towering above me, his monstrous erection projecting out above my head.

I had known it was the Green Man, not thought, but known, only for that instant, but if for that instant, why not longer? Why shouldn't he be drawn into Magog's body, here and now, to chase me and possess me on the ground, as it should be? Everything was right, the time right, the lonely woods coming into spring, the place right, a pagan temple in an overgrown garden, the people right.

Lily continued to chant, louder than before, and clear, but in no language I knew. Her voice was higher, full of longing, and as it rose to a crescendo something seemed to pass, maybe just a breeze, making the torches in the processional way flutter and jerk as my eyes came wide at a bass grumble from Magog.

I saw his face and it had changed. It was now human only in outline, his features taking on the lines and knots of wood, his eyes blazing with rude earthy vitality. His hand had gone down and he was holding his penis, which was no longer limp but straining upwards in blatant raging virility. He turned to me, his eyes burning into mine, and I ran stumbling out through the temple door and into the night.

A bass growl sounded from behind me and I knew he was coming, to take me, to ravish me. It was going to happen, and I couldn't stop it. Everything seemed to slow, the twin row of torches moving back to either side, one after another. Every instant I was expecting his great clutching hands to pull me down, but the last torches passed and I was on the lawn, racing out into the blackness of the night, to stumble, and trip.

I twisted my body as I went down, landing on my side and rolling further, onto my back, to find him towering over me, his bulk black against the stars. Through no will of my own my knees came up and he was on top of me, my thighs opening to the pressure, the split of my combinations open, my sex bare to the night and to him. I felt his monstrous erection probing at me, pressing between my legs and to my sex.

He grunted, pushed, and I had accepted him, deep in my body, utterly helpless beneath his weight as he began to move inside me, deep and firm. My hands were clutching at his body, my mouth came wide and I heard my own ecstatic scream in reaction to what seemed an impossible bulk within me, on top of me too, and impossibly hard. He was invisible in the darkness, his hair in my face, but as he began to come, and to fill my body with his precious seed, it no longer felt like hair, but leaves.

9

What had I done?

What I had done was indulge myself without compromise, giving up my pleasure in worship as freely and openly as any one of Elgar Vaughan's acolytes had ever done. I was now well and truly a pagan and a follower of Vaughan, not simply through holding a set of beliefs, but as an initiate into a wonderful secret that made the rites and beliefs I'd been brought up in seem cold and sterile. What had happened between Magog and me was so far beyond any religious experience I had known before that it simply could not be compared.

As I'd come I had felt the leaves in my face, and it had drawn me up to an orgasm so intense I had been crying my ecstasy into the night and had then briefly fainted. I'd come round with him still moving inside me, slower, and it had no longer been the Green Man, but Magog. As the long thrusts of his erection grew less frenzied and my orgasm slowly subsided my arms had come around his broad back and we had kissed, he and I, his flesh now firm but pliant, that beast of a man. I'd been shaking badly and needed to be held, so clung on, but I was not frightened.

We had walked back to the temple, hand in hand, silent until we reached the others. I was full of a crazy exultance and a sense of triumph, Magog quiet. He could remember nothing, from listening to Lily chanting to the moment he had come around on top of me on the lawn. It was real, without question, and for me a true epiphany. I had seen the change in Magog's face as the wild spirit entered him. I had felt the hardness of his body as he pounded into me and I had clutched at him in helpless ecstasy. I had been chased and taken by the Green Man, an experience more real and more intense than I could possibly have hoped for. Now I was truly what I had always longed to be, and I wanted to celebrate until I could celebrate no more.

Richard, Lily and Nathan were standing between the torches, she still stark naked, both of them with their arms around her. I walked to them, ignoring their hurried, concerned questions, to press my lips to hers in a kiss that was as much gratitude as affection or lust. She responded, her mouth opening under mine, warm and eager. Her breasts were pressing against me and my hands were reaching out to either side, to pull down the men's flies and free them from their material confines.

From that moment on the night was one of uninhibited lust. Each of us indulged as we pleased, enjoying our own bodies and each other's without restraint. I tongued Richard's anus together with Lily, declaring him the Great God Pan. I brought her to orgasm under my tongue, both at her feet and entwined together head to tail on the moonlit grass. I took all three of the men into me more than once, in a dozen different ways, mounting high on the altar with my legs straddled wide across Richard's body, kneeling across it with Magog in my mouth and Nathan pushed into me from behind, and more, so much more, until at last I collapsed from sheer drunken exhaustion.

By then I was naked, and my last memory of the evening was of being lifted across Richard's shoulder and carried back to the house. At some point during the hours of orgiastic sex and drinking Lily had led me through a little ceremony of renunciation, kneeling to kiss Pan's arse once more, and hers. I'd been giggling with pleasure and sheer naughtiness as I'd done it, and was glad I had. Despite having done it before I now felt I'd burnt my bridges with a vengeance, and the first time I had still been a doubter. Now I was sure, and I was equally sure in the morning.

If I was exulting mentally, then physically I was completely drained. Even to stir myself from bed was a serious effort, but it had to be done. I seemed to have shared my bed with Lily rather than Richard, although I couldn't remember getting in with her, and she was still asleep. She was also nude, as she had been for most of the evening, and so was I. That meant our clothes might still be in the temple, not to mention the pentacle, candles, cups, empty bottles and all the paraphernalia of our rite. There was also the pentagram on the floor, clear evidence of what was sure to be seen as a Satanic orgy by anyone who came across it.

They'd have been right, and I hurried into the first clothes I could find before running downstairs and around to the lawn. I was half expecting to find Lorna Meadows standing disapprovingly among the debris, but there was only Magog, squatting down with a sponge in one hand as he wiped away the last traces of the pentagram. Everything else was gone, but there was a good deal of wax on the floor, and I went to help him.

'Hi, you were up early.'

'Haven't been to sleep. Nor's Richard.'

'Oh. Where is he?'

'Off into town, getting food.'

'He's tough, you too. Did you take my clothes and everything in?'

'Yes.'

'Thanks. Look, let me finish off. You must need some sleep.'

He nodded, terse as ever, slightly shy, as he always

was. What we'd done together didn't seem to have affected him at all, which made it easy to ask the crucial question.

'Last night, how did you feel?'

'Great. You?'

'I mean, while you were possessed?'

'Don't remember.'

'Nothing?'

'One moment I'm sitting there. The next we're at it on the lawn.'

I felt myself colour a little at his words, a reaction that never seemed to go no matter what I did. He'd seemed a little scared too, but it seemed best not to mention that, and I could easily understand it. My fear had come beforehand, but it had not stopped me, and I couldn't imagine his own fear stopping him from doing it again.

When there was no trace of the pentagram left he began to collect the cleaning things together. I carried on working as he thanked me for taking over, and watched him lumber away towards the house. Before long I'd picked off the last of the wax, and while a close observer might have realised that something had happened, they would have no idea what. Satisfied, I started back, hoping no visitors would arrive, or at least not until I'd had breakfast.

Nathan and Lily were in the kitchen, he dapper in his black suit, she bleary-eyed and yawning in my pjs. They'd made toast and coffee and I helped myself to both before sitting down beside her.

'You look wrecked. Did you know Richard and Magog stayed up all night? They've cleared everything away too. Where did you sleep, Nathan?'

'In my car.'

'Oh. We'll have to do something about accommodation, but it's hard to see what.'

'Why not set up one or two of the empty rooms as they'd have been in Vaughan's time?'

'That's a great idea. I'm not sure the Trustees would accept it, but maybe if I keep the costs down.'

Lily looked up from her coffee.

'Which was Elgar Vaughan's own room?'

'It was in the tower. A staircase led up to the gallery which joined the first floors of the two wings and his room was on the next floor.'

I heard Richard's voice before I saw him, and instantly felt a little jump in my stomach.

'He had his bed made specially, a four-poster big enough to fit at least six people. You can still see bits of it in among the rubble.'

'Now that's what we needed last night. I'll talk to the Trustees about the rooms, but we must be careful about drawing attention to ourselves. Lorna Meadows is quite likely to turn up on a Sunday morning and might wonder what's going on.'

Richard seemed to ponder for a second.

'I went out and came back along the back lane, and I think it's best we use it as much as possible.'

'Have you got my key then?' I asked. 'And did you unchain the front gate?'

'Yes I have and yes I did.'

'Good. For a moment there I thought that was why we hadn't had any visitors yet!'

'No. Don't worry,' said Richard. 'I've seen to everything.'

'Thanks. You make me feel completely useless!'

'Don't worry. You had a harder time of it than I did last night, after all, as the sacrifice, and you certainly drank more.'

'I felt I needed to, but I'm beginning to regret it.'

'Take it easy. I'll cope with any visitors.'

'But you haven't even had any sleep!'

'I'm fine, really.'

I just smiled in answer. It was so easy to just let him take charge.

In the end I went back to bed with Lily, not for sex but to sleep, and cuddle a little, and talk. She was as delighted as me with what we'd achieved, and full of ideas for the future. Most I agreed with, because it was becoming plain that she had a great deal more experience than I did when it came to actual occult practice.

She also told me more about herself and how she'd started out by rebelling against her parents as a teenager. They'd been members of some modern Christian sect, one of those that seem to take a peculiar delight in ensuring their members have as miserable and restricted a life as possible. She'd been forced to attend services every Sunday and a good many weekdays, to give up her time to social functions and her money to supposedly good causes, which meant the Church.

At first she'd merely wanted out, until she discovered just how much outrage she could cause by as small a thing as wearing pentacle earrings. From there it had escalated, with every effort to change her attitude making her more determined still. By the time she was eighteen she'd been wearing full blown Goth gear and flatly refusing to have anything to do with the Church. Finally she'd left home, but by then her interest had taken hold and shifted from simple antagonism to the Church to devotion to its opposite.

Once she'd managed to establish herself in a flat there had been nothing to hold her back. She'd studied every aspect of paganism, the occult, witchcraft and more, dismissing some and accepting others, but with an increasing focus on Lilitu. Like me she had not really believed in summoning until she'd seen it done, but afterwards she had become determined to do the same herself. I could see it would have required immense courage, but that seemed to be typical of her.

Elgar Vaughan had fascinated her because his belief system was at once all-embracing and unusually pure, with none of the commercial attitude which had so disgusted her about her parents' Church. He was also one of those who had developed the idea of creating an egregore, something I had always assumed to be a delusion, albeit an intense one, but no more. Now I knew, as she did, although she simply accepted it as fact, and I wanted to know more.

The old answer provided by theologists and spiritualists alike – 'it is beyond our understanding' – has never been good enough for me. As we sat talking around the kitchen table on the Sunday evening, all four of the others accepted it, regarding an element of mystery as inevitable to what we were doing. Even after I'd sent Richard home at one in the morning with a satisfied smile on his face, I was still thinking about it, and him.

Monday morning was strange, surreal almost. With everybody gone and no evidence of what had happened, it was as if it had been a dream. The weather had broken the previous afternoon, and with nothing to do I went to the library, hoping to find links between Richard and Elgar Vaughan, or to break them. Already my attitude to him was something approaching awe, and very different to what I'd felt for other partners.

Despite my experience with Magog, there was still a lot of scepticism in my mind about Richard. I had come to accept the possibility of his being Elgar Vaughan, but I still felt I needed proof. Only if I got that proof would I then be able to give in to my feelings and truly worship him. That was my aim, but there could be no compromise.

If the library held a clue, I couldn't find it, and when

it came down to it I didn't even know if Richard Fox was his real name. In fact, if my suspicions were correct I knew it wasn't. His borrowed flat didn't seem to offer much either, although he presumably had some documents with him. Not that they would necessarily tell me anything, and the idea of looking through his private things made me feel bad, but I knew I was going to do it.

The opportunity came sooner than I expected. He called me on the Wednesday, to say he had another potential occult playmate to interview and asking if I could come in. It was practical as long as I got up early, and I agreed. He collected me from Paddington, explaining as we drove west through the evening traffic.

'. . . I think he'll be your type, but he's not an obvious choice like Magog and Nathan, so I felt showing you a picture wouldn't be enough.'

'Thanks. What's his background then?'

'That's the thing. He picked up on one of the message board threads where I was discussing Vaughan with Nathan. The idea fascinates him, but he's new to it. In fact, I think you may be a little surprised, and perhaps tempted.'

'Why's that?'

'You'll see. Just think of yourself as a succubus.'

'A succubus? Why?'

'You'll see.'

'Richard! You have to tell me more than that!'

'Oh no, I don't. Anyway, we're here.'

'Here! Are you mad?'

He'd turned left into a side road, and immediately left again into the parking space outside a large red-brick church. A sign announced it as St Barnabas Hall-field, in the care of the Rev. James Langdon. I got out, still half-expecting Richard to start laughing and admit it was all a joke. He didn't. To one side of us was the church door, to the other a comfortable-looking Victorian villa, built in the same red brick and flint mix as the church, and with a gnarled wisteria growing thick over the porch. Richard stepped towards it and we were bathed in the brilliant white of a security light. I followed, somewhat doubtfully, reaching Richard's side as he rang the bell.

A moment later the door opened revealing a tall slender man whose calm handsome features shifted to a worried look as he saw us. We were ushered inside without speaking, and he closed the door purposefully behind us, his every movement full of nervous energy. Richard was wearing his little amused smile and spoke as soon as the door was firmly closed.

'James, this is my priestess, Dr Sophie Page. Sophie, meet the Reverend James Langdon, vicar of this parish.'

Langdon nodded, his mouth twisting between a smile and a grimace.

'Come in, come in.'

We followed him into a comfortably furnished living room, with a well stuffed three-piece suite in a floral cover, two bookcases, various ornaments, pictures, a pair of crossed oars above a stone fireplace. I'd never been into a vicar's house before, but it was much as I'd have expected: cosy, refined, with a touch of the scholarly. There was another touch too, a woman's.

'Will your wife be joining us?'

His face was distinctly red as he responded.

'No ... no, not at all. Eleanor is chairing a women's group this evening and is not expected back until late. Do sit down.'

I sat on the sofa beside Richard, who'd had made himself comfortable without waiting to be asked. The Reverend Langdon was clearly in a state and it was impossible not to feel a little amused, also curious. Richard began to talk.

'James here had been developing his interest in Elgar Vaughan and wanted to ask you a few questions, Sophie.'

There was more to it than that, as I could tell from the amused tone of Richard's voice, and the colour of James Langdon's face as he answered.

'I, ah ... understand that you live at Elmcote Hall?'

'I do, yes.'

'And you are effectively the curator of Elgar Vaughan's effects, his library included?'

'Yes.'

'I see, I see. You must have seen his extraordinary prints then?'

'Yes. The entire collection. Some of the originals are framed on the library walls.'

He stopped and steepled his fingers, his face now distinctly red. Richard spoke.

'I was telling James that they are supposed to have been drawn from life. He doesn't believe me, of course –'

James interrupted.

'I would not go quite that far. There must be some degree of artistic interpretation, yes, but at least the human elements ...'

I paused before answering, and wondering what an observer would have seen as I lay beneath Magog on the Elmcote lawn.

'There must have been some interpretation, yes, and the pictures are supposed to have been drawn after their rites rather than during them, but such things inspire very intense emotions, and more, blurring the lines between what is there and what appears to be there.'

Richard broke in.

'I think James is more interested in what's going on.'

Now thoroughly pink-faced, James went on.

'Yes, quite. I shall be frank. Lately I have been having what might be called a crisis of conscience. In two years' time I will be fifty years old, and while it is always said that the Devil has all the best tunes, I cannot help but feel my life has been rather devoid of, shall we say, the more earthly pleasures. By contrast you pagans seem to have a thoroughly jolly time.'

'We do. Why, do you wish to convert?'

It was very hard to keep the smile from my face as I waited for his reply. He was so full of repressed lust and eagerness, leaving me feeling delightfully wicked, as Richard had said, a succubus, intent on seducing a man from the straight and narrow path. Finally he found his words.

'Convert might, perhaps, be rather a strong word. I am certainly curious though and, I confess, doubtful, which was why I asked Richard to bring you here tonight. I trust you excuse what might seem to be cynicism, but it had occurred to me that your claims might be vain . . .'

'. . . or some sordid commercial scam, no doubt.'

Richard had interrupted, and at his words James went redder still, stammering a reply.

'No, no, not at all, nothing like that, merely . . .'

Richard held up a hand.

'Don't apologise, please. Yes, I might have been lying or, for all you knew, a pimp. I am neither, just a practising pagan, as you are a practising Christian. It really is as simple as that, and if we celebrate in a rather more earthy way, as you put it, then I can only recommend it to you.'

James nodded earnestly. We were a little too close to admitting what we actually did, and where, for my liking, and I shot Richard a warning glance as James went on.

'I see. Well, I must say that I would be very grateful indeed if at some point I might be permitted to – to attend one such ceremony. If of course that is at all appropriate? I mean to say – that is, if this is not simply something you do between yourselves, which is, er, rather the impression I got?'

His face was bright pink with embarrassment, leaving me feeling more mischievous than ever. Richard gave a calm, easy response.

'You impression is correct, absolutely. We celebrate nature, the turning of the seasons, life itself, and, if we take joy in our bodies, what could be more natural?'

'Quite, quite, that is what I have always thought.'

His voice was hoarse with earnest passion and lust, his eyes flicking to my face, my chest, and the curve of my hip where I'd curled myself onto the sofa. It was all highly amusing, and exciting too, but there was one thing I wanted to know.

'What about your wife?'

'Eleanor knows nothing of my feelings on this subject. She has many virtues, but is perhaps a trifle staid in her ways.'

'So she would object? Wouldn't you feel unfaithful to her?'

His face filled with sudden dejection as he answered.

'In the physical sense, no, I confess not. My wife and I have not had sexual relations in over ten years.'

'Ten years?'

'Almost twelve, since an unfortunate misunderstanding over my brother's *au pair*, of which I assure you I was completely innocent. May I ask, then, if your rites reflect, at all, those scenes depicted in Elgar Vaughan's prints?'

I laughed.

'We've yet to summon a giant goat-headed hermaphrodite, but we're trying our best.'

His expression wavered, perhaps trying to decide if I was being serious or not, and he went on.

'This is essentially what Richard and I were discussing

online, along with your friend Nathan. Yet I confess to being sceptical. Can you really be so open in the expression of your sexuality?'

There was only one answer, and a glance to Richard confirmed that it was what he wanted of me. I stood, walked to James' chair and got down on my knees in front of him. The look on his face was truly comic as I took the hem of his robe and lifted it, but he made no effort to stop me. A moment later I had him released from his trousers and in my hands, and he had rolled his eyes up in bliss, or possibly prayer.

A brief adjustment to my jumper and bra and my breasts were naked, something men always seem to appreciate if a woman is going to pay court to his manhood, and I'd begun, taking him in my mouth as Richard watched with amusement and delight. Possibly having Richard watch was a little off-putting, because James took ages to grow erect, despite my best efforts, and even longer to come, although I was spurred on to see it through thoroughly. It felt so wrong and deliciously forbidden – to take this man of the cloth into my mouth and give him pleasure. My job at Elmcote had led me down the most extraordinary path!

When he had finished he was full of embarrassed thanks, and concern that I hadn't really enjoyed it. I assured him I had, which was true, and went to sit by Richard again, feeling extremely naughty.

I'd have gone further, but Richard seemed content, and after a little more conversation we left, with James already getting nervous in case for any reason his wife returned early. Back in the car I could barely contain myself and would happily have indulged Richard then and there. He was rather cooler, contenting himself with stroking my very obviously erect nipples through my jumper before starting off.

'What do you think?'

'Wonderful!'

'Do we take him then?'

I tried to put aside my needs and be serious for a moment.

'I'd like to, and I genuinely feel it would be a kindness, for all his worries. But could he cope? If he's had one crisis of conscience, why not another?'

'True, true. But I just like the idea of having a vicar as a member. According to some schools of thought, a cult like ours should be led by a defrocked priest.'

'Not according to Vaughan, and James Langdon's not defrocked.'

'Not yet. He soon will be if he carries on like that.'

'Exactly my point. He's a risk, but he is tempting. Would you make him kiss your arse?'

'Oh, I think so. Obviously I'd prefer it with a woman, but in the circumstances, I rather think it would be necessary.'

'Do you think he'd do it?'

'Maybe. Perhaps we'd have to put a little temptation in his way first, but I'm sure you and Lily could see to that.'

'With pleasure! Yes, Lily and I, but that's another problem. We need to keep the number of men and women equal, and if James comes that will be four to two.'

'I couldn't agree more and, seriously, I am concerned that James might lose his nerve. Perhaps we should invite him to something, an initiation ritual comes to mind, but not at the Hall. Nathan is keen to host something at his farm, for instance, in the woods.'

'Sounds perfect, but what about female members?'

'It's difficult. Most women on the internet are cautious of men, and pagans are no exception. Perhaps you should come down on Sunday night and you can spend Monday surfing at my flat?'

'Perfect.'

It was perfect, absolutely, although I felt distinctly guilty about my intentions.

By the time we'd got back to his flat I'd decided what to do. A hurried search in the morning, as I'd planned, wasn't enough. I needed time, and that meant waiting until Monday, but first, I needed to resolve my conscience and finish what we'd begun with the Reverend James Langdon. As we entered the kitchen Richard made straight for the coffee apparatus, but I stepped in front of him.

'Just sit down.'

He sat, his face showing a flicker of revolt at me telling him what to do, but not after I'd sat on his lap and put my arms around his neck.

'I've been a very bad girl indeed, haven't I?'

'I suppose you have.'

'No question. I mean, sucking off a vicar? I think something should be done, don't you? I think I should have my bottom smacked.'

His face lit up.

'Undoubtedly.'

The next moment I'd been lifted and placed across his knee, so easily. I closed my eyes in bliss as he began to disarrange my clothes, taking my top and bra up, my jeans down, and finally my knickers, eased all the way to my ankles, to leave me feeling delightfully exposed. He set to work, hard enough to make me squeak and wriggle, and to feel I was being punished as well as to grow ever more aroused, only it wasn't what I'd done to James he was punishing me for, but for what I was about to do to him.

It didn't last very long. No sooner had my bottom begun to grow warm and rosy than he stopped and lifted my body once more, this time to lower me onto the floor. I moved into a kneeling position by instinct, knowing exactly what was going to happen. Sure enough, he pushed his lower clothes to the floor, opened his knees wide, and fed himself into my mouth.

I took him in, sucking with my eyes closed in bliss and very much aware of the warmth of my spanked bottom behind me. Unlike James Langdon, Richard was soon erect, and as I licked and kissed at his beautiful smooth skin I was thinking of how I'd been made to take two men in my mouth in one evening, and how good that felt. After a while I'd put a hand back, to stroke the hot skin of my bottom and to play with myself. I was no longer merely sucking him but worshipping him, his big smooth erection a living idol, to be knelt to in adoration.

Taking his cock in hand, I planted a firm, purposeful kiss right between his buttocks, letting him know just how deeply I worshipped him. He gave an amused chuckle in response, which broke to a sigh as I began to lick once more, giving him the unrestrained pleasure of my tongue as I masturbated to bring us to ecstasy at the same perfect moment.

As it turned out I wouldn't have had a chance to search the flat anyway, because Richard insisted on seeing me into a Paddington-bound cab before heading for work himself. I got back to the Hall in good time, opening only a few minutes after I technically should have done. After a quick coffee I made my rounds of the temples, still not one hundred per cent sure that we'd sorted out the problem of the intruders. There was no sign anyone had been there, much less attempted to tamper with anything, and I was smiling for my own suspicious nature as I walked back to the Hall.

With nobody about I set to work calculating Elgar Vaughan's exact height. Various photos showed him next to objects I could measure, and even allowing for the difficulties of scale I'd soon managed to pin him down to between six-three and six-four. Richard claimed to be six-three, and even if men have been known to exaggerate he had to be close.

I also used a lens to make a minute examination of Vaughan's face for tell-tale marks. Everybody, you'd have thought, would have small but distinct features, even if just a particular pattern of freckles. Elgar Vaughan seemed remarkably fresh-faced, or so I thought until I managed to pick out a tiny irregularity to the side of his left eye.

It was there in every one of the pictures, at least, those in which there was any chance of me picking out anything at all. I put the photos back with a renewed sense of expectation. Now I could make sure and, while I wasn't entirely certain I actually wanted to know, I knew I would do it. Despite the voice of reason in the back of my head still telling me I was being silly, I knew that if Richard Fox proved to be plain old Richard Fox I would be disappointed. If he proved to be Elgar Vaughan I didn't know how I'd feel, but the very thought was enough to fill me with awe, and not a little dread.

For the rest of the day my thoughts were swinging between telling myself I was being ridiculous and a burning desire for it to be true. I couldn't concentrate on anything else, and kept going back to the library just to stare at Vaughan's face, my obsession stronger than ever before. Again and again I tried to find a fault with my logic, but there wasn't one. Everything made sense, including his interest in me. After all, if he had decided to revive the Sabbat Aceras, what better way to begin than to seduce the woman who was looking after the house?

It was driving me to distraction, but there was nothing I could do about it until I saw him again. When closing time came I very nearly went straight back to the station. Only my fear of disappointment prevented me, but I was still feeling tense and completely unable to relax. I wanted something to do, and it had been a warm day, so I went down to the lake, stripped off and plunged in from the bridge.

The water was cool, soothing my body, but doing nothing to calm my seething mind. Just to picture myself floating naked in the pool in Elgar Vaughan's woods was enough to stop me thinking about anything but him, and fantasising about how he might come across me, watching me swim naked with his cool smile, before lifting me from the water and putting me on my knees to fill me with his huge smooth cock.

I was going to masturbate over it, I simply couldn't help myself, but had no sooner got out of the pool and begun to tease myself as I dried off than a voice called my name from the direction of the house. It was Julie, unmistakably, but it still made me jump out of my skin. I called back and quickly gathered up my clothes, walking up to the lawn in just my shoes and towel.

She was waiting almost exactly on the spot where Magog had taken me during the ritual, bringing a flush to my cheeks as I kissed her in welcome. Nobody could have been better company, her sensible, down-to-earth manner the perfect antidote to the state I'd worked myself into. She'd brought wine too, and an offer I couldn't refuse.

'You just slip into something comfortable and let me take charge. I'm going to cook for you.'

'Thanks. What have I done to deserve that?'

'Been a friend, honey, that's all. Now come on with you.'

I came, allowing her to steer me back to the house and running upstairs to change while she began to cook. There didn't seem any point in putting on more than a T-shirt and a pair of knickers, and I was soon back downstairs. Julie had my pinny on over her smart bottle-green business suit, and was chopping aubergines. A full glass of red wine stood beside her, another on the table. I took a drink as I sat down.

'This is really good of you. What are you making?'

'Just a bake, home-style, from whatever I can find in the cupboard. So, honey, any scandalous confessions this week?'

'Nothing I can't handle.'

'You're going to tell Auntie Julie though, huh?'

'Maybe. Are you religious?'

'Hell no.'

'Good. Richard took me to see a vicar on Wednesday.'

'And that's supposed to be scandalous?'

'Richard made me suck him off.'

That had her attention.

'He made you suck him off, in front of the vicar!'

'No. He made me suck the vicar off.'

'Now that is scandalous. You are one bad girl, Sophie Page.'

'That's what I told Richard. He spanked my bottom.'

I was going pink and trying not to laugh at the same time. Julie turned, one hand on her hip, her eyebrows raised.

'If you want to know, honey, I reckon you got just what you deserved! Why, maybe I ought to do the same myself?'

She was joking, and I stuck my tongue out as she turned back to the chopping board. It was fun confessing to her, and always made what I'd been up to seem that little bit naughtier, not that I needed much help in this case. She carried on cooking, and drinking, putting everything together in a dish and sliding it into the oven before sitting down across from me.

'Maybe I ought to meet this guy Richard?'

'Maybe you should. He's great, just the sort of man I always wanted, strong without being up himself.'

I could hardly admit the full details of my desire or she'd have thought I was mad, but as always I felt the need to talk.

'Sounds perfect. You're lucky.'

'I suppose I am. Not that I mind being single, but when a man like that comes along...'

'Take it while it's hot, honey.'

'...somebody who thinks the same way I do, who wants the same things I do. I've never met anyone like him.'

'Me neither, which is a crying shame.'

'Don't you start. You know it's only because you work too hard, and you're too fussy.'

She gave a wry smile and reached for the bottle. There was only enough to half fill our glasses and I went to fetch one of the ones Richard had brought. Already I felt far more relaxed and ready for an evening of Julie's company, good food and good drink. The pasta bake needed an hour, but I didn't mind, happy to let my appetite build while we talked about every subject under the sun.

By the time dinner was ready I was drunk, too drunk to think that opening yet another bottle might not be a good idea. I didn't care and, after all, we had to have something to wash our food down with. It was delicious too, despite being put together from the bits and pieces in my larder, and left us feeling replete and completely at ease, giggling together over increasingly dirty stories, of which Julie seemed to have an endless supply.

'...oh but you should have seen it. The guy's standing there with his pants around his ankles and his dick sticking up in the air, and the officer does not look happy, like he's smacking his night-stick on his hand. So the guy says, "You've got this all wrong, officer, I only needed a leak", and this with me still down in front of him!'

'Oh no! What happened?'

'We got busted, that's what happened. The officer calls

up a wagon, and down we go to the precinct house, only they didn't know which cells to put me in ...'

She stopped, suddenly, and if she hadn't I wouldn't have realised anything was amiss. As it was I could hardly fail to, because she'd gone bright red and was looking at me with her mouth open. Suddenly I realised, and my own mouth had come open, my jaw slowly dropping as it all sank into place. She saw, and put her hand to her face.

'Oh shit!'

I couldn't find words. My head was spinning, my eyes were refusing to focus and I was having serious difficulty taking it in, feeling angry and amused, and betrayed and delighted, all at the same time. Only when I realised that she was crying did I finally find my voice.

'No, Julie, don't, please ...'

She looked up, her eyes wet with tears, shaking her head as she began to rise, and to talk.

'No, I'm sorry, Sophie, I'm so sorry – I never meant to –'

'No, Julie, stop! Come back, you're being silly!'

'No. Now you're going to hate me –'

'No!'

She'd made for the door. I followed, keeping up with her easily and grabbing her by the arm before she could leave. She turned, her face set in utter misery with the tears streaming down her cheeks as she looked down at my face.

'Don't go, Julie! We can talk about it, we –'

Again she shook her head.

'No. It's no good, Sophie, it could never be the same. I'm so sorry, but ... I never meant to lie to you. I love you, Sophie, I love you more than any ...'

She tried to pull away, but I clung on.

'Shut up and come here!'

I pulled her back inside and towards the library. She

came, reluctantly, and still crying bitterly, and I had to hold her shoulders to make her look at the picture of Elgar Vaughan seated beside the blatantly erect and blatantly hermaphrodite figure of Baphomet.

'Look at that, Julie. Do you think I mind?'

'Of course you mind. Everybody minds, outside of –'

'OK, OK, I mind, and you might have told me, but it's not bad, it's – it's –'

'No. You're so sweet, Sophie, but –'

'Oh shut up! Come here.'

I took her in my arms, going up on tiptoe to kiss her face. She tried to turn away, but as my lips took the tears from her cheeks I could feel the tension slowly starting to drain from her body. I held on, pushing her back towards where I'd left Vaughan's chair, and into it. She went, now pliant, but with a sudden gasp as my hands went to her skirt.

'Sophie, no!'

'Uh, uh, shut up, Julie. I'm going to do this.'

Her answer was a weak moan as I tugged her skirt up around her hips. Underneath she had stockings on, supported by suspenders to leave twin rings of pale smooth thigh at the tops of her legs and either side of a pair of loose silk camiknickers. As I got down on my knees I felt every bit as excited and every bit as rude as the first time I'd ever taken out a man's cock to play with.

I hadn't hesitated then and I didn't hesitate now, reaching out to pull the crotch of Julie's camiknickers aside and free the little pink cock and rounded balls within, straight into my mouth. She sighed as I began to suck on her, an exhalation of complete bliss, but she had the sense not to say anything that might have broken the moment, simply allowing me to go to work and enjoying my efforts. I didn't want to talk. I didn't want to think. I simply wanted to enjoy her little penis and revel in the feeling of being so thoroughly rude with a transsexual, beneath the print of Elgar Vaughan, and with her in his chair.

Not a word was spoken as I brought Julie slowly and gently to erection, sucking and teasing with my tongue, determined to show that I had no reservations whatsoever. I was on my knees too, the way I like to be, and as I finally let her straining erection free of my mouth I looked up, eager to surrender completely.

'Do whatever you want, but do it here.'

She nodded, and once again there was something of the old spark in her eyes. Her arms came down and she lifted me, pulling my body to hers. Our mouths met and we were kissing, even as she made quick work of my top, pulling it high to bare my breasts, and off. My knickers followed, eased down my legs and kicked free, and I was nude in her arms. She stood, lifting me easily, and set me down in the chair again, kneeling. I pushed out my bottom, my breathing deep as I looked back over my shoulder.

Now she was in charge, firmly, and my eyes were fixed on her erection, sticking straight up from the pale silk of her camiknickers, ready for my body. She quickly shrugged off her jacket and opened her blouse. In her bra her heavy breasts looked perfectly real, and she didn't take it off, but stepped close to take me firmly but gently by the hips. I was shaking badly as I felt her little cock press to my sex and ease in, fucking me, but only briefly.

A few firm pushes and she'd pulled out to once again press the firmly rounded tip to my body, but higher, and my mouth came open in a little gasp as I realised I was to be sodomised. A denial came to my lips, but I bit it back, and then it was too late. I'd accepted her, and as she pushed herself in up my bottom I put a hand back to masturbate over the exquisite experience of having my girlfriend bugger me with Elgar Vaughan looking down on us from his picture.

10

I knew I should have realised, because with hindsight it was obvious. Julie's height alone should have given the game away, along with the way she dressed, the way she walked, the way she made up – everything about her behaviour. It had simply never occurred to me, anymore than it might have occurred to me that the Reverend James Langdon harboured a desire to indulge in pagan orgies, had I not known it. Unless there's good reason to do otherwise, we tend to accept people as they represent themselves to us. I'd put the way Julie was down to her New York background, and if that makes me naïve, then so be it.

What I was not going to do was get in a state over it. I'd made the right choice in the first place, and I intended to stick to it. I liked her, or him – whatever – and I refused to let the fact that she was a he spoil that. That didn't mean it was easy to come to terms with, and it was true that our relationship wouldn't be the same, but that didn't mean it couldn't be good. Better, in fact, because being taken by her from behind, with her body on mine and her heavy breasts pressed to my back while her penis was inside me, felt bizarre in the extreme and absolutely delightful. I've always enjoyed *outré* sexual experiences, and Julie had plenty to give in that line.

After she'd had me in the library we'd gone to bed and thoroughly indulged ourselves. Or rather, Julie had enjoyed doing all the things to me she'd been fantasising over since the day we'd met. I'd let her lead, enjoying being told what to do and enjoying being rude. Not that

I missed out either, as she had a compulsion to enjoy my body and had made me come more times than I could count.

We'd spoken very little, both aware that there were inevitable unresolved issues between us. Those had been put to one side, and remained unresolved in the morning, as she'd left before I was really awake. We'd parted with a kiss and shared reassurances, so I was very sure she'd be back, and looking forward to it.

If my head had been full the day before, now it was worse. I had an awful lot to resolve, not least telling my boyfriend that I'd been to bed with a transsexual – that was, if Richard could be counted as my boyfriend rather than the object of my worship. It was almost too much to take in, and the aftereffect of sharing four bottles of strong red wine hadn't done a great deal for my ability to think clearly in any case. I also had several visitors, and when the time came to close up I was immensely relieved. A few mouthfuls of cold pasta bake topped with tomato ketchup and I was ready for bed, without even enough energy to get into my pyjamas.

When I awoke it was to the touch of Richard's lips against mine, which was quite a shock. He now had his own keys, but there was a moment when I really wasn't sure if I was dreaming and that Richard was kissing me, that I was dreaming and Elgar Vaughan was kissing me, or that I was awake and one or the other was kissing me. With that thought my eyes flicked to his face, and there it was, a tiny mole, just a centimetre clear of his left eyebrow.

Or was it? Elgar Vaughan's mark was pale, Richard's was dark. Only that might have changed, or not, as the case might be, and I could only stare, my mouth working as I struggled to find words. Finally he spoke.

'Are you OK, Sophie?'

'Yes – no – sorry . . . I had a dream. Elgar Vaughan was

kissing me, and then you were, and – and – look, Richard,
I –'

'I think you'd better have some breakfast. It's nearly
nine o'clock.'

'Shit. You couldn't do the gates could you? I've got a
German coach party coming at half past.'

'Already done.'

'Thank you. You are so wonderful, and I am so
hopeless.'

I hauled myself out of bed, ignoring the pleased
expression on Richard's face as he realised I was stark
naked. There was no time for messing about. While I
was feeling so mixed up I wouldn't have been sure what
to do anyway, other than what I was told. Fortunately
he didn't press the issue but went downstairs to make
coffee while I showered and dressed. I'd had twelve
hours' solid sleep, so at least my head felt clear, and I
managed to find the energy to dress properly, corset and
all, while I listened out for the noise of the coach.

I made it, coming downstairs to accept my coffee from
Richard, and even to drink it before the German party
arrived fifteen minutes late. There were thirty of them,
including a guide who seemed to know what he was
doing and even had a basic knowledge of the estate.
They were also determined to get their money's worth,
and it was nearly noon before they left. Richard had
gone off about his own affairs, but reappeared as the
coach moved off down the driveway, walking around
the side of the house.

'Are you done for the day?'

'Maybe. That was the only booking, but people are
quite likely to turn up.'

'That's a shame, because with you dressed like that . . .'

'Later, just as you like, as long as you still want to. I
have a confession to make.'

His eyebrows rose a little.

'Something worthwhile, I hope?'

'I think so, yes. I told you about my friend Julie didn't I?'

His smile grew broader.

'The New Yorker, yes. Do I judge from the pretty pink colour your face is taking on that you've been up to no good with her? Let her take you to bed, perhaps, to indulge your new-found passion for pussy?'

'Um ... sort of.'

'Sort of?'

'Sort of. Yes and no.'

'Yes and no?'

'Yes, we went to bed together, but not for that.'

'Something kinky then? I do hope so.'

'Yes. The thing is, Richard, Julie's not Julie, she's ... a man.'

For one awful moment I thought he was angry, but it was merely sinking in. He laughed, rich and loud.

'A man! Really? Tell me you're not joking, please!?'

'I'm not. I don't know why I didn't realise it before, but ...'

'And he took you to bed? Superb! I trust he thoroughly enjoyed you?'

'Oh yes. So – so you really don't mind?'

'Mind? Why should I mind? It's wonderful, priceless! I wish I'd been there!'

'Really?'

'Of course! What could be better?'

'I am so glad you feel that way. I thought you might be angry.'

'Not at all. I trust you, Sophie, and hope you return that trust. Still, I do think you might have asked, or even invited me along.'

I hung my head.

'Sorry.'

'Don't be. I'm just looking for an excuse to turn you across my knee and spank your delectable bottom.'

'If you wish it . . .'

'I do. Come on.'

He'd sat down on one of the square blocks of stone from the tower, his eyes glittering with mischief and lust as he patted his lap.

'Over you go, my dear.'

'Richard!'

'Come on, buns up.'

'Not here. What if somebody comes down the drive? They'll have a fine view!'

'Very fine indeed, I'd say, but don't worry, we can pretend it's all part of the Elmcote Hall experience.'

'What, watching you spank me?'

'Why not? I'm sure those Germans would have been more than happy to pass you around, and merely thought it was a bit of English eccentricity.'

'I bet they wouldn't! Come on, Richard, be sensible. You know I love to be punished by you, but not here. It's too risky.'

'Very well, if you're going to be difficult, we must take sterner measures. Come with me.'

'Where?'

'To that little temple in among the rhododendrons, the one where you first played with yourself over me.'

'The arboretum temple.'

I'd already been going pink, and my blushes grew hotter still at his words. He stood up and took me by the hand to lead me unresisting across the carriage sweep and into the arboretum. My heart was hammering at the thought of being punished, and at the thought of being caught. The Hall was open, anyone might come in, and there was nothing to stop them exploring the arboretum. If I made a fuss over my spanking somebody might even hear and come to investigate, maybe even Lorna Meadows.

The thought of her finding me laid bare-bottomed over Richard's lap set my face redder than ever, but I did nothing to stop it as Richard led me into the little classical temple and pointed to the same squat pentagonal cylinder of black stone I'd knelt across as I brought myself to a bitter-sweet climax over he and Elgar Vaughan sharing my virginity.

'Kneel down. Prepare yourself.'

I hesitated.

'I . . . thought you were going to spank me over your knee? I like that.'

'No. I'm going to switch you. Now do as you are told.'

I swallowed hard, but I got down, my legs trembling as I bunched my skirts up and knelt on the cold marble, just as I had once before. My fear was growing with my arousal and Richard stepped outside to pick up a long whippy twig from the Tree of Heaven, then a second. As I began to gather up my skirts behind I really didn't know if I wanted to do it or not, ever more nervous as Richard added to his growing bundle of twigs and I prepared my bottom for whipping.

With my skirt and petticoat on my back I hesitated for a last moment before opening the split of my combinations and laying myself bare. Richard saw and gave a low chuckle as he once more stepped into the temple, now with a big bunch of the supple green Tree of Heaven twigs in his hand. Coming close he tapped them to my bottom, sending tiny stinging thrills across my skin. It was going to hurt.

'I – I think you'll have to hold me.'

He nodded, understanding, and paused to take my arms up behind my back, holding my wrists together with just a little pressure to keep me down over the altar, or, as it had become, the whipping block. I closed my eyes, my whole body shaking, determined not to scream. His grip tightened. I heard the swish of the wands and a smack as they landed, a stinging blow that made me gasp and kick my legs.

Another followed, and a third, hard, but not unbearably hard, pushing all thoughts of trying to hold still right out of my head as I wriggled in his grip. It really only took me a moment to get over the pain and I was growing warm behind, and desperately, urgently keen to have him inside me. Not that it mattered what I wanted. He had me, and he could do as he pleased.

What he pleased was to take out his cock and feed himself into my mouth as he continued to whip my bottom. I struggled to suck, my muscles jumping each time the twigs touched down on my tender skin. He'd let go of my wrists and I couldn't stop myself from reaching back to play with myself, thoroughly enjoying my punishment. He merely laughed to see the state I was in, and a moment later he had pulled out of my mouth, fully erect.

The whipping stopped as he threw down the twigs, his cock in his hand as he got behind me. I felt him between my reddened bottom cheeks, and in, eased deep with one easy push, and it was done. I just lay there, shivering in bliss, utterly surrendered to his will as he pumped himself into me, my fingers working lazily at my sex. He was going to come, deep in me, the man who'd just whipped me across an altar, as no doubt he had whipped many a girl before. As I screamed out my ecstasy without the slightest thought for who might hear, I was once more thinking of both Richard and Elgar Vaughan as one.

Being whipped had been wonderfully intense and left me with my bottom tingling pleasantly. It was only by luck that my yells of ecstasy hadn't been heard, and I was quite busy for the rest of the day, leaving Richard to the grounds and the library. Halfway through the afternoon I brought him a coffee as he sat musing over a map of the estate made during the construction of the temples. It was the perfect opportunity, and I pretended to make a casual inspection of the photos of Vaughan, comparing their faces.

Still it was impossible to be sure. Certainly they were remarkably similar, but in every single photo Vaughan either had a hat, side-whiskers, or was in a hooded robe. The tiny marks by their eyes were also impossible to decide on; they were very similar, perhaps too similar to be coincidence, but not absolutely identical. It was immensely frustrating, and the urge to ask him straight out close to unbearable, yet I knew it was useless, while to judge from the faint sardonic smile on his face as he studied the map, he might have been reading my mind.

Nor was his identity the only mystery. I was sure I'd never told Richard about my little bit of misbehaviour in the temple among the rhododendrons, let alone that at the final ecstatic moment I imagined receiving both his attentions and Vaughan's. Yet he'd known. It was just conceivable that in his supreme arrogance he automatically assumed that when I played with myself it was him I thought about, even before we'd been together, and also that he had somehow observed me.

An awful possibility entered my head that the entire estate might be set up with hidden CCTV cameras, for who knew what bizarre or sinister purpose. Pretending I'd heard a car approaching, I left the library and hurried to the temple, my head full of visions of internet porn movies of me *in flagrante*, on my own, with Richard, with Magog, with Lily, with Julie, with several of them at once in assorted combinations.

It was, inevitably, only my overactive imagination. There were no cameras, although I spent the best part of an hour searching, until my next group of visitors arrived. By the end I was more puzzled than ever, but also relieved. I wanted Richard to be not merely my perfect man, but something beyond that, somebody I truly worshipped, body and soul. To have discovered that he had feet of clay would have been agonising, but nothing beside the pain and humiliation of discovering that he was in fact a pornographer intent on providing the world with a range of voyeuristic occult sex videos featuring me as the star.

He, as always, was blissfully unaware of my uncertainties, and I tried my best to put them from my mind in an effort to enjoy the weekend. Julie called in the early evening, wanting to see me, but was reluctant to come up while Richard was there. He was disappointed, and began to tease me about what might have happened, which inevitably led us to bed and several hours of gloriously rude naughty sex.

It was much the same in the morning with Richard in high spirits from the start, demanding his morning erection sucked and sending me out to greet my first coach party with a warm bottom, which kept me on my toes for the day. That afternoon there was a minor function, the launch of a book on the famous buildings of the area, but as it wasn't an exclusive booking I had to cope with people in the grounds and the reception room at the same time, both of whom managed to run me ragged.

There was no opportunity at all for misbehaviour, sadly, because Magog had chosen that day to continue with the gardening. He decided to open a proper way to the Temple of Gaia, which would have been an excellent place to play, although risky, because when I went to look at the end of the day some unknown person had picked a bunch of bluebells and laid them out, although not on the altar, but on the plaque for Florence Zeals' grave.

By then Magog had gone and Richard and I were left to put supper together from what was left in my fridge, then head back to London. I was exhausted and also distracted, but he was in the best of moods, teasing me and discussing the possibilities for Sabbat Aceras rituals. Only back at his flat did I perk up at all, over a shared bottle of Champagne with which I gave him a fizzy blow-job as I knelt in worship to him at the end of his bed.

In the morning I was still in bed when he left, propped up with a cup of his elaborately made coffee. I took my time, feeling more than a little guilty about what I was about to do. His trust in me was casual to say the least, perhaps more an assumption that I would do no wrong, but I was still betraying it. That didn't stop me as I slipped on his huge bathrobe and padded into his study to turn the computer on.

I was going to search for possible female acolytes, both because I genuinely wanted some and to show that I'd been busy with what I'd said I was doing. A few trial searches revealed even more listings for Elgar Vaughan than before, and I began to copy down possible leads and refine my search. Richard had left a list of the discussion groups he'd been on, and I joined as many as I could without waiting, adopting the screen name Elgar's Girl to make my interest and gender plain without giving too much away.

Having sent out a dozen messages designed to draw in enthusiasts I began the more secretive part of my day's work. There was still very little of Richard in the flat, basic personal possessions and a few things he bought recently. Even looking through his clothes made me feel extremely guilty, and I'd soon given up and gone back to the computer.

Two of my messages had generated replies, but both had gone off on tangents, one comparing Vaughan's belief system with others from the same period and the other a long diatribe against mixing pagan and occult ideas from somebody calling himself Mithras. I replied to both, adding a little of the knowledge drawn from my thesis to the first and putting together a long refutation for the second in the hope that an argument might draw in some true Vaughan enthusiasts.

I had decided to be methodical in my search, doing one room at a time and putting everything back exactly as I found it. Having started with the bedroom I completed it, returning each neatly folded item of Richard's clothing to its original place. There was nothing even remotely unusual, not only no clues to support or contradict his identity, but nothing to suggest his interest in the occult, let alone Elgar Vaughan. I knew he tended to keep it all in his head, and there were plenty of his posts on the discussion groups, but it still struck me as odd, or at the least, as very different to my own attitude.

Back in virtual space the argument was hotting up nicely. The belief system thread had gone on to Crowley and personification of the Devil, interesting but irrelevant, while the other had been joined by a Christian claiming that paganism and the occult were inextricably mixed, while condemning both me and Mithras. I waded in, thoroughly enjoying myself, with deliberately provocative quotes from the Bible, Golden Dawn philosophy and historical witchcraft cases.

Typing out my replies had kept me busy for very nearly an hour, and as I went back to searching the flat my head was full of directions the discussions might take and how I would in turn respond. The kitchen and bathroom didn't seem very likely to yield anything worthwhile, but I did both properly in the interests of thoroughness. They were blank and I returned to the computer.

Mithras and the Christian had both worked themselves into fine states, neither one prepared to give an inch and both accusing the other of having been brainwashed into inherently nonsensical beliefs, and more. Unfortunately nobody else had joined in, but it was more than I could resist not to add petrol to the fire by arguing that the only real difference between them was in the names they applied to the deities they worshipped.

I went through the other groups too, but there was very little of interest. Nearly everyone involved seemed to be a modernist, at least among those who took any real interest in the subject at all. There were also several Christians around, most intent either on preaching or condemnation, one or two genuinely worried for other people's souls, and also trolls, there purely to cause dissent or mock people for their beliefs.

Another hour had passed before I went back to my search, this time in the living room. Again, there was very little of anything, let alone what I was after. It did seem to show that Richard was not somebody to whom possessions meant a great deal, which was in itself interesting, but hardly conclusive. His love of neatness and organisation also showed, but again, not to any good purpose.

The internet discussion was now a blazing row, without the slightest resemblance to reasoned discussion. Both Mithras and the Christian had given up trying to persuade the other to change his viewpoint and resorted to raw insult, including the wonderful expression 'spawn of Beelzebub'. My own posts had been overlooked in the fracas, but I added a few more anyway, and on other groups, still hoping to draw out some beautiful and splendid woman.

Only the study and various nooks and crannies remained to be searched. I began with the cupboards, which yielded next to nothing, significant or otherwise. The owner of the flat had evidently moved out with a vengeance, taking with him just about everything he owned. That seemed a trifle peculiar but told me nothing, and before long I was back in the computer chair reading about how Mithras was not only damned for eternity but was also quite obviously a bearded geek too stupid to accept the truth and who badly needed to first take a bath and then get a life.

The beautiful and splendid Lily had turned up and kept me busy chatting for so long that I finally had to excuse myself or risk Richard coming back before I'd finished my dubious task. I'd left the study until last because I knew it would take the longest. There was a lot of paper around – books, files, neatly arranged bills and so forth. I worked with extreme care, replacing each item exactly as I found it and feeling gradually worse as I went along. Richard had spanked me and whipped me with twigs, but I knew that if I finished and found nothing, I was going to need the same again, or more.

Still there was nothing, only the mundane by-products of everyday life and work. Had I not known Richard for who he was, I would have been putting him down as the most boring person on earth, and it was really hard to believe that the man whose belongings I was looking through was the same one who shared so much of my belief system, and who'd indulged me in so much glorious and curious sex.

It was gone five o'clock by the time I reached the bottom drawer of the cabinet in which most of his papers were held. It contained files, as did many of the others, each a different colour and neatly labelled with a printed sticker. There were four, relating to an accident claim, a dispute over the management costs for the flats, an estimate for some plumbing work, and right at the bottom a slim green one with two words on the label – VAUGHAN IDENTITY.

I pulled it out with trembling fingers and opened it. Within were several papers, some new, some old. More than one were official certificates, and I'd caught my breath as I tipped the file. Something fell out, a tiny badly rusted tag. I hadn't done my research for nothing, and my heart jumped as I recognised a military identification tag from the Great War. I picked it gently from the floor and examined it. It was barely more than a scrap of rust, the number illegible, but the letters were plain enough – E. Vaughan. At that instant I heard the grate of Richard's key in the door.

11

The rest of the day passed in a haze. I managed to get everything away in time and was sitting at the computer when Richard appeared, but I didn't know what to say or what to do. No words and no actions could encompass the situation. He was, as ever, calm, self-assured and full of mischief, barely settled into a comfy chair before he asked me to go down on him. I did it, but with none of the profound worship I'd imagined, only a sort of dazed awe.

I was the same as we ate at a nearby Thai restaurant, answering his questions about my computer researches with monosyllables. He kept asking me what was wrong and I had to pretend I didn't feel very well, so eventually he drove me to Paddington and put me on a train, making me promise to get a cab at the far end. All the way to Elmcote I sat staring out at the night, but with Richard no longer with me I finally managed to bring my mind into some sort of focus.

He had Elgar Vaughan's identity tags, supposedly lost with his body somewhere in the mud of Ypres. By the look of it he also had various original certificates, most of which were missing, or rather, had been. It was still too much to take in and yet, try as I might, I could think of no other explanation. Richard Fox and Elgar Vaughan were one and the same.

The tags alone were otherwise inexplicable. At the time they'd been made of thin iron and so had quickly rusted away. Ignoring the difficulty, or chance, of finding such a tiny thing buried in a huge area of fields and among tens of thousands of other bits of scrap, the tags would undoubtedly have rusted away decades before. I was wishing I'd had a chance to try and copy the number, to make absolutely sure, but it would have been superfluous. That, combined with the certificates, their striking resemblance, his extraordinary knowledge of all things to do with Elgar Vaughan and Elmcote Hall, all added up to certainty.

It didn't even seem irrational anymore. Elgar Vaughan had claimed to be able to summon spirits and I had doubted him. Lily had shown me that it was perfectly possible to summon spirits, and I no longer doubted. Elgar Vaughan had claimed eternal youth, and I had doubted him. Now it seemed that both his claims had been no more than simple fact.

Still my mind rebelled at the idea, refusing to accept something so completely at odds with everything I had come to accept as certainty. Back at the Hall I went straight to the Temple of Baphomet, got down on my knees and prayed, hoping for some spark of enlightenment. Nothing came, and the moonlit carvings now seemed to be staring at me, demanding to know who I was, and what I was.

I went back in, to undress and lie awake on top of my covers, my mind working in an endless loop between rejection and acceptance. Eventually I must have slept, because it seemed to be suddenly light, but if I might have expected the light of day to make things any clearer, I was wrong. The facts remained, and the only possible conclusion that could be drawn from those facts.

Even Richard's behaviour fitted, the absolute self-confidence, the sardonic mirth, the casual assumption of superiority. That was as far as it needed to go, because there was no reason for a man of one hundred and twenty-four but still youthful to behave oddly, to dress in old-fashioned styles, or anything of the sort. He was more than simply eternally young too, because the plane had crashed, without doubt, and yet here he was, without a mark on him.

It was terrifying, but it was also wonderful, and over the next few days all sorts of bizarre and sometimes macabre possibilities occurred to me. At first I couldn't even bear to see anybody, and pretended to be ill. Fortunately there were no big events, but the resilience of the human mind is an amazing thing and by the Wednesday I was showing people around as if nothing had happened. In practical terms nothing had, and that evening I even managed to hold a reasonably sensible phone conversation with Richard.

He had been talking to the Reverend James Langdon, also Nathan, who was keen on the idea of us meeting at his farm. It was so easy to just slip back into the way I'd always behaved with him before. Deep down I knew it would never be the same, but I suppose instinct just takes over, rather as if I'd summoned the Devil and he'd asked my opinion of the train service to London. I'm sure I'd have given him a straight answer.

I'd agreed the farm idea was good, but timing was difficult. Some of us could only manage the weekend, others, including James Langdon and myself, could only manage weekdays. With advance planning it was clearly practical, but not for quite some time. Richard was still keen to get something together sooner rather than later, and I found myself more in thrall to his desires than ever.

He was particularly keen for me to find new female members, and there I would have agreed anyway. Unfortunately my computer search hadn't yielded anyone worthwhile, with everyone I'd talked to being either male or obviously unsuitable, Lily excepted. Therefore I was doubly surprised when the doorbell went on the

Friday evening and I answered it to find Richard standing outside.

'I have another possible woman member,' he said.

'Yes?'

He stepped inside and handed me his coat which was wet from the rain. Just him being there had started my feelings of awe off again, and I walked meekly behind him as he made for the kitchen. I hung his coat up as he opened the briefcase he was carrying and threw a handful of printouts on the table.

'Here we are. What do you think?'

I picked up the top piece of paper which was a photo of a tall slender young woman, very pale. She was standing by a whitewashed cottage overlooking a craggy coastline with her simple black dress and long Titian hair blowing in the wind. Her expression was serene, detached even, and her eyes a strange pale green. Around her neck was a beautiful silver Baphomet, a Vaughan's Baphomet, on a long chain. Beside her a great black dog squatted on his haunches, his jaws wide to show impressive teeth and a lolling pink tongue. There was a name in the text underneath: Alice Kyteller.

'She's named herself for the witch of Kilkenny!'

'She claims to be her reincarnation, but she's not in Ireland. That's her cottage on the western tip of Mull. Her dog is called Robin, her familiar.'

'Wonderful. But how does she relate to you – to Elgar Vaughan, and how is she supposed to attend rites here if she lives on Mull?'

'That's the wonderful thing about it. Apparently she moved up there thinking she'd be able to live in peace somewhere so remote. Because it's such a small community, and everyone knows everyone else, the opposite is true. So she's planning to move down to the south, probably London. As for Elgar Vaughan, she considers him the focus of pagan and occult concepts. Look here.'

He pushed another of the sheets towards me, a printed message board conversation between Alice Kyteller and himself, which I read with rising excitement. They discussed me too, in the most flattering terms, and it ended with Alice requesting that I come up and see her in Scotland. By the time I'd finished I was shaking my head in wonder and delight.

'She is perfect! I have to go, but how do I get to Mull, in time, anyway?'

'Don't worry, I've got it all worked out. Find an excuse for the Trustees, and Magog and I can cope with one Sunday. That way you can take a night train north on Saturday and be in Oban by the morning. There's a ferry from Oban to Mull, and a bus to take you out to Tobermory. You'll have to get a cab the last couple of miles, because she's right out at the tip, or nearly. The house is called Sorne Point Cottage and you can't miss it, apparently. I've printed out maps for you, made all your bookings, and I'll pay for all your fares.'

For a moment I was speechless with pleasure and gratitude and expressed my feelings with a lingering kiss. I was going to Mull.

It is a long, long journey from Oxfordshire to Mull. First into London and then north, the train clattering the full length of England and beyond, up through the Scottish lowlands. Then changing trains at dawn among cold damp platforms in Glasgow. Yet another train, moving up through the Highlands, among ever more magnificent scenery with the sun now breaking through fast-moving ragged cloud. By the time I'd reached Oban I felt as if I'd spent half my life staring out of train windows, and I was extremely pleased to be able to stretch my legs and make an early lunch from a seafood stall on the quay.

For no obvious reason I'd pictured the ferry as much like the larger river boats on the Thames, rather than the great blue thing loading up with cars and even lorries. It was also impressively tall, towering high above the docks and the waterfront stores. As soon as I was on board I climbed up to the observation deck, to find myself looking out over the broad silver sea and the distant masses of the islands.

I stayed there during the crossing, enjoying the view and simply being there, doing just the sort of thing I had imagined so often in romantic childhood daydreams, travelling to some beautiful lonely spot to meet a witch. Now it was real, and not only was I going to see her, but to offer her the chance to indulge in elaborate orgiastic rituals with Elgar Vaughan himself.

As Mull grew larger and more solid, with the huge mound of what could only be an extinct volcano rising up above the clouds, my sense of adventure and unreality grew ever stronger. It seemed a magical place, regardless of the mundane nature of the crowds and the cars at the tiny village where the ferry came in. Even the ancient bus that took me towards Tobermory seemed to fit perfectly with the setting, and the dark woods and mist-covered moors to either side of the road were places of mystery, concealing strange creatures and even stranger goings-on.

Tobermory was perfect, a ring of brightly coloured houses set on the steep slopes of an almost circular bay. Taking a cab would have broken the spell and I hired a bicycle instead, asking the way out to Sorne Point. As I peddled and pushed my way out from the town and up onto the bleak rocky hills the enchantment grew stronger still, until when I finally came out onto a ridge overlooking the Atlantic it was as if I was walking on air.

It could not have been more perfect. The sky was a mass of swirling broken cloud with the sun breaking through in places to light the leaden sea brilliant gold or turn the drab landscape briefly to rich deep colour. Two long jagged headlands pushed out to either side of a rocky bay and on the nearer stood the cottage, unmistakably the one in the picture. As I began to pedal down the track a break in the clouds sent a single shaft of sunlight briefly down, bathing Alice Kyteller's cottage in brilliant light. Perfection.

Only it wasn't. When I knocked at the cottage door it was answered by an old man in a woolly hat, who claimed to live on his own. I showed him the picture, but he denied ever having met Alice, or recognising her, despite having lived all his life on Mull and in the same cottage for ten years. For a moment I thought it was some simple mistake, but he confirmed that I was on Sorne Point, and that there was no other house within a half-mile, which I could see anyway. He also claimed to know every neighbour nearer than Tobermory.

Yet I had a picture of Alice standing outside his cottage, which I showed him. He admitted it was his cottage, but still denied ever having seen her, even inviting me inside to look around if I didn't believe him. By then I did believe him. His voice had the ring of truth about it. I left, feeling extremely sheepish. Two separate neighbours confirmed what the old man had said, and I found myself with no option but to cycle back to Tobermory, determined to continue my enquiries.

Only then did I realise that I had a serious problem. There was no earthly use in asking the locals where Alice Kyteller lived, as it wasn't her real name. I was immediately cursing myself for my stupidity, but there was nothing to be done. It had been meant to be simple, and it wasn't. Perhaps there was another Sorne Point, but a glance at a map ruled out that idea. Perhaps Richard had got the address wrong, and yet there she was, standing outside the cottage.

Or perhaps she wasn't who she claimed to be at all, but some fantasist who had created a romantic pretend life for herself, living as a witch on Mull. It made sense. The photo taken on holiday, the details picked up from her imagination and the internet. Richard, who lived a yet more extraordinary life for real, would never have thought to question her, and nor had I.

Still I didn't want to give up, and spent the rest of the day asking if anyone in the town recognised her picture. Not one person did and I was finally forced to accept defeat and leave, now angry, tired and thoroughly fed up instead of elated. The journey back seemed to take three times as long, and it was dark before I was once more back in Oban.

I was cursing bitterly as I boarded the train. It had begun to rain again and I spent the journey staring at the droplets running backwards along the window and thinking black thoughts about the woman who called herself Alice Kyteller. Thanks to her, I had wasted a whole weekend, much of which might have been spent in Richard's arms, or enjoying myself being rude with him and Magog.

Ironically, she too might have had the same, if only she'd been honest with us. After all, she appreciated Elgar Vaughan and everything he stood for, she had got on well with Richard, to judge by the transcripts of their message board discussions, and she was beautiful. At least, the woman in the picture was beautiful. Possibly it wasn't her at all. Possibly 'Alice Kyteller' wasn't even a woman.

The thought made me more fed up than ever. As I waited in Glasgow with sheets of lamp-lit rain coming down beyond the platforms I was brooding on the nature of the internet and reality. Magog, Nathan, Lily, all represented themselves as they were; indeed, they revealed elements of their personalities normally kept hidden. Then there was 'Alice Kyteller', in sharp contrast, who had appeared every bit as real, but didn't exist at all.

I needed company, something to drink, and a cuddle. Not being very good at chatting up complete strangers on trains, I was left with buying myself several miniatures of vodka and a carton of orange juice to make up a particularly nasty cocktail. It did at least put me to sleep, and when I woke up again we were pulling into Watford.

The train was supposed to take around six hours, but seemed to have overrun, leaving me coming in not so very long before Richard would be getting up for work. I was determined to see him, even if it was only for a few minutes, just to vent my feelings about 'Alice Kyteller'. It was pushing seven by the time we pulled in at Euston. I was sure I had time and managed to grab a cab almost immediately. By 7.15 I was outside his door, looking forward to a soothing hug, his fancy coffee and perhaps a doorstep-sized bacon sandwich oozing with butter. Possibly I'd even stay and could gaze in rapture at his identity tags and take a proper look at the certificates.

Unfortunately I'd missed him, probably by just minutes, although all the other times I'd been there he'd left at shortly before eight. Evidently I was going to get two bad days in a row, and I turned for Paddington feeling thoroughly dejected. It was at least dry, and as I was in no rush to get to the Hall I treated myself to my much-needed bacon sandwich at a café before walking to the station.

In fact it didn't seem to have rained at all and Elmcote looked as picturesque as I'd ever seen it, and a striking change to Scotland. I walked to the Hall, cheering myself up by imagining what the six of us could get up to at Nathan's farm, and before. The gates were closed, as they should have been, but as I walked up the drive I realised that something wasn't right. At first I couldn't put my finger on it, but as I drew closer I realised. The outline of the huge pile of rubble from the tower was no longer the same: the great stone gargoyle now stood close to the upright instead of at a drunken angle.

Immediately I was running forward, my bag dropped on the drive, fervently hoping I was wrong. I wasn't. The rubble had been moved, and it was no chance collapse. It had been done deliberately, the ground marked with scratches and the indentations of caterpillar tracks. Yet it made no sense. The rubble was much as before, covering the same ground, only not quite right, a change perhaps not even noticeable to somebody who didn't know the position of just about every block. Not only had some of it been cleared, but it had been put back afterwards.

Nor was that the only mystery. Heavy machinery had been used. At least one bulldozer and some kind of extremely powerful digger. Yet short of smashing either the front or rear gates from their hinges there was no way to get such huge machines onto the estate. With that I was running again, to the tradesmen's track and the rear gate, which stood as usual, closed and chained shut. Only two people had the key, myself and Richard.

I could have screamed. Still I didn't want to believe it and I was searching desperately for alternatives as I ran back to the house, any alternative that wasn't completely crushing. When I got to the rubble pile I climbed up once more, cautiously, balancing on the stone blocks until I was above the centre of the hall. Beneath me I could see the old floor, which I'd never been able to do before. I could see the edge of the pentagonal slab too, cracked and out of true to its neighbours.

Now I screamed, choking back tears, but laughing too, unable to control my raw emotion, until I realised I was having hysterics and forced myself to breathe calmly. Still streaming tears and biting back crazy laughter, I picked my way down the pile of rubble and sat down on a block. There really was no other option. Richard had been there, perhaps with others, to move the rubble and lift the pentagonal slab at the heart of the old Sabbat Aceras temple.

Again and again I tried to find a way to deny the truth. Possibly somebody else had done it, cutting the chain and replacing it with a new one. Possibly Richard had been caught and forced to open the gate. Possibly somebody had stolen his keys. I wanted to believe each and every explanation, anything that left Richard who I had supposed him to be, but there was no denying the facts.

He had tricked me from the first, seduced me, learnt my dreams and exploited them, in detail. Nor was it just Richard. I could see it all, how I'd been carefully led into their trap. Richard's task had been to get to know me, and to get me out of the way. Meanwhile, Magog and Lily had tried to lift the slab in the Temple of Baphomet. In my naïve eagerness to be with somebody who understood me I'd been so easy to manipulate, pathetically easy, even explaining to them why they were trying the wrong slab.

The other slab, hidden beneath tons of rubble, had not been so easy. More elaborate plans had been needed, something that got me out of the way for long periods. I'd fallen for it, hook, line and sinker. Indulging myself in a fake ritual so intimate it now made me blush purple just to think about it. How they must have laughed, the three of them, or four, because Nathan was presumably involved as well, over how they'd shared me. I'd even been with another woman!

It didn't bear thinking about, and for the second time I had to choke back hysterics. I succeeded, but that didn't stop the images coming unbidden into my head, of me grovelling on my knees as I licked and sucked at Richard's erection or kissed his anus, of me letting three men take turns in my mouth, of me masturbating as Lily settled her bottom into my face, of me being fucked and spanked and – and basically, used.

Now they'd lifted the slab, and that was that. They'd be gone. Now I knew why Richard's flat was so Spartan, and why there was no evidence of the man he'd supposedly borrowed it from. It would be rented, and he'd be gone, taking everything with him, everything in the green file included. No doubt it had all been faked, even the tags, somehow, put together in order to lure me in, but never used because it hadn't been needed, because I'd proved to be ridiculously easy.

Yet if I'd been a dupe, so had he, to me. I desperately wanted to find him, to tell him exactly what I thought of him, and to laugh in his face. Only I couldn't. I didn't even know where he worked. The same was true for Magog. I had an address, but I'd never been there and, just like Alice Kyteller, it was sure to be a fake. The same was true for Nathan, while the incident with James Langdon had presumably been genuine, and just an excuse to watch me suck another stranger's cock. How he would have laughed once I'd gone!

What I did know was Lily's address. Her flat had been far too elaborate, far too lived in, to be a set-up. Somehow they'd made a mistake, perhaps through Richard's eagerness to get me together with another woman. After all, he'd always been keen on the idea and, ironically, the bizarre and extreme fantasies we'd so often talked about were probably the only genuine part of himself he'd allowed me to see. A lot of them had involved me with other women and no doubt he'd had Lily in mind from the start.

It was a mistake he was going to regret because I was not allowing myself to be trampled on so easily. I was going to Lily's flat. What I'd do once I got there I wasn't quite sure, except give her a piece of my mind and maybe smack her stupid painted face, but I was going.

I was no longer on the edge, but grim and determined as I retrieved my bag and got myself together. A change of clothes, a quick strong coffee to steady my nerves, and I was ready. One last glance at the rubble pile and I set off, down to the station, into London and north on the tube, the whole journey seeming to pass in a flash. As I approached Lily's block I was stoking my anger by thinking what a dupe she'd made of me, and the things she'd made me to do to her.

No, the things we'd done together, because I'd enjoyed every single moment of it. By the time I got up to her floor my eyes were filled with bitter tears and my teeth set in fury. I pounded on the door, yelling for her to come out and face me, and kicked it, just as it opened. Lily stood there, a black velvet robe clutched across her chest, her eyes wide in surprise.

'Sophie? What's the matter?'

I pushed past her, slamming the door and the security gate aside.

'Don't you give me that bullshit. I know the whole story.'

'Sophie! Calm down! What are you talking about?'

'No, I will not calm down. I really liked you, Lily, maybe I even fell in love with you a little, so how could you do this to me, you evil fucking bitch!'

'Sophie! Stop it! Hey!'

She'd tried to come towards me as we'd entered her living room. I pushed back, sending her sprawling on the golden cushions where we'd first made love. That memory, and the frightened look in her eyes, calmed me down just a little but I went on, my voice an angry hiss.

'Why did you have to do that, Lily? Why did you have to hurt me so badly? You could have asked, couldn't you? Couldn't you?'

'Sophie, stop it! I don't know what you're talking about!'

'Don't give me that crap, Lily. I've seen it, the way the rubble's been moved, the cracked slab, and I may be stupid but I'm not a complete idiot.'

'I don't know what you're talking about.'

'Oh don't you? Setting me up so you could get me out of the way long enough to bring heavy equipment in and lift the slab under the fallen tower at Elmcote. No, I don't suppose you know a thing about it, do you!?'

'No! I swear! Is that what's happened? When?'

'Last night, as you perfectly well know.'

'Well it wasn't me then, was it!? I was at my Gran's this weekend, in Brighton. You can check if you don't believe me.'

I stopped, not knowing what to say in the face of her flat denial. She sounded scared, and completely genuine. I drew a deep breath and closed my eyes, trying to calm down and to think clearly as Lily went on, stumbling over her words in her eagerness to placate me.

'I swear it, Sophie, it's nothing to do with me, it really isn't. I wasn't there. I don't know anything about it, only that I wanted to come up and play with you, but Richard said it wasn't convenient this weekend, and so I went to my Gran's.'

'What? When? When did Richard call you?'

'Thursday. He said you were going up to Scotland to contact a woman who might be good for our group.'

'I did. Alice Kyteller she called herself, only she was a fake.'

A fake created by Richard, as I now realised. Even the picture of her by the cottage had probably been done with a graphics program. It was still in my bag, and I pulled it out. I wasn't sure now, but I wanted her not to be part of it so badly it hurt. She took the picture, her expression immediately changing to surprise.

'That's my friend Celine!'

'Are you sure?'

'Yes, I was there, at Glastonbury last year. I remember the photo being taken, and I gave her the Baphomet for her birthday. We were on top of the Tor, and it was really windy.'

'You mean it's been doctored?'

'And then some!'

I drew my breath in again, trying to think. If she was lying she was very, very good at it, but I had to be sure.

'I don't mean to doubt you, Lily, but can I ring Celine?'

'You can ring Celine, you can ring my Gran, anyone. Whatever's happened, Sophie, I'm not part of it. I swear it, and no, I wouldn't do that to you. Here.'

She rolled to reach for her bag and drew out a little black book, holding it up to me.

'She's Celine Robertson. Try her work number first, then her mobile if she's not there, and you can ask her anything you like.'

I took the book and leafed through it. There was a Celine Robertson, with a tiny neatly drawn pentagram by her name, just as there was beside mine on the page before. Lily spoke as I reached for the phone.

'I'd been wanting to talk to you about Celine anyway. She'd be great for us.'

'I can't think about that now.'

I dialled, waited, and a female voice answered, her tone detached, professional.

'Celine Robertson, how may I help you?'

'Celine? Hi, you don't know me, but I'm a friend of Lily's, Sophie Page –'

'Sophie!? Oh wow, I have so wanted to talk to you . . .'

The change in her tone couldn't have been greater, one moment cool, the next full of enthusiasm and friendliness. She carried on too, asking straight out if we could meet up, along with Lily, so that it took me a moment to get a word in.

'Fine . . . yes . . . that would be great. Hang on a second,

Celine. I just need to ask a couple of questions. Lily says you missed Glastonbury last year?'

'Last year? No, she was there with me, the daft cow!'

'Do you remember anyone taking a picture of you, on the Tor?'

'Yeah, loads. Dave had his digital, and –'

'Great, thanks, Celine, and I'd love to meet up, but just now I have to go.'

'OK. Talk to you soon then.'

I put the phone down, still wondering if the whole thing could be a set-up. If so it was extraordinarily elaborate, but I still had doubts. Lily spread her hands, now looking a little cross.

'See?'

'OK, but how would Richard have got hold of this picture?'

'It's probably on the net.'

I nodded. She was right. If Lily had been in on it she'd hardly have admitted to knowing the girl in the fake picture. She was genuine, and now I'd spoiled everything by shouting at her. I could already feel my tears coming again, but she was holding her arms out.

'Come on, come here.'

My knees seemed to have turned to jelly as I sank down on the floor, letting her take me into her arms and cuddle me as I sobbed my heart out against her chest.

I spent the night at Lily's because I couldn't bear to go back to Elmcote Hall. To me, it had been desecrated, while I badly needed to be held. She was perfect, looking after me without a thought for herself, and even turning visitors away. Only late at night, as we lay together in the warmth of her bed, did she gently ease me down between her thighs. I obliged, taking as much comfort as sexual pleasure in the act, and in the climax I gave myself under my own fingers as I did it.

In the morning I felt immeasurably better. Whatever else had happened, I at least had Lily. With a little care it might even be possible to conceal the way the rubble had been moved. I knew how it lay, but the only other person who was even likely to notice was Lorna Meadows. She and I got on well, and I even considered the possibility of telling her, only to dismiss the idea. As Richard had no doubt anticipated as he'd drawn me deeper into his scheme, any official investigation was going to mean I had a lot of explaining to do. Even if Lorna did support me at first, I would end up losing my job.

As soon as I arrived at the Hall I began to erase all remaining traces of what had happened. It was hard work, and I could just imagine Richard laughing at the thought of me slaving away to repair what he'd done, but there was no choice. By noon I'd removed all evidence of caterpillar tracks, which fortunately had made little impression on the hard-packed gravel. An hour more and I felt I could reasonably claim that the pile had merely subsided during the night, a story I was sure would be more readily accepted than the truth.

There was a letter for me, from Penzance, so presumably about the brass pentacle, but I'd left it unopened on the kitchen table. It no longer mattered, just one more symptom of how foolish I'd been. Yet there was no way it could have been planted, as neither Richard, nor anyone else, could have anticipated me going to that particular antiques shop in Penzance. I let my mind dwell on the problem as I worked, as that was a marked improvement on thinking how easily I'd been tricked, or how rude I'd been with the tricksters.

Only when I'd done everything I possibly could, taken a shower and changed my clothes did I sit down in the kitchen with a badly needed coffee and open the letter. Sure enough, it was from the antiques shop, and the contents were very peculiar indeed. There was a letter, in itself fairly straightforward. He'd picked up the pentacle a couple of years before at an auction in Paris, as part of the stock from a bankrupt magic shop, along with my tarot and various other things. It had come in a box with a note, which he enclosed, with a yellowing envelope. In it was a pawnbroker's receipt, in French, dated December 1918 and made out in the name of Elgar Vaughan.

I sat staring at it for a good ten minutes before I even moved. Elgar Vaughan had been dead in 1918, and definitely should not have been pawning occult goods in Paris. The implications made my head hurt, because they supported everything Richard Fox had carefully fed to me, except for the fact that if he really was Elgar Vaughan after all, then he had no reason whatsoever to want to lift the slab under the rubble. Either he was a con artist and had tricked me in the hope of gaining Vaughan's lost fortune, or he was Vaughan and he'd have known perfectly well there was no lost fortune. There was a third option: that Elgar Vaughan had survived the crash but wasn't Richard; and others, each more insane than the last, leaving me clutching my head in utter confusion.

Somehow it had to make sense. It always does, and yet there wasn't much evidence of that at the moment. As I'd lain in bed with Lily I'd tried to make a joke of how Magog had taken us in by pretending to become the egregore of the Green Man, but she'd sworn it had been genuine. Maybe then Magog hadn't been involved either, and the summoning had been genuine? Yet to the best of my knowledge Magog was the only person who either knew how to operate or had access to the kind of heavy machinery that had been used to move the rubble. He was also the only person big enough to have made the tell-tale footprints in the frost.

Not that he'd ever admitted it, and there was still the problem of his giant disappearing girlfriend. The female footprints had been another thing I'd thought I could lay at Lily's feet, but her feet were nothing like big enough. Whoever had been with Magog that night had to have been over six foot tall, and the only person I knew who fitted that description was Julie, which was ridiculous.

Or was it? Julie always wore heels. Julie never, ever allowed herself/himself to be seen in anything that projected even a hint of masculinity, at least, not consciously. It still made no sense, as she wasn't even interested in Elgar Vaughan, and yet otherwise her presence fitted rather well with the theory of me being tricked. Despite her supposedly busy job, she always seemed to be around. In fact, my efforts to contact her at work had failed.

There was something else too. I'd told Julie about my fantasy in the classical temple, every detail, including that I'd come over Richard as well as Elgar Vaughan. That explained how Richard had known. There was even a sneaking suspicion that Julie had mentioned Lily's name before I had. It seemed to make sense, but I was not about to barge in on her the way I had on Lily. Assuming she was even still at the house in Elmcote, I would be careful, pretending I'd been too busy to notice anything amiss at the Hall and was merely worried Richard had dumped me.

I had nothing to gain, but I still had to find out what I could. Assuming she did work, and in London, she was likely to arrive back in Elmcote fairly shortly after it was time for me to lock up. That was less than an hour, and I spent the time pacing fretfully around the house, trying to ignore the implications of her being involved with the con. It didn't work. To have done all the things I had with Richard and the others was bad enough, but to have allowed myself to be sodomised by a brash American transsexual really took the biscuit, along with the cheese, and the pickle on top.

As I walked down the hill I was feeling distinctly rueful, and hoping I was wrong. Julie was still a she in my mind, despite what I knew, and also my friend. I didn't want what had happened between us to be false, especially after her show of emotion when I'd realised the truth. Like Lily, she was an extremely good actress if it had been put on, but that was no consolation at all.

I went straight to her house and rang the bell. There was no answer and my heart sank, but as I turned away from the door I saw her, coming across the bridge. She was, as ever, flamboyant in a cerise skirt suit and matching heels, big and brash and brassy. I started towards her and as I reached the little piece of grass by the river where we'd first spoken she saw me. She must have read my face, because the change in her expression was immediate, from calm to intense embarrassment, yet she continued walking, and I held my ground. She seemed unable to meet my eye, and when she was close enough to speak her voice was full of distress.

'Sophie, I am so sorry it had to come to this, I –'

'I don't want your apologies, Julie – or whatever your real name is – I want an explanation.'

She nodded, tight-lipped.

'That's the least you're entitled to.'

'We'll sit here then, it's as good as anywhere else. And what should I call you, Jules? John?'

'That hurt, Sophie.'

'How do you think I feel!?'

I felt I was being a bitch because the distress in her face was genuine, but I sat down on the bench, saying nothing. She spread her hands in a gesture of resignation as she too sat down, and there was a long pause before she spoke.

'It wasn't supposed to be like this.'

'Oh? How was it supposed to be then? I suppose I wasn't supposed to realise, and continue to get shagged senseless by half the con artists in the country!'

'No, Sophie, it's not like that. I really like you. You're the first woman who's ever accepted me for who I really am.'

'Why trick me then? If I really meant anything to you, even as a friend, why not tell me?'

'I wanted to! Richard wouldn't let me –'

'So you do know Richard?'

'Yes. I don't expect you to believe this, but I had to play along 'cause it was the only way I had a chance of staying close to you when it was done, which was what Richard wanted as well.'

'Why?'

'So that he'd know what happened afterwards. If you noticed, or, if you wanted to go to the police, I was supposed to talk you out of it.'

'Oh, right. That's what you've been all along, isn't it? Pretending to be my friend so you could manipulate me, and have your fun with me, telling me it was OK to go with Lily, and with Magog and Nathan.'

I cut myself off, because my voice had begun to rise with my temper and people were starting to stare. Julie just looked more miserable than ever and I forced myself to keep my voice low and even as I spoke again.

'Who was in on it?'

'Richard and I, at first. Then, when we found we'd got the wrong slab, we needed somebody who had access to heavy plant, so we recruited Magog.'

'Don't lie to me, Julie. I saw Magog's footprints in the frost before I told Richard about the slab.'

'No. That was Richard and I. The night after the wedding. You slept through the lot.'

I looked at her aghast. 'No. How could it have been

you? The male footprints were bigger, much bigger, maybe the female ones too.'

'It was us, and we got lucky there. When there's a footprint in snow, or frost, the sides start to melt first, making it seem bigger. Don't you know about the Abominable Snowman?'

'Never mind the Abominable Snowman. So that was you, and before?'

'Yes.'

'And Nathan?'

'No.'

I had to ask.

'And Lily?'

'No.'

'And the vicar, James Langdon?'

'No. Just the three of us.'

'So why ... why the rituals?'

'It all got kind of complicated. At first we just wanted you out of the way for a short while so we could lift the slab, but we couldn't do it alone. We couldn't do it together either, after the wedding, and then we found out it was the wrong one anyhow.'

'But the slab was tampered with after I'd told Richard, and while I was with him.'

'We figured you might be starting to catch on, so I snuck up and made it look like there'd been another go. By that time Richard was getting well into the stuff you liked to do with him –'

'Bastard!'

'– and he knew you were up for more. We needed access to the grounds too –'

'Like getting me to let him have keys?'

'Yeah. The cult was the perfect way to do it.'

'And Magog, was he faking that night? I suppose you know about that too?'

'No, he wasn't faking. Lily scared the shit out of the guy.'

'Good. So why the vicar?'

'For a laugh. Sorry. He started chatting to Richard on the net, and so . . .'

'I get the idea, no need to go into detail. And all that stuff about the woman on Mull, Alice Kyteller?'

'Richard faked it, completely. He found some picture of a Goth girl on the web and Photoshopped it onto one of a cottage in Mull. We didn't think you'd realise.'

'I didn't, not until afterwards.'

I stopped, seeing no reason to explain what I knew about the picture. Inside I was absolutely seething, and yet more and more my anger was coming to focus on Richard. He was the one who had organised it all, who had made the decisions, who had seduced me to himself, and for other people. The only thing I couldn't blame him for was me thinking he was really Elgar Vaughan, because in that instance I hadn't needed any help to make a complete fool of myself. I was just very glad I'd never told him. Yet there had been the identity tags, and the pentacle.

'Tell me about Elgar Vaughan's identity tags from the war. What were you going to use those for?'

'You've seen the dog tags?'

'Yes, I've seen the dog tags, and don't start, because if I've been a bit sneaky, I'm not in your league.'

'OK, I don't suppose it matters anyway, not now.'

'It does to me. It matters a great deal.'

'They're his grandfather's.'

'His grandfather's? Elgar Vaughan is Richard's grandfather!'

I'd have called her a liar, but the resemblance was there, undeniably, and atavism was a lot easier to accept than immortality. Still it made no sense.

'How could that be? Even if Elgar Vaughan had children, his tags would have been lost at Ypres.'

'No. Richard's grandfather was called Elgar Vaughan, but he wasn't your Elgar Vaughan. He was his son, by the nurse, Florence Zeals.'

'But she died –'

'Of pneumonia, when her son was four. Elgar Vaughan senior had been seventeen when the child was conceived, so his Trustees removed the child to cover up any scandal. Florence called him Elgar and managed to have his surname registered as Vaughan. He served in the Great War, and survived, moving to the States in the early 'twenties.'

'So you're telling me Richard is Elgar Vaughan's – my Elgar Vaughan's great-grandson?'

'That's right.'

'How do you know all this?'

'That was how it started. Richard wanted to trace his family. His mother was a Vaughan and she had papers, but you've seen those?'

'Only a glimpse.'

'There's his birth certificate, and others too, and letters from Florence Zeals. He got well into it, and even more when he found out he was descended from a famous Satanist. Then, when he read your paper –'

'– he got a bee in his bonnet about Vaughan's missing fortune. Yes, I worked that out for myself. So how do you come into it? And what about the pentacle?'

'The brass one you showed me? I don't know.'

'There was a ticket with it, from a Parisian pawn shop, dated 1918.'

'Elgar Vaughan junior must have pawned it. I suppose he had it from his dad.'

'Could be. And you?'

'Me? I'm just a ladyboy Richard picked up one night in a bar in Greenwich Village.'

'He what!?'

'Just that. Four years ago, that was. He even gave me

that scent you spotted. Believe me, honey, there is nothing that man has had you do he wouldn't do himself, and ten times more, only you've got different equipment.'

'Right. Well I don't suppose that should surprise me too much. So – so why not just ask me?'

''Cause you'd have said no, right? By the time you maybe wouldn't have said no, we'd got in way too deep.'

'Yes, I'd have said no. I'd have – never mind.'

I still couldn't bring myself to admit the truth, not when withholding it was my sole tiny piece of revenge on Richard Fox.

12

Nobody keeps me down for long, not even Richard Fox. He might have tricked me, he might have led me into doing things I'd never have done otherwise, but I'd gained a great deal more than I'd lost. After the initial shock and embarrassment I had quickly got over my feelings about the things I'd done with Richard, and for his sake. After all, there was no use in denying that I'd enjoyed myself; it was only a shame that so much of my experience had in the end turned out to be false. My only real regret was to lose that aura of wickedness I'd always enjoyed because, when it came to kissing the Devil's arse, there was really no substitute for Richard Fox, or so I thought.

Yes, without doubt I had gained more than I'd lost.

I'd gained Lily, my beautiful warm friend, and my lover. She and I had grown steadily closer over the months, sharing an intimate relationship far beyond the usual in that we enjoyed each other sexually much as more conventional friends might have enjoyed confidences. At Elmcote Hall, when we came together in one temple or another late at night, she was something more akin to a priestess.

I'd gained James, whose nervous excitement and enthusiasm never failed to inspire deliciously naughty feelings within me. A simple kiss or a caress to his cheek was enough to set him shaking, with the light of adoration in his eyes. Of his own choice he had taken his place as servant to the rest of us, a position he clearly craved.

I'd gained Celine, who was everything her picture had

promised, and more. Her Titian hair and slender beauty lent a fey touch to our rites, while she had taken her place among us with a refreshingly simple pleasure. She had fitted in immediately, quickly attaching herself to James, whose take on life, and on religion, delighted her.

Best of all I'd gained Nathan, a genuine pagan with a feel for the wild wood, and more importantly still, a man I could trust. He had quickly taken over Richard's role as the male head of our group, complementing Lily, with his old-fashioned paganism in balance to her love of the occult. Before long he had also taken Richard's place as my lover, both in the Sabbat and in a more conventional sense, taking me out to see films or go to concerts, something I'd not really done since university. From then on I was truly happy, and Richard no longer important. After all, if he'd been Elgar Vaughan for me, Nathan was one better, the Devil.

That was the group who gathered together on the first of August to celebrate Lammas and the turning of summer with the fifth meeting of the new Sabbat Aceras. We'd met at Nathan's farm a month and more before, running naked in the woods in a joyful disorganised celebration of the solstice. Before that, we had met at Lily's flat, with her chained by the ankle as she became Lilitu, an experience which left me scratched, bruised and blissfully happy for days. Now it was my turn once more, and with the Hall booked for the day we could do more or less as we pleased during the day, and exactly as we pleased during the night.

Our covering excuse was a small informal engagement party, which allowed us to set the kitchen table out on the grass of the lime walk and take a leisurely lunch, talking, nibbling delicacies and sipping Champagne. We still had to be a little cautious, but that made little difference to me, as I could enjoy the slow gentle arousal of being in full Victorian dress without needing to worry about the Trustees.

Not quite full, as it was too warm for my heavy dress and petticoats, but in my combinations beneath a light summer dress, with a wasp-waist corset Lily had bought me for my birthday. I was barefoot too, adding to the pleasantly liberated feeling it all gave, and yet with the repeated touch of lace or cotton on my skin as I moved serving to keep me constantly in mind of my body.

I was ever so slightly drunk, and smiling, very pleased with what I'd created. As I sat back in my chair and put my glass to my lips I was watching the others and thinking how well they suited the setting, with the great trees rising to either side and the Temple of Baphomet beyond.

Lily was perhaps best of all, in a loose dress of green velvet, cut low to show the full pale swell of her breasts, between which hung a dozen pieces of occult jewellery. She was talking to James, whose face was set in an expression of pure worship as she casually explained the symbolism of letting him suckle at her breast. He wore his cassock and dog collar, which the rest of us had decided was obligatory.

Nathan was in immaculate black, as always on any occasion that did not involve hard physical work, with Celine standing behind him, bright-eyed and giggling in a thin summer dress that did very little to conceal the fact that she was naked underneath.

One thing I could be certain of: Elgar Vaughan would have thoroughly approved.

Only when James began to grow over-eager did Lily give him a playful back-handed cuff and turn to sit in a position that left a little less leg and cleavage on display.

'Down, boy. Behave, and maybe I'll allow you a little something later, once everybody else has had their fill.'

I knew she had something special lined up for me, but she'd refused to say exactly what, merely hinting that I needed to be in my most receptive frame of mind to cope with it. Knowing what she liked, and what she was capable of, just that had been enough to keep me on my toes all week, and I urgently wanted to know.

'I suppose you'd better tell me what's happening now, if you want my help preparing.'

She returned an amused smile.

'You'll find out in due time, Sophie. I just hope you're ready.'

'I am, but at least give me a hint. Is it to be like Solstice at all? Will I need to be naked?'

'Oh no, you know me, I'm more of a goats' skulls and candles sort of girl. What you're wearing now will do very nicely, or at least, your underwear will.'

'Will you whip me?'

'Maybe, maybe not, but if you don't stop asking questions I might be tempted to spank you, right now.'

'OK. Name the four nearest planets to the sun? How do you calculate the radius of a circle? Who was Tycho Brahe?'

'Right!'

She snatched out for my wrist. I was laughing too much to do anything about it, even had I wanted to, as she hauled me unceremoniously across her lap. An instant later my dress was on my back, my combinations had been pulled apart and I was squealing in half-mock protest as my bare bottom was spanked, and still laughing.

'Hey, no! No, Lily! Somebody might see! No!'

The smacks stopped, but only to let her adjust the split of my combinations to make sure all three of them had an unobstructed view. She was talking to me too, trying her best to sound stern.

'I want people to see. That's the whole idea, silly.

What's the good of getting you bare if there's nobody to see?'

She'd set to work again, hard enough to make me kick my legs and leave my words coming between gasps and yelps.

'Strangers! I meant strangers! Or Lorna might come!'

'Well I'm sure she'd be glad to see that you get proper discipline. OK though, just ten more, because I think James is going to burst. Count them out loud.'

I did, blushing furiously as I was made to call out each of ten smacks delivered at long intervals to make sure everyone got a good look. When she finally let me up I spent a moment rubbing my warm bottom, deliberately turned to give James the best view, because his eyes looked as if they were about to come out on stalks.

After Richard had done it to me I'd developed a taste for having my bottom smacked, so Nathan and Lily had taken over his duty. It always gave me a delicious glow behind, and between my legs, especially when it was done in front of other people, but there was no denying it had been better from him. He was no stronger than Nathan, or more skilled than Lily, but there was something in the way he had done it, as if it was his automatic right, that really got to me.

Lily knew, because I confided everything in her, but she seemed more than happy to get me warm when I needed it, or just to do it for fun. She also knew it made me want to do as I was told, something she took advantage of without the slightest protest from me. Now, as I retrieved my spilt Champagne glass and settled back onto my chair, what Lily then said made me start, because it was as if she'd read my mind.

'Could you forgive Richard, completely?'

I shrugged, quickly adjusting gear from the playful images of how the two of them spanked me to a more serious question.

'No, not completely. I don't hate him, but I don't want to be with him either. It's a shame though, I just wish he'd approached it differently. Obviously he had no idea what I was like as a person, but if he'd taken a little time . . .'

Celine laughed.

'That's men all over, always in a rush.'

'I'd have explained everything to him and everything would have been fine. Wouldn't it have been great to have Elgar Vaughan's great-grandson among us? I liked Magog too.'

Nathan made an airy gesture with his fingers.

'Genuine people are rare, as we know. Disappointments are inevitable.'

'He wasn't a disappointment, that's the trouble, but never mind Richard Fox. He's gone, and we're here.'

I'd refilled my glass as I spoke, and held it forward, to touch against Nathan's as I toasted the five of us, then spoke again.

'There is one other thing, which I wish he'd known. Maybe he does, now. There wasn't anything under the slab.'

Both Nathan and Lily looked surprised, but she spoke first.

'How can you be so sure? In fact, you said there was, or at least implied it.'

Nathan nodded his agreement.

'Yes. It's quite clear from your interview with Alice Scott that you believed that Elgar Vaughan concealed everything that was of importance to him under a pentagonal slab in the main temple. OK, so they got the wrong temple, but –'

'No.'

'How do you mean "no"?'

I couldn't help but laugh.

'What I say. When I went to interview Alice Scott she

was one hundred and four years old. She was a delightful old lady and amazing for her age, but her time at
Elmcote Hall meant almost nothing to her at all. Oh she
remembered it all right, in broad outline, but as a brief
folly of her youth, something at once amusing, and yet
rather improper. If she had any details, let alone anything new, or insights into Elgar Vaughan, she wasn't
prepared to give them away, but I honestly don't think
she did. She'd had a long life, and her time with him
was just one incident, and far less important than either
of her marriages, her children, her grandchildren and
great-grandchildren. That was what she wanted to talk
about, not Elgar Vaughan. By the time the nurse at the
home chivvied me out, I had precisely nothing.'

Now Nathan was really staring, and I was imagining
how Richard would have looked.

'Nothing? What do you mean nothing? You based your
whole thesis around the interview!'

'I mean nothing. You see, Elgar Vaughan gave so little
away, and my supervisor was so impressed with me for
tracking Alice down and interviewing her.'

He was laughing too as he replied.

'You said she told you about Vaughan's papers, and
the possibility of a great deal more!'

'Yes, I know I did. That's just it, you see. Everyone
thought I was so clever, and it was going to make all the
difference to my thesis to have a first-hand account of
Elmcote Hall in Vaughan's day, so when she died just a
few days later, and knowing, thinking, the slab would
never be lifted, I – I made it all up.'

Lily held up her mobile phone.

'I've still got his email. Shall I send him a text?'

'Yes. Why not?'

Visit the Black Lace website at
www.blacklace-books.co.uk

**FIND OUT THE LATEST INFORMATION AND TAKE
ADVANTAGE OF OUR FANTASTIC FREE BOOK OFFER!
ALSO VISIT THE SITE FOR . . .**

- All Black Lace titles currently available
  and how to order online

- Great new offers

- Writers' guidelines

- Author interviews

- An erotica newsletter

- Features

- Cool links

BLACK LACE — THE LEADING IMPRINT OF WOMEN'S SEXY FICTION

TAKING YOUR EROTIC READING PLEASURE TO NEW HORIZONS

LOOK OUT FOR THE ALL-NEW BLACK LACE BOOKS – AVAILABLE NOW!

All new books priced £7.99 in the UK. Please note publication dates apply to the UK only. For other territories, please contact your retailer.

THE POWER GAME
Carrera Devonshire
ISBN 0 352 33990 X

The only thing Luke and Cassandra have in common is that they both work for the Government – he as a Director of Communications for the New Spectrum Party, she significantly lower down in the ranks. Serious and ambitious, he wants to change the world. She just wants to have fun. Cassandra, whose fondness for sexy shoes is exceeded only by her fondness for sexy men, is a woman who knows where she's going, and she certainly isn't going after Luke. But as Cassandra learns more about his mysterious past, her fascination with her new boss grows. She falls hopelessly in lust and vows that she will have him. Luke, however, is not hers for the taking, but knowing what she does about his private life, something has to give.

PASSION OF ISIS
Madelynne Ellis
ISBN O 352 33993 4

Adie Hamilton is young, ambitious and wants to make a name for herself in Egyptology, but when Killiam Carmichael invites her to join his prestigious research term at the desert necropolis of Saqqara it's not all dusty tombs and broken pots. Whilst Adie is drawn into the search for the vital missing fragment of an erotic mural, Dareth Sadler, the charismatic leader of a cult hooked on sex magic, and Killiam's bitter rival, arrives to threaten the future of the project. Sadler knows a whole range of erotic dirty tricks, so it's up to Adie to keep one step ahead. The result is a sultry journey of discovery and naked ambition set in the stormy desert landscape of Egyptian monuments and ancient sybaritic secrets.

CONFESSIONAL
Judith Roycroft
ISBN O 352 33421 5

Faren Lonsdale is an ambitious young reporter, always searching for the scoop that will rocket her to journalistic fame. In search of a story she infiltrates St Peter's, a seminary for young men who are about to sacrifice earthly pleasures for a life of devotion and abstinence. What she unveils are nocturnal shenanigans in a cloistered world that is anything but chaste. But will she reveal the secrets of St Peter's to the outside world, or will she be complicit in keeping quiet about the activities of the gentleman priests?

Black Lace Booklist

Information is correct at time of printing. To avoid disappointment check availability before ordering. Go to www.blacklace-books.co.uk. All books are priced £6.99 unless another price is given.

BLACK LACE BOOKS WITH A CONTEMPORARY SETTING

☐ SHAMELESS Stella Black	ISBN 0 352 33485 1	£5.99
☐ INTENSE BLUE Lyn Wood	ISBN 0 352 33496 7	£5.99
☐ A SPORTING CHANCE Susie Raymond	ISBN 0 352 33501 7	£5.99
☐ TAKING LIBERTIES Susie Raymond	ISBN 0 352 33357 X	£5.99
☐ ON THE EDGE Laura Hamilton	ISBN 0 352 33534 3	£5.99
☐ LURED BY LUST Tania Picarda	ISBN 0 352 33533 5	£5.99
☐ THE NINETY DAYS OF GENEVIEVE Lucinda Carrington	ISBN 0 352 33070 8	£5.99
☐ DREAMING SPIRES Juliet Hastings	ISBN 0 352 33584 X	
☐ THE TRANSFORMATION Natasha Rostova	ISBN 0 352 33311 1	
☐ SIN.NET Helena Ravenscroft	ISBN 0 352 33598 X	
☐ TWO WEEKS IN TANGIER Annabel Lee	ISBN 0 352 33599 8	
☐ PLAYING HARD Tina Troy	ISBN 0 352 33617 X	
☐ SYMPHONY X Jasmine Stone	ISBN 0 352 33629 3	
☐ SUMMER FEVER Anna Ricci	ISBN 0 352 33625 0	
☐ CONTINUUM Portia Da Costa	ISBN 0 352 33120 8	
☐ FULL STEAM AHEAD Tabitha Flyte	ISBN 0 352 33637 4	
☐ A SECRET PLACE Ella Broussard	ISBN 0 352 33307 3	
☐ GAME FOR ANYTHING Lyn Wood	ISBN 0 352 33639 0	
☐ CHEAP TRICK Astrid Fox	ISBN 0 352 33640 4	
☐ THE GIFT OF SHAME Sara Hope-Walker	ISBN 0 352 29935 1	
☐ COMING UP ROSES Crystalle Valentino	ISBN 0 352 33658 7	
☐ GOING TOO FAR Laura Hamilton	ISBN 0 352 33657 9	
☐ THE STALLION Georgina Brown	ISBN 0 352 33005 8	
☐ DOWN UNDER Juliet Hastings	ISBN 0 352 33663 3	
☐ ODALISQUE Fleur Reynolds	ISBN 0 352 32887 8	
☐ SWEET THING Alison Tyler	ISBN 0 352 33682 X	
☐ TIGER LILY Kimberly Dean	ISBN 0 352 33685 4	

☐ RELEASE ME Suki Cunningham   ISBN 0 352 33671 4
☐ KING'S PAWN Ruth Fox   ISBN 0 352 33684 6
☐ FULL EXPOSURE Robyn Russell   ISBN 0 352 33688 9
☐ SLAVE TO SUCCESS Kimberley Raines   ISBN 0 352 33687 0
☐ STRIPPED TO THE BONE Jasmine Stone   ISBN 0 352 33463 0
☐ SHADOWPLAY Portia Da Costa   ISBN 0 352 33313 8
☐ I KNOW YOU, JOANNA Ruth Fox   ISBN 0 352 33727 3
☐ THE HOUSE IN NEW ORLEANS Fleur Reynolds   ISBN 0 352 32951 3
☐ HEAT OF THE MOMENT Tesni Morgan   ISBN 0 352 33742 7
☐ THE WICKED STEPDAUGHTER Wendy Harris   ISBN 0 352 33777 X
☐ DRAWN TOGETHER Robyn Russell   ISBN 0 352 33269 7
☐ LEARNING THE HARD WAY Jasmine Archer   ISBN 0 352 33782 6
☐ VELVET GLOVE Emma Holly   ISBN 0 352 33448 7
☐ UNKNOWN TERRITORY Annie O'Neill   ISBN 0 352 33794 X
☐ VIRTUOSO Katrina Vincenzi-Thyre   ISBN 0 352 32907 6
☐ FIGHTING OVER YOU Laura Hamilton   ISBN 0 352 33795 8
☐ ARIA APPASSIONATA Juliet Hastings   ISBN 0 352 33056 2
☐ THE RELUCTANT PRINCESS Patty Glenn   ISBN 0 352 33809 1
☐ ALWAYS THE BRIDEGROOM Tesni Morgan   ISBN 0 352 33855 5
☐ COMING ROUND THE MOUNTAIN Tabitha Flyte   ISBN 0 352 33873 3
☐ FEMININE WILES Karina Moore   ISBN 0 352 33235 2
☐ MIXED SIGNALS Anna Clare   ISBN 0 352 33889 X
☐ BLACK LIPSTICK KISSES Monica Belle   ISBN 0 352 33885 7
☐ HOT GOSSIP Savannah Smythe   ISBN 0 352 33880 6
☐ GOING DEEP Kimberly Dean   ISBN 0 352 33876 8
☐ PACKING HEAT Karina Moore   ISBN 0 352 33356 1
☐ MIXED DOUBLES Zoe le Verdier   ISBN 0 352 33312 X
☐ WILD BY NATURE Monica Belle   ISBN 0 352 33915 2
☐ UP TO NO GOOD Karen S. Smith   ISBN 0 352 33589 0
☐ CLUB CRÈME Primula Bond   ISBN 0 352 33907 1
☐ BONDED Fleur Reynolds   ISBN 0 352 33192 5
☐ SWITCHING HANDS Alaine Hood   ISBN 0 352 33896 2
☐ BEDDING THE BURGLAR Gabrielle Marcola   ISBN 0 352 33911 X
☐ EDEN'S FLESH Robyn Russell   ISBN 0 352 33923 3
☐ CREAM OF THE CROP Savannah Smythe   ISBN 0 352 33920 9 £7.99
☐ PEEP SHOW Mathilde Madden   ISBN 0 352 33924 1 £7.99

☐ RISKY BUSINESS Lisette Allen	ISBN 0 352 33280 8	£7.99
☐ OFFICE PERKS Monica Belle	ISBN 0 352 33939 X	£7.99
☐ CAMPAIGN HEAT Gabrielle Marcola	ISBN 0 352 33941 1	£7.99
☐ MS BEHAVIOUR Mini Lee	ISBN 0 352 33962 4	£7.99
☐ FIRE AND ICE Laura Hamilton	ISBN 0 352 33486 X	£7.99
☐ SLEAZY RIDER Karen S. Smith	ISBN 0 352 33964 0	£7.99
☐ VILLAGE OF SECRETS Mercedes Kelly	ISBN 0 352 33344 8	£7.99

BLACK LACE BOOKS WITH AN HISTORICAL SETTING

☐ PRIMAL SKIN Leona Benkt Rhys	ISBN 0 352 33500 9	£5.99
☐ DARKER THAN LOVE Kristina Lloyd	ISBN 0 352 33279 4	
☐ THE CAPTIVATION Natasha Rostova	ISBN 0 352 33234 4	
☐ MINX Megan Blythe	ISBN 0 352 33638 2	
☐ DIVINE TORMENT Janine Ashbless	ISBN 0 352 33719 2	
☐ SATAN'S ANGEL Melissa MacNeal	ISBN 0 352 33726 5	
☐ THE INTIMATE EYE Georgia Angelis	ISBN 0 352 33004 X	
☐ SILKEN CHAINS Jodi Nicol	ISBN 0 352 33143 7	
☐ THE LION LOVER Mercedes Kelly	ISBN 0 352 33162 3	
☐ THE AMULET Lisette Allen	ISBN 0 352 33019 8	
☐ WHITE ROSE ENSNARED Juliet Hastings	ISBN 0 352 33052 X	
☐ UNHALLOWED RITES Martine Marquand	ISBN 0 352 33222 0	
☐ LA BASQUAISE Angel Strand	ISBN 0 352 32988 2	
☐ THE HAND OF AMUN Juliet Hastings	ISBN 0 352 33144 5	
☐ THE SENSES BEJEWELLED Cleo Cordell	ISBN 0 352 32904 1	
☐ UNDRESSING THE DEVIL Angel Strand	ISBN 0 352 33938 1	£7.99
☐ THE BARBARIAN GEISHA Charlotte Royal	ISBN 0 352 33267 0	£7.99
☐ FRENCH MANNERS Olivia Christie	ISBN 0 352 33214 X	£7.99

BLACK LACE ANTHOLOGIES

☐ WICKED WORDS Various	ISBN 0 352 33363 4
☐ MORE WICKED WORDS Various	ISBN 0 352 33487 8
☐ WICKED WORDS 3 Various	ISBN 0 352 33522 X
☐ WICKED WORDS 4 Various	ISBN 0 352 33603 X
☐ WICKED WORDS 5 Various	ISBN 0 352 33642 0
☐ WICKED WORDS 6 Various	ISBN 0 352 33690 0
☐ WICKED WORDS 7 Various	ISBN 0 352 33743 5

☐ WICKED WORDS 8 Various   ISBN O 352 33787 7

☐ WICKED WORDS 9 Various   ISBN O 352 33860 1

☐ WICKED WORDS 10 Various   ISBN O 352 33893 8

☐ THE BEST OF BLACK LACE 2 Various   ISBN O 352 33718 4

☐ WICKED WORDS: SEX IN THE OFFICE Various   ISBN O 352 33944 6 £7.99

☐ WICKED WORDS: SEX ON HOLIDAY Various   ISBN O 352 33961 6 £7.99

BLACK LACE NON-FICTION

☐ THE BLACK LACE BOOK OF WOMEN'S SEXUAL   ISBN O 352 33793 1
   FANTASIES Ed. Kerri Sharp

☐ THE BLACK LACE SEXY QUIZ BOOK Maddie Saxon   ISBN O 352 33884 9

To find out the latest information about Black Lace titles, check out the website: www.blacklace-books.co.uk or send for a booklist with complete synopses by writing to:

> Black Lace Booklist, Virgin Books Ltd
> Thames Wharf Studios
> Rainville Road
> London W6 9HA

Please include an SAE of decent size. Please note only British stamps are valid.

Our privacy policy
We will not disclose information you supply us to any other parties. We will not disclose any information which identifies you personally to any person without your express consent.

From time to time we may send out information about Black Lace books and special offers. Please tick here if you do <u>not</u> wish to receive Black Lace information.   ☐